Algernon Blackwood
THE MAGIC MIRROR

MIKE ASHLEY is a highly respected editor and anthologist in the supernatural and horror fiction field. His publications include *Who's Who in Horror and Fantasy Fiction* and *The Mammoth Book of Short Horror Novels*. For the past ten years he has been researching and writing a complete biography of Algernon Blackwood and is the author of *Algernon Blackwood: A Bio-Bibliography*. Mike writes regularly on horror, fantasy, and science fiction for British and American magazines. He lives in Kent.

Also available in this series

The Flint Knife: Further Spook Stories by E.F. Benson
Selected and introduced by Jack Adrian

In the Dark: Tales of Terror by E. Nesbit
Selected and introduced by Hugh Lamb

Warning Whispers: Weird Tales by A.M. Burrage
Selected and introduced by Jack Adrian

Stories in the Dark: Tales of Terror by Jerome K. Jerome, Robert Barr, and Barry Pain
Selected and introduced by Hugh Lamb

Bone To His Bone: The Stoneground Ghost Tales of E.G. Swain
Introduced by Michael Cox

The Black Reaper: Tales of Terror by Bernard Capes
Introduced by Hugh Lamb

Dracula's Brood: Rare Vampire Stories
Selected and introduced by Richard Dalby

THE MAGIC MIRROR

Lost Supernatural and Mystery Stories by Algernon Blackwood

Compiled with an Introduction and Story Notes by
MIKE ASHLEY

This selection first published 1989

Blackwood text copyright © Sheila Reeves
Editorial copyright © 1989 by Mike Ashley

All rights reserved. No part of this publication may be reproduced, stored in a retrieval system or transmitted, in any form or by any means, electronic, mechanical, photocopying, recording or otherwise, without prior permission from the publishers.

British Library Cataloguing in Publication Data

Blackwood, Algernon, *1869-1951*
The magic mirror: lost supernatural and
mystery stories.
I. Title II. Ashley, Michael, *1948-*
823'.912 [F]

ISBN 1-85336-117-8

Equation is part of the Thorsons Publishing Group Limited, Wellingborough, Northamptonshire, NN8 2RQ, England

Printed in Great Britain by Richard Clay Limited, Bungay, Suffolk
Typeset by MJL Limited, Hitchin, Hertfordshire

1 3 5 7 9 10 8 6 4 2

CONTENTS

Introduction   7

The Early Years
A Mysterious House   17
The Kit-bag   27
The Laying of a Red-haired Ghost   38
The Message of the Clock   48
The Singular Death of Morton   53
La Mauvaise Riche   62
The Soldier's Visitor   68
The Memory of Beauty   73
Onanonanon   78

The Novels
The First Flight [from *Jimbo*]   87
The Vision of the Winds [from *The Education of Uncle Paul*]   98
The Call of the Urwelt [from *The Centaur*]   110
The Summoning [from *Julius LeVallon*]   126

Radio Talks
The Blackmailers   143
The Wig   152

King's Evidence	154
Lock Your Door	161
Five Strange Stories	166

Later Stories

At a Mayfair Luncheon	177
The Man-eater	184
By Proxy	197
The Voice	205
The Magic Mirror	209
Roman Remains	218
Wishful Thinking	227
Bibliography and Acknowledgements	233

INTRODUCTION

IN the early pedigree of the supernatural story a few names stand out in letters of fire: Joseph Sheridan Le Fanu, Lord Bulwer Lytton, Arthur Machen, M.R. James, and Algernon Blackwood. You may name others, but it is likely that any gathering of horror and fantasy *aficionados* would agree that the above five were the creators and shapers of the modern ghost story. One of them, however, stands apart from the other four. Bulwer Lytton, after all, developed the haunted house story into a distinct genre with 'The Haunted and the Haunters' and brought the occult sciences into modern horror and away from alchemy. Arthur Machen developed this trend. Sheridan Le Fanu drew the supernatural story away from its popular gothic trappings and established the more personalized sinister psychological horror story which was to mature under M.R. James. All of these writers heavily influenced others of their day and those who followed.

But what of Algernon Blackwood? He was certainly influenced by Lytton and Le Fanu and by the gothic writers, but he soon shed those skins in developing a style and approach of his own which became so unique and such a trademark that few have been able to follow in his footsteps. Many may have been inspired to write by reading his work, but few have been able to capture the spirit of his best stories. He ploughed a lonesome furrow from which sprouted a rare fruit—the uniquely super-Natural tale.

For Blackwood explored the world of horrors in the wide outdoors. Seldom did he turn to the haunted house—though he did occasionally, and a couple will be found in this book. Blackwood was at his best writing about the world of nature. He was himself a nature mystic and spent his life travelling and sleeping beneath the stars in the wild parts of the world. 'I have slept in strange places,' he later recorded, 'high in the Caucasus, on the shores of the Black Sea, on the Egyptian desert, on the banks of the Danube, in the Black Forest and Hungary ...', and each time would be a source of wonder and inspiration:

> Here I lay and communed ... There were no signs of men, no sounds of human life ... nothing but a sighing wind and a sort of earth-murmur under the trees, and I used to think that God, whatever He was, or the great spiritual forces that I believed lay behind all phenomena ... must be nearer to one's consciousness in places like this than among the bustling of men in the towns and houses. As the material world faded away among the shadows, I felt dimly the real spiritual world behind shining through ... I meditated on the meaning of these dreams till the veil over outer things seemed very thin; diving down into my inner consciousness as deeply as I could till a stream of tremendous yearning for the realities that lay beyond appearances poured out of me into the night.

Blackwood became possessed by nature:

> When possession was at its full height, the ordinary world, and my particular little troubles with it, fell away like so much dust; the whole fabric of men and women, commerce and politics, even the destinies of nations, became a passing show of shadows, while the visible and tangible world showed itself as but a temporary and limited representation of a real world elsewhere whose threshold I had for a moment touched.

Blackwood's creative faculties were thus open to channels of inspiration denied many writers through their own suffocation by humanity. Blackwood was able to reach beyond the human world into the real world of Nature, the one few eyes see. 'Do we possess faculties which, under exceptional stimulus, register beyond the normal gamut of seeing, hearing, feeling?' Blackwood wrote in 1938. 'Such exceptional stimulus may be pathogenic, or due to some dynamic flash of terror or beauty which strikes a Man in the Street.'

Blackwood's own stimulation came from his communion with Nature. This he did to an extent unequalled by other writers of weird fiction, which is what makes him unique, and what makes the best of his fiction examples of rare distinction. The American scholar Jack Sullivan, commenting on two of Blackwood's best-known stories, 'The Willows' and 'The Wendigo', stated that they 'sustain an atmosphere of dread that no one has bettered'. There are many who regard 'The Willows' as the single best story in the history of supernatural fiction, a reputation which is in many ways justifiable.

Blackwood was at his creative peak in the decade prior to the First World War. One might well question how much Blackwood was stimulated by his communion with nature or how much the powers of nature used him as their medium. He himself observed how 'these tales poured from me spontaneously, as though a tap were turned on'. Often the best stories are those that write themselves as they are not the product of laboured effort, but of inner power, direct from the soul, perhaps divinely inspired. It is fortunate that Blackwood led such an itinerant and adventurous life that he found himself in a sufficient variety of places to produce a wide range of nature-inspired, 'pantheistic' stories. Without dwelling too deeply on biographical details it might be useful for a better appreciation of Blackwood's stories, to know something of his life and travels.

Algernon Blackwood was born in Shooter's Hill in Kent on 14 March 1869. His father was then a clerk to the Treasury and he would rise to be Permanent Secretary to the Post Office. His mother was, through her first marriage, the Dowager Duchess of Manchester. Through his father, Blackwood was related to Sir Frederick Blackwood, Lord Dufferin. Blackwood was thus never far from aristocratic circles. Both his parents were ardent evangelists and young Blackwood was reared under constant threat of hellfire and damnation. It was this rigidly restricted view of the world that made Blackwood a rather naïve and gullible youth, but it also kept about him an unspoilt air of innocence that even in his later years manifested itself in his ability to talk to children as their equal. The repression also found release in his discovery of eastern religions and the realization that the spirit world might have powers other than those taught by the Bible.

Thus as he grew to manhood Blackwood became a keen student of eastern wisdom and of the occult. He became a theosophist and a Buddhist. Although sent to Edinburgh University to study agriculture he preferred the pathology lectures and closely explored the world of medicine, both physical and mental. He learned hypnotism and yoga, attended seances and investigated haunted houses.

He never graduated in agriculture, but having reached the age of twenty-one, Blackwood was despatched by his father to Canada with the idea that he would establish a farm. Although he received an allowance he was expected to work and, after initial employment in an insurance office and his spare-time teaching of French and German—he was fluent in both—and giving violin lessons, he became assistant editor on the *Methodist Magazine* where some of his early writings appeared. This job lasted only four or five months as his main allowance arrived and Blackwood went into partnership on a dairy farm. It was successful at first but come summer both milk and prospects soured and Blackwood cut his losses. After a summer in the Canadian backwoods he invested what money he had salvaged in a hotel, another fruitless enterprise. By early 1892 Blackwood had dissolved his latest partnership and headed off again for the backwoods.

Adventures followed thick and fast. October 1892 found him in New York working as a reporter. These years are described in graphic detail in his autobiography *Episodes Before Thirty* (1923) which concentrates on his friendship with a petty criminal and how Blackwood was himself forced to track down and arrest the man during the harsh winter of 1892-3. The book also covers his days of illness and privation, working when he could as an actor, an artist's model and again as a reporter. His abortive trip to the Rainy Lake goldfields, the period working for a perfume manufacturer who also turned criminal, were further experiences on his eventual rise to the role of private secretary to the millionaire banker James Speyer.

Blackwood returned to England in 1899 to work in a newly established dried milk concern. At this time he also joined the Hermetic Order of the Golden Dawn and though he rose to the grade of Philosophus his interests in magical studies waned in favour of his more mystical interests. But he continued to investigate haunted houses and other psychic matters.

It was now that he found the need to write: 'I guess that the accumulated horror of the years in New York was seeking expression.' Some were published in magazines but he gave no thought to their book publication until a friend, the journalist Angus Hamilton, sent a selection to the publisher Eveleigh Nash and they were published in 1906 as Blackwood's first collection *The Empty House*. These were mostly traditional ghost and horror stories but they attracted some critical attention, not least from Hilaire Belloc, whose review encouraged Blackwood to try a second book. This became *The Listener* (1907) which includes the masterpiece 'The Willows'. This story had been directly inspired by a trip Blackwood had made in 1900 with his friend Wilfred Wilson down the Danube from its source in the Black Forest to Budapest. Blackwood made two further trips down the Danube and travelled extensively through Europe during the summers of 1900 to 1907. France, Sweden, Italy, Germany, Hungary, and Switzerland were just some of the countries he visited, never the cities or towns, but always the remote areas where the powers of nature had yet to release their hold.

When in 1908 his third book, *John Silence*—a collection of stories about an investigator of the paranormal—proved both a critical and financial success, Blackwood realized he could survive on the income from his writing and this freed him from his London office. He settled in Switzerland, only visiting England, and still travelling widely. In 1910 he journeyed deep into the heart of the Caucasian mountains, an experience that inspired what I believe to be his greatest work, *The Centaur* (1911), one of the profoundest novels in all fantastic literature. In 1912 he made his first trip to Egypt, which he would visit regularly, thereafter.

His travels were only temporarily curtailed by the First World War. He turned his creative skills to propaganda, little of which is worth reading. Inwardly, though, he felt the troubles of the world might be solved by the power of love if everyone concentrated on generating benign thoughts. This rather naïve concept had been the basis of his novel *A Prisoner in Fairyland* (1913) and with the help of Violet Pearn he endeavoured to adapt it for the stage as a children's Christmas musical play. The result, *The Starlight Express*, performed at the Kingsway Theatre in London during December and January 1915-16, was a commercial failure, though many children who saw it loved it dearly. It is remembered today more for its incidental music by Sir Edward Elgar and as the source of the title of Andrew Lloyd Webber's musical.

In 1916 Blackwood was approached with the offer to work as an undercover agent in Switzerland, which he felt was his patriotic duty. He served successfully as an agent during 1917 till his cover was blown and he retreated into France where he worked as a searcher with the Red Cross.

After the war, Blackwood never quite recaptured the full range of his past inspiration. Perhaps the horrors of war had stifled the creative channels. The occasional story as of old appeared, but the majority of his adult stories were of a mundane nature. For the most part he concentrated on writing book reviews and critical essays, working on plays for the stage and in particular writing for children. As his sixties approached he contented himself visiting his many friends, travelling through Europe, and enjoying the company of children. He studied under Gurdjieff and Ouspensky in France, but this seems not to have inspired any new stories. Neither did a final trip to New York in 1933.

In 1934 his career took a new turn. He was interviewed on the popular BBC radio programme *In Town Tonight*. Rather than succumb to the usual interview Blackwood chose to narrate a story. It proved such a success that Cecil Madden, a pioneer radio and television producer, asked Blackwood to tell another story in a special feature spot. His innate skill as a story-teller was ideally suited to the medium of radio. His broadcasts became a regular feature and he also appeared on the first television programme broadcast from London on 2 November 1936.

At the outbreak of the Second World War Blackwood again volunteered for military intelligence, but his services were not wanted. With Europe denied him Blackwood found Britain somewhat restricting. His London lodgings were bombed during the Blitz and he only narrowly escaped though most of his papers and records were destroyed. He settled for a while in Devon and later in Sussex where he continued to write talks and plays for the BBC.

After the war, with the return of television, Blackwood established himself as a regular broadcaster relating his Saturday Night Story. These were never scripted but only mentally rehearsed on his way to the studio. As a result they were broadcast spontaneously, just as if he was bringing the audience into his conversation at the fireside. This knack, combined with his rather spooky appearance—a weather-beaten, highly wrinkled, gaunt visage—made him extremely popular. In 1949 he was awarded both the CBE and the Television Society Medal for services to television. It is probably true that despite the early success of his books, he was better known as a radio and television personality at the time of his death than as an author. He died on 10 December 1951 of cerebral thrombosis and arterio-sclerosis, aged 82.

During his lifetime Blackwood had forty-eight books published. Of these, thirteen were original collections of stories and another nine were retrospective selections of his best stories (a further eight of these have been published since his death—this book is the ninth). It will probably be a surprise to many to find that another thirteen of his books were novels—he wrote as many novels as he did original collections, and yet today his novels are neglected. For that reason I have selected four self-contained extracts from his novels to present to modern readers some of his most powerful writing. Of his novels, *The Centaur* is the most original and imaginative and remains his masterpiece, though *Julius LeVallon* (1916) runs it a close second. Excerpts from both works are included here.

But it is as a short story writer that Blackwood's reputation in the field of supernatural fiction has survived. The thirteen original collections mentioned above—there is a full bibliography at the back of this book—contain a total of 151 stories. In my researches toward a biography of Blackwood I have so far traced over 220 stories, with over 130 more essays and reviews, plus radio talks and plays and other writings. Blackwood was a prolific author and it is perhaps surprising that more collections of his work were not published, especially during his resurgence in the late 1940s. There are a number of reasons why the stories now included here were not previously collected. One was simply that Blackwood lost track of them. He kept little record of his writings relying instead on his literary agents and his friends, but he was so prolific and diverse that many stories were published and forgotten, and when Blackwood's papers were destroyed in the Blitz what little record he had kept was lost. It has taken me nearly ten years to unearth most of the items included here, and I firmly believe there are other writings hidden for future rediscovery.

Another reason is that Blackwood lost his own desire to write. Of his 220 known published stories, around a hundred were written during the eight inspired years between 1907 and the outbreak of war. The second hundred were spread over thirty years—the muse had certainly rationed its gifts. The creative urge had gone. There was no longer the need to express his innermost sentiments. He had said it all. Instead it was replaced by the thrill of story-telling, the oldest art of all. Blackwood now developed his skills not as a writer but as a raconteur. Firstly to children, and then to adults on radio and television. His talent was honed at the many house parties and homes to which he was invited as a 'professional guest', as he liked to call himself.

Writing and story-telling are two distinct talents and Blackwood possessed them both in good measure. None of his masterpieces was written as a story to tell around a camp-fire and though one might try this with 'The Willows', 'The Wendigo' or 'Ancient Sorceries', their length and complexity inhibit the intimacy that is the core of story-telling. This collection includes both kinds of stories. Some of the early tales, written out of the inner desire for expression, and those later tales written down only after having been shaped and reshaped from many after-dinner and pre-bedtime narrations. Some of these were broadcast over the radio only and never published. This volume contains four unpublished stories, one of which, 'Wishful Thinking', so far as I can determine, has never been published or broadcast. It is a shame that the stories cannot now be read aloud by Blackwood, late at night, his cragged face lit only by the firelight and his steel-blue eyes penetrating through to your very soul.

I cannot promise that the stories published here will be on a par with Blackwood's very best, but neither are they his worst. Some of the stories in his later collections, such as *Day and Night Stories, Tongues of Fire* and especially *Ten Minute Stories* are trivia scarcely worthy of attention. Why they should have been published instead of such highly atmospheric tales as 'The Singular Death of Morton', 'La Mauvaise Riche' or 'Onanonanon', I do not know. I can guess that Blackwood's poor memory and inadequate records caused them to be overlooked. I think he just forgot them.

The stories and extracts are presented here in the order they were first published or broadcast, though I have grouped them for reasons of orderliness into his early tales, novels, radio stories and later tales. They span from his very first story published in 1889 to his last written for the adult market and published nearly sixty years later in 1948. Few writers have had longer or more productive careers, and fewer still can be said to have created an entirely new field in literature and made it distinctly his own.

MIKE ASHLEY
Walderslade, Kent
August 1988

THE EARLY YEARS

A MYSTERIOUS HOUSE

So far as I can tell this is Blackwood's first published story. It appeared in *Belgravia* for July 1889 probably fairly soon after it was written. Blackwood was then just twenty years old and was studying at Edinburgh University. There may have been several sources for the story. Blackwood had been investigating haunted houses for a couple of years. He was even encouraged by his father who was acquainted with Frank Podmore who also worked at the Post Office headquarters in London. Podmore was one of the pioneering members of the Society for Psychical Research and Blackwood accompanied him on a number of investigations. Whether one of these was a house in Norfolk, I know not, but Blackwood used Norfolk as a setting in several stories including 'Old Clothes' and the radio talk 'Pistol Against a Ghost'. Two more immediate influences may have been acquaintances Blackwood made at Edinburgh University. One was a certain 'Dr H——', whose wife was a spiritualist medium. Blackwood attended many of their seances and the doctor taught Blackwood how to use hypnotism. Then there was a Hindu medical student who taught Blackwood yoga. 'We made curious and interesting experiments together....' Blackwood enticingly recalls, but he says no more on the matter. We shall encounter this student again.

EXPLANATIONS are usually very tedious, and so without any introduction or preambulation I will plunge right into the midst of this uncanny story I am about to tell.... When, some fifteen years before the time of which I write, I was a schoolboy at Eton I made close friends with a fellow above me in the school, named Pellham. We were very great chums, and later on we went to Cambridge together, where my friend spent money and time in wasting both, while I read for holy orders, though I never actually entered the Church. Since that time I had completely lost sight of him and he of me, and, with the exception of seeing his marriage in the papers, had no news at all of his whereabouts. One morning, however, towards the close of September 1857, I received a letter from him, short, precise, and evidently written in a great hurry, asking me to go down and see him at his family seat just outside Norwich. I packed my bag and went that very same evening. He met me himself at the station and drove me home. We hardly recognized each other at first sight, so much had we changed in appearance, both being on the dark side of thirty-five, but our individual characters had remained much the same and we were still to all appearances the best of friends. My friend was not very talkatively disposed, and I kept up a fire of questions until we drew up at the park gates. Going up the drive to the house he brightened up considerably, and gave me plenty of information about himself and family. He was quite alone, I was surprised to hear, his wife and two daughters with an uncle of his having left for the Continent two days previously. After dinner he seemed quite the old 'Cambridge Undergrad' again, and once settled round the old-fashioned hearth, with cheroots and coffee, we talked on over the days spent at Eton and Cambridge. We were just discussing our third edition of tobacco, when Pellham suddenly changed the subject, and said he would tell me now why he had written so shortly to me to pay him this unexpected visit. His face grew grave as he began by asking me if I was still a sceptic as regards ghostly manifestations.

'Indeed I am,' was my answer; 'I have had no reason to change my views on the subject, and think exactly as I used to at Cambridge, when we so strongly differed; but I remember you then saying that, if ever in after years you should come across an opportunity of proving to me your ideas on the subject, you would write to me at once, and I also recollect giving my word that, if possible, I would come. But during the fifteen years that have since passed by I have bestowed little, if any, thought on the subject.'

'Exactly,' answered Pellham, with a grave smile that did not please me; 'but now I have at last heard of a case which will satisfy us both, I think, so I wrote to you to come down and fulfil your old promise by investigating it.'

'Well! Let me hear all about it first', I said cautiously. I certainly was not overjoyed to hear this news, for, though a sceptic to all intents and purposes, still 'ghosts' was a subject for which I had a certain fear, and the highest ambition of my life was not to investigate haunted houses and the like just because I had years ago promised I would should a chance occur. But I repressed my feelings and tried to look interested, which I was, and delighted, which I certainly was not. Pellham then gave me a long account—thrilling enough too it was—of the case, which I have somewhat condensed in the following form. Some three or four years before, my friend had bought up a house which stood on the moorland about eight miles off. One morning before breakfast the tenant of the house, a Mr Sherleigh (who was there with his family), suddenly burst into my friend's study without any ceremony, and, in great heat and excitement, shouted out the following words:

'You shall suffer for it, Lord Pellham, my wife mad, and the little boy killed with fright, because you didn't choose to warn us of the room next to the drawing-room, but you shall——' Here the footman entered, and at a sign from his master led the excited and evidently cracked old man from the room, but not before he had crashed down some gold pieces on the table, with: 'That's the last rent you'll get for that house, as sure as I am the last tenant.'

'Well,' continued my friend, 'that very day, now two years ago, I rode over there myself and the house was empty. The Sherleighs had left it, and since that day I have never been able to let it to anyone. Mr Sherleigh, who was quite mad, poor fellow, threw himself before a train, and was cut to pieces, and Mrs Sherleigh spread a report that it was haunted, and now no one will take it or even go near it, though it stands high and is in a very healthy position. Two nights ago,' he went on gravely, 'I was riding past the road which leads up to it, and through the trees I could see light in one of the upper rooms, and figures, or rather shadows, of a woman's figure, with something in her arms, kept crossing to and fro before the window-blind. I determined to go in and see what on earth it was, and tying my horse just outside I went in. In a minute or two I was close underneath the window where the light was still visible, and the shadow still moving to and fro with a horrible regularity. As I stood there, undecided, a feeling within warned me not to enter the house, so vivid, it was almost a soft voice that whispered in my ear. I heard no noise inside, the night air was moaning gently through the fir trees which surrounded the house on one side and nearly obscured the upper part of the window from view. I stooped down and picked up a large stone—it was a sharp-edged flint—and without any hesitation hurled it with all my might at the window pane, some eight or ten feet from the ground. The stone went straight and struck the window on one of the wooden partitions, smashing the whole framework, glass and all, into a thousand splinters, many of which struck me where I stood. The result was awful and unexpected. The moment the stone touched the glass the lights quite disappeared, and in the blackness in which I was shrouded, the next minute, I could see hiding behind the broken corners of glass a dark face and form for a short instant, and then it went and all was pitch dark again. There I was among those gloomy pine trees hardly knowing which way to turn. The face I had caught a momentary glimpse of was the face of Mr Sherleigh, whom I knew to be dead! My knees trembled. I tried to grope my way out of the wood, and stumbled from tree to tree, often striking my head against the low branches. In vain. With the weird light in the window as a guide, I had taken but a few minutes to come, but now all was dark and I could not find my way back again. I felt as if the dismal tree trunks were living things, which seemed to move. Suddenly I heard a noise on my left. I stopped and listened. Horror! I was still close to the window, and what I heard was a cracking and splintering of broken glass, as if some one from inside were slowly forcing their way out through the hole made by my stone! Was it he? The fir tree next to me suddenly shook violently, as if agitated by a powerful gust of wind, and then in a gleam of weird light I saw a long dark body hanging half-way out of the window, with black hair streaming down the shoulders. It raised one arm and slammed down something at my feet which fell with a rattle, and then hissed out: "There's the last rent you'll ever have for this house." I stood literally stupefied with horror, then a cold numb sensation came over me and I fell fainting on my face, but not until I had heard my horse give a prolonged neigh and then his footsteps dying away in the distance on the hard moorland road.

...When I recovered consciousness it was broad daylight. I was cold and damp; all night I had lain where I fell. I rose and limped, stiff and tired, to the place where I had tied my horse the night before, but no horse was there. And the horrible sound of his hoofs echoing away in the distance came back to me, and I shuddered as I thought of what I had seen. After a terrible trudge of three hours I reached home. A tremendous search had been made for me, of course, but no one dreamt of looking for me where I really was. The horse had found his way home, and I have never found out what frightened him so.'

My friend's account was over. He lit his cigar, which had gone out during the narrative, and settling himself comfortably in his chair, said, 'Well, old boy, that's a case I don't feel at all inclined to investigate by myself, but I'll do it with your aid. You know, a genuine sceptic is a great addition in such things, so we'll get to the bottom of it somehow.'

My feelings at that moment were not difficult to describe. I disliked the whole affair, and wanted heartily to get out of it; and yet something urged me to go through with it and show my friend that the house was all right, that imagination did it all, that the horse may have taken fright at anything, and that very possibly there really was someone in the house all the time, and imagination had done the rest. Such were the somewhat mixed thoughts in my mind at the time. However, in a few moments all was settled and we had agreed to go the following night, search the house first, and then sit up all night in the room next to the drawing-room. Then we both went to our separate bedrooms to think the matter over and get a long sleep, as we neither expected to get any the following night.

Next morning at breakfast we both talked cheerfully about the coming night and how best to meet its requirements as regards food, etc. We agreed to take pistols for weapons, horses as a means of conveyance, and abundant food wherewith to fortify ourselves against a possible attack of ghosts.

The day drew on towards its close. It was very hot and sultry weather, and not a breath of wind stirred the murky atmosphere, as at 4.30 p.m. we bestrode our horses and made off in the direction of the 'White House'. A long gravel road, lonely in the extreme, led us across the wild uncultivated moorland for six or seven miles, then we saw a copse of fir trees which, my friend informed me, were the trees which sheltered one side of the house. In a few minutes we had passed through the front garden gate and were among the dark fir trees, and then as we turned a sharp corner the house burst full upon us. It was square and ugly. Great staring windows in regular rows met our eyes and conveyed an unpleasant impression to the brain—at least, they did to mine. From the very moment we had passed the front gate till I left the house next morning, I felt a nasty sick sensation creep over me, a feeling of numbness and torpor which seemed to make the blood run thick and sluggish in my veins. The events of that night have remained engraven on my brain as with fire, and, though they happened years ago, I can see them now as vividly as then. Only an eye-witness can possibly describe them, should he wish to do justice to them, and so my feeble pen shall make the attempt.

It was about 6.30, and we had settled our horses in a barn outside for the night. There were only two walls to keep the barn in position, and these were simply a row of rotten posts, half-decayed in places, so we securely tied the horses and, with a good supply of hay, left them for the night. We then approached the door and, after fumbling in the lock for some time, Pellham succeeded in opening it. A sickly, musty odour pervaded the hall, and the first thing we did after a thorough search, which revealed nothing, was to open all the doors and windows all over the house, so as to let in what little air there was. Then we went upstairs into the little room next to the drawing-room, where, according to Sherleigh, strange things had occurred. But the window was in pieces, and hardly an entire pane of glass was left, and we were forced to select another room on the same floor (i.e., the second) and looking out on the same copse of pine trees, whose branches almost touched the glass, so close were they. It was a very ordinary room; a fireplace, no furniture but a rickety table and three chairs, one of which was broken. The only disagreeable feature we noticed about the room was its gloominess; it was so very dark. The trees outside, as I have already said, were so close that the slightest breath of wind rustled their twigs against the window. We soon had six candles fixed and burning in different parts of the little room, and the blaze of light was still further increased by a roaring fire, on which a kettle was singing for tea, and eggs boiling in a saucepan, and at half-past seven we were in the middle of our first tea in a haunted house. It was, indeed, less luxurious than the dinners I had been used to lately, but otherwise there was nothing to find fault with, and a little later the tea things were cleared away in a heap in a corner (where, by-the-by, they are to this day), and we were sitting round an empty table, smoking in silence. The door out into the passage was fast shut, but the window was wide open. The sun had sunk out of sight in a beautiful sky of wonderful colouring. Small fleecy clouds floating about caught the soft after-glow and looked unearthly as seen through the thick fir branches. The faint red hue of the western sky looked like the reflection of some huge and distant conflagration, growing dimmer and fainter as the dark engines of the night played upon it, extinguishing the leaping flames and suffusing the sky with a red reflected glow. Not a breath of air stirred the trees. My friend had left the window and was poking and arranging the fire, with his back turned towards me. I was standing close to the window, looking at the fast-fading colours, when it seemed to me that the window sash was moving. I looked closer. Yes!

I was not mistaken. The lower half was gradually sinking; gradually and very quietly it went down. At first I thought the weight had slipped and gone wrong, and the window was slipping down of its own accord; but when I saw the bolt pulled across and fastened as by an invisible hand, I thought differently. My first impulse was to immediately undo the bolt again and open the window, but on trying to move—good heavens! I found I had lost all power of motion and could not move a muscle of my body. I was literally rooted to the ground. Neither could I move the muscles of my tongue or mouth; I could not speak or utter a sound. Pellham was still doing something to the fire, and I could hear him muttering to himself, though I could not distinguish any words. Suddenly, then, I felt the power of motion returning to me; my muscles were relaxing, and turning, though not without a considerable effort, I walked to the fireplace. Pellham, then, for the first time noticed that the window was shut, and he made a remark about the closeness of the night, asking me why I had closed it.

'Hulloa,' he went on, before I had time to answer, 'by the gods above! What is happening to that window? Look—why it's moving!'

I turned. *The window was slowly being opened again.*

Yes, sure enough it was. Slowly and steadily it moved or was pushed up.

We could but believe our eyes; in half a minute the window was wide open again. I turned and looked at Pellham and he looked at me, and in dead silence we stared at one another, neither knowing what to say or wishing to break the silence. But at length my friend spoke.

'I wish I were a sceptic, old man, like you are; sceptics are always safer in a place like this.'

'Yes,' I said, as cheerfully as I could, 'I feel safe enough, and what's more, I am convinced that the window was opened by human agency from outside.'

Pellham smiled, he knew as well as I that no human fingers could have fastened the bolt from outside. 'Well,' he said briskly, 'perhaps you are right; come, let's examine the window.'

We rose and approached it, and my friend put his head and shoulders out into the air. It was very dark, and a strange oppressive stillness reigned outside, only broken by the gentle moaning sound of the night wind as it rustled through the trees and swept their branches like the strings of a lyre. I followed my friend's example, and together we peered out into the night. Soon my eyes rested on the ground below us, and at the base of one of the nearer pines I thought I could distinguish a black form, clinging, as it seemed, to the tree. I pointed it out to Pellham, who failed to see anything, or at least said so; anyhow, I was glad to believe that my excited imagination was the real cause. We were still leaning out of the window in silence, when several of the trees, especially the one where I imagined I had seen the shape, were most violently agitated, as though by a mighty wind; but we felt not the slightest breath on our faces. At the same instant we heard a subdued shuffling sound in the room behind us, which seemed to come from the direction of the chimney. But neither of us referred to it as we slowly walked back to the fire and took up our places on either side on the two chairs, which were at the best very rickety.

'It isn't wise to leave the window open,' said my friend, suddenly, 'for if there really is anyone outside, they can see all and everything we do; while we, for our part, can see absolutely nothing of what goes on outside.'

I agreed, and walked up to the window, shutting it with a bang and firmly drawing the bolt.

'I've brought a book,' he went on, 'which I thought we might read out aloud in turn to relieve the dullness and the silence.'

He stopped speaking and looked at me, and at the same moment I raised my eyes to his face. To my intense horror and surprise I noticed for the first time a long smear of blood, wet and crimson, across his forehead. My horror was so great that for some seconds I could not find my tongue, and sat stupidly staring at him. At last I gasped out:

'My dear fellow, what has happened to you, have you cut yourself?'

'Where? What do you mean?' he replied, looking round him with surprise.

For answer I took out my handkerchief, and wiping his brow, showed him the red stains. But as I stood there showing him this proof and as he was expressing his utter astonishment, I distinctly saw something that for the moment made the blood rush from the extremities and crowd into my head. Something seemed to tighten round my heart. I saw a large, gleaming knife and hand disappear into the air in the direction of the window. It was too much; my nerves failed me, and I dropped fainting to the floor.

When I came to myself I was lying where I fell by the fireplace. Pellham was sitting beside me.

'I thought you were dead,' he said, 'you've been unconscious for over an hour.' He said this in such a queer manner and laughed so fiendishly that I wondered what had happened to him during the interval. Had he seen something awful and gone mad? There was a strange light in his dark eyes and a leer on his lips. Just then he took up his book quite naturally and began to read aloud, every now and then he made a comment on what he was reading, quite sensibly too, and soon I began to think, as I sipped my brandy out of our flask, that I must have had a frightful dream. But there at my feet lay the blood-stained handkerchief, and I could not get over that. I glanced at his face; the smear had disappeared, and no scratch or wound was visible.

Pellham had not been reading long, perhaps some five or ten minutes, when we heard a strange noise outside among the trees, just audible above the death-like stillness of the autumn night. It was a confused voice like the low whispering of several persons, and as I listened, still weak from the last shock, the blood stood still in my veins. Pellham went on reading as usual. This struck me as very curious, for he must have heard the noise plainly; but I said nothing, and glancing at him I saw the same light in his eyes and the evil leer on his mouth, looking ugly in the flickering glare of the candles and firelight.

Suddenly we heard a tremendous noise outside, altogether drowning the first. The horses had broken loose and were tearing wildly past the house. Long and wild neighs rang out and died away, and we knew our horses were gone. Pellham was still reading, and as I looked at him a sudden and horrid thought flashed through my brain. It was this: had he anything to do with this? Was it possible? Before I had time to answer my question Pellham threw down the book and made for the door, locked it, drew out the key, and opening the window threw it far away among the trees. I then recognized the awful fact that I was alone with a madman. I glanced at my watch, it was a quarter to one. Instead of one hour I must have been unconscious two at least. This was terrible in the extreme. He was a man of far more powerful physique than I. What was to be done? Pellham strode grinning up to the fire, went down on both knees and commenced blowing between the bars with all his might. I saw my chance, and quietly walking to the window, without a word I climbed out, and letting myself as far down as my arms would allow I then let go and dropped. It was a distance of four or five feet, but in the darkness I tumbled forward on my face. As I rose, uninjured, I distinctly heard the sound of running feet close to me, but in my bewilderment I could not make out clearly in which direction they were going; they only lasted a moment or two. But what a terrific sight met my gaze as I turned the corner of the house, and saw volumes of smoke pouring steadily out of the windows and roof of the back portion of the house. Now and again a long flame, too, shot up to heaven.

'Good God!' I cried, 'the house is on fire.'

No wonder the horses had taken flight. But my poor friend, what could I do for him? The window was too high for me to climb in again, and the doors were locked. In a few minutes the flames would spread to this side of the house and the poor fellow would be burnt to death unless he had enough sense left to jump out of the window.

I hurried back to the spot where I had let myself down from the window, just in time to see the last scene of the most ghastly experience I have ever witnessed. Pellham was standing at the window. In his hand was a red-hot poker, and it was pointed at his throat, but the strain was too great for my nervous system and with a violent start *I woke up!*

After our heavy tea we had both fallen asleep, just as we were in our chairs. Pellham was still snoring opposite me, and the light was stealing in through the window. It was morning, about half-past six. All the candles had burnt themselves out, and it was a wonder they had not set fire to the dry wood near them.

Twenty minutes later we had re-lit the fire and were discussing the remnant of eggs and coffee. Half an hour later we were riding home in the bright, crisp, morning air, and an hour and a half later we were in the middle of a second and far superior breakfast, during which I did *not* tell my dream, but during which we *did* agree that it had been the dullest and most uncomfortable night we had ever spent away from home.

THE KIT-BAG

There is a span of almost 20 years between 'A Mysterious House' and this story which appeared in *Pall Mall Magazine* for December 1908. By now Blackwood was a published author with over thirty stories and three books to his credit. There were other uncollected stories published in magazines during this period but none that I have found with supernatural or mysterious themes. The most interesting is 'How Garnier Broke the Logjam' (1904), a tale of derring-do amongst the Canadian lumberjacks. I suspect that 'The Kit-bag' was written at the same time as the other stories that make up *The Listener*. It's set in Bloomsbury, the same locale as that title story and others, which Blackwood frequented at that time, and has much the same mood about it. Blackwood was still shaking off the shackles of the traditional ghost story and had yet to unleash the power of his nature stories.

WHEN the words 'Not Guilty' sounded through the crowded courtroom that dark December afternoon, Arthur Wilbraham, the great criminal KC, and leader for the triumphant defence, was represented by his junior; but Johnson, his private secretary, carried the verdict across to his chambers like lightning.

'It's what we expected, I think,' said the barrister, without emotion; 'and, personally, I am glad the case is over.' There was no particular sign of pleasure that his defence of John Turk, the murderer, on a plea of insanity, had been successful, for no doubt he felt, as everybody who had watched the case felt, that no man had ever better deserved the gallows.

'I'm glad too,' said Johnson. He had sat in the court for ten days watching the face of the man who had carried out with callous detail one of the most brutal and cold-blooded murders of recent years.

The counsel glanced up at his secretary. They were more than employer and employed; for family and other reasons, they were friends. 'Ah, I remember; yes,' he said with a kind smile, 'and you want to get away for Christmas? You're going to skate and ski in the Alps, aren't you? If I was your age I'd come with you.'

Johnson laughed shortly. He was a young man of twenty-six, with a delicate face like a girl's. 'I can catch the morning boat now,' he said; 'but that's not the reason I'm glad the trial is over. I'm glad it's over because I've seen the last of that man's dreadful face. It positively haunted me. That white skin, with the black hair brushed low over the forehead, is a thing I shall never forget, and the description of the way the dismembered body was crammed and packed with lime into that——'

'Don't dwell on it, my dear fellow,' interrupted the other, looking at him curiously out of his keen eyes, 'don't think about it. Such pictures have a trick of coming back when one least wants them.' He paused a moment. 'Now go,' he added presently, 'and enjoy your holiday. I shall want all your energy for my Parliamentary work when you get back. And don't break your neck skiing.'

Johnson shook hands and took his leave. At the door he turned suddenly.

'I knew there was something I wanted to ask you,' he said. 'Would you mind lending me one of your kit-bags? It's too late to get one tonight, and I leave in the morning before the shops are open.'

'Of course; I'll send Henry over with it to your rooms. You shall have it the moment I get home.'

'I promise to take great care of it,' said Johnson gratefully, delighted to think that within thirty hours he would be nearing the brilliant sunshine of the high Alps in winter. The thought of that criminal court was like an evil dream in his mind.

He dined at his club and went on to Bloomsbury, where he occupied the top floor in one of those old, gaunt houses in which the rooms are large and lofty. The floor below his own was vacant and unfurnished, and below that were other lodgers whom he did not know. It was cheerless, and he looked forward heartily to a change. The night was even more cheerless: it was miserable, and few people were about. A cold, sleety rain was driving down the streets before the keenest east wind he had ever felt. It howled dismally among the big, gloomy houses of the great squares, and when he reached his rooms he heard it whistling and shouting over the world of black roofs beyond his windows.

In the hall he met his landlady, shading a candle from the draughts with her thin hand. 'This come by a man from Mr Wilbr'im's, sir.'

She pointed to what was evidently the kit-bag, and Johnson thanked her and took it upstairs with him. 'I shall be going abroad in the morning for ten days, Mrs Monks,' he said. 'I'll leave an address for letters.'

'And I hope you'll 'ave a merry Christmas, sir,' she said, in a raucous, wheezy voice that suggested spirits, 'and better weather than this.'

'I hope so too,' replied her lodger, shuddering a little as the wind went roaring down the street outside.

When he got upstairs he heard the sleet volleying against the window panes. He put his kettle on to make a cup of hot coffee, and then set about putting a few things in order for his absence. 'And now I must pack—such as my packing is,' he laughed to himself, and set to work at once.

He liked the packing, for it brought the snow mountains so vividly before him, and made him forget the unpleasant scenes of the past ten days. Besides, it was not elaborate in nature. His friend had lent him the very thing—a stout canvas kit-bag, sack-shaped, with holes round the neck for the brass bar and padlock. It was a bit shapeless, true, and not much to look at, but its capacity was unlimited, and there was no need to pack carefully. He shoved in his waterproof coat, his fur cap and gloves, his skates and climbing boots, his sweaters, snow-boots, and ear-caps; and then on the top of these he piled his woollen shirts and underwear, his thick socks, puttees, and knickerbockers. The dress suit came next, in case the hotel people dressed for dinner, and then, thinking of the best way to pack his white shirts, he paused a moment to reflect. 'That's the worst of these kit-bags,' he mused vaguely, standing in the centre of the sitting-room, where he had come to fetch some string.

It was after ten o'clock. A furious gust of wind rattled the windows as though to hurry him up, and he thought with pity of the poor Londoners whose Christmas would be spent in such a climate, whilst he was skimming over snowy slopes in bright sunshine, and dancing in the evening with rosy-cheeked girls—— Ah! that reminded him; he must put in his dancing-pumps and evening socks. He crossed over from his sitting-room to the cupboard on the landing where he kept his linen.

And as he did so he heard someone coming softly up the stairs. He stood still a moment on the landing to listen. It was Mrs Monks's step, he thought; she must be coming up with the last post. But then the steps ceased suddenly, and he heard no more. They were at least two flights down, and he came to the conclusion they were too heavy to be those of his bibulous landlady. No doubt they belonged to a late lodger who had mistaken his floor. He went into his bedroom and packed his pumps and dress-shirts as best he could.

The kit-bag by this time was two-thirds full, and stood upright on its own base like a sack of flour. For the first time he noticed that it was old and dirty, the canvas faded and worn, and that it had obviously been subjected to rather rough treatment. It was not a very nice bag to have sent him—certainly not a new one, or one that his chief valued. He gave the matter a passing thought, and went on with his packing. Once or twice, however, he caught himself wondering who it could have been wandering down below, for Mrs Monks had not come up with letters, and the floor was empty and unfurnished. From time to time, moreover, he was almost certain he heard a soft tread of someone padding about over the bare boards—cautiously, stealthily, as silently as possible—and, further, that the sounds had been lately coming distinctly nearer.

For the first time in his life he began to feel a little creepy. Then, as though to emphasize this feeling, an odd thing happened: as he left the bedroom, having just packed his recalcitrant white shirts, he noticed that the top of the kit-bag lopped over towards him with an extraordinary resemblance to a human face. The canvas fell into a fold like a nose and forehead, and the brass rings for the padlock just filled the position of the eyes. A shadow—or was it a travel stain? for he could not tell exactly—looked like hair. It gave him rather a turn, for it was so absurdly, so outrageously, like the face of John Turk, the murderer.

He laughed, and went into the front room, where the light was stronger.

'That horrid case has got on my mind,' he thought; 'I shall be glad of a change of scene and air.' In the sitting-room, however, he was not pleased to hear again that stealthy tread upon the stairs, and to realize that it was much closer than before, as well as unmistakably real. And this time he got up and went out to see who it could be creeping about on the upper staircase at so late an hour.

But the sound ceased; there was no one visible on the stairs. He went to the floor below, not without trepidation, and turned on the electric light to make sure that no one was hiding in the empty rooms of the unoccupied suite. There was not a stick of furniture large enough to hide a dog. Then he called over the banisters to Mrs Monks, but there was no answer, and his voice echoed down into the dark vault of the house, and was lost in the roar of the gale that howled outside. Everyone was in bed and asleep—everyone except himself and the owner of this soft and stealthy tread.

'My absurd imagination, I suppose,' he thought. 'It must have been the wind after all, although—it seemed so *very* real and close, I thought.' He went back to his packing. It was by this time getting on towards midnight. He drank his coffee up and lit another pipe—the last before turning in.

It is difficult to say exactly at what point fear begins, when the causes of that fear are not plainly before the eyes. Impressions gather on the surface of the mind, film by film, as ice gathers upon the surface of still water, but often so lightly that they claim no definite recognition from the consciousness. Then a point is reached where the accumulated impressions become a definite emotion, and the mind realizes that something has happened. With something of a start, Johnson suddenly recognized that he felt nervous—oddly nervous; also, that for some time past the causes of this feeling had been gathering slowly in his mind, but that he had only just reached the point where he was forced to acknowledge them.

It was a singular and curious malaise that had come over him, and he hardly knew what to make of it. He felt as though he were doing something that was strongly objected to by another person, another person, moreover, who had some right to object. It was a most disturbing and disagreeable feeling, not unlike the persistent promptings of conscience: almost, in fact, as if he were doing something he knew to be wrong. Yet, though he searched vigorously and honestly in his mind, he could nowhere lay his finger upon the secret of this growing uneasiness, and it perplexed him. More, it distressed and frightened him.

'Pure nerves, I suppose,' he said aloud with a forced laugh. 'Mountain air will cure all that! Ah,' he added, still speaking to himself, 'and that reminds me—my snow-glasses.'

He was standing by the door of the bedroom during this brief soliloquy, and as he passed quickly towards the sitting-room to fetch them from the cupboard he saw out of the corner of his eye the indistinct outline of a figure standing on the stairs, a few feet from the top. It was someone in a stooping position, with one hand on the banisters, and the face peering up towards the landing. And at the same moment he heard a shuffling footstep. The person who had been creeping about below all this time had at last come up to his own floor. Who in the world could it be? And what in the name of Heaven did he want?

Johnson caught his breath sharply and stood stock still. Then, after a few seconds' hesitation, he found his courage, and turned to investigate. The stairs, he saw to his utter amazement, were empty; there was no one. He felt a series of cold shivers run over him, and something about the muscles of his legs gave a little and grew weak. For the space of several minutes he peered steadily into the shadows that congregated about the top of the staircase where he had seen the figure, and then he walked fast—almost ran, in fact—into the light of the front room; but hardly had he passed inside the doorway when he heard someone come up the stairs behind him with a quick bound and go swiftly into his bedroom. It was a heavy, but at the same time a stealthy footstep—the tread of somebody who did not wish to be seen. And it was at this precise moment that the nervousness he had hitherto experienced leaped the boundary line, and entered the state of fear, almost of acute, unreasoning fear. Before it turned into terror there was a further boundary to cross, and beyond that again lay the region of pure horror. Johnson's position was an unenviable one.

'By Jove! That *was* someone on the stairs, then,' he muttered, his flesh crawling all over; 'and whoever it was has now gone into my bedroom.' His delicate, pale face turned absolutely white, and for some minutes he hardly knew what to think or do. Then he realized intuitively that delay only set a premium upon fear; and he crossed the landing boldly and went straight into the other room, where, a few seconds before, the steps had disappeared.

'Who's there? Is that you, Mrs Monks?' he called aloud, as he went, and heard the first half of his words echo down the empty stairs, while the second half fell dead against the curtains in a room that apparently held no other human figure than his own.

'Who's there?' he called again, in a voice unnecessarily loud and that only just held firm. 'What do you want here?'

The curtains swayed very slightly, and, as he saw it, his heart felt as if it almost missed a beat; yet he dashed forward and drew them aside with a rush. A window, streaming with rain, was all that met his gaze. He continued his search, but in vain; the cupboards held nothing but rows of clothes, hanging motionless; and under the bed there was no sign of anyone hiding. He stepped backwards into the middle of the room, and, as he did so, something all but tripped him up. Turning with a sudden spring of alarm he saw—the kit-bag.

'Odd!' he thought. 'That's not where I left it!' A few moments before it had surely been on his right, between the bed and the bath; he did not remember having moved it. It was very curious. What in the world was the matter with everything? Were all his senses gone queer? A terrific gust of wind tore at the windows, dashing the sleet against the glass with the force of small gunshot, and then fled away howling dismally over the waste of Bloomsbury roofs. A sudden vision of the Channel next day rose in his mind and recalled him sharply to realities.

'There's no one here at any rate; that's quite clear!' he exclaimed aloud. Yet at the time he uttered them he knew perfectly well that his words were not true and that he did not believe them himself. He felt exactly as though someone was hiding close about him, watching all his movements, trying to hinder his packing in some way. 'And two of my senses,' he added, keeping up the pretence, 'have played me the most absurd tricks: the steps I heard and the figure I saw were both entirely imaginary.'

He went back to the front room, poked the fire into a blaze, and sat down before it to think. What impressed him more than anything else was the fact that the kit-bag was no longer where he had left it. It had been dragged nearer to the door.

What happened afterwards that night happened, of course, to a man already excited by fear, and was perceived by a mind that had not the full and proper control, therefore, of the senses. Outwardly, Johnson remained calm and master of himself to the end, pretending to the very last that everything he witnessed had a natural explanation, or was merely delusions of his tired nerves. But inwardly, in his very heart, he knew all along that someone had been hiding downstairs in the empty suite when he came in, that this person had watched his opportunity and then stealthily made his way up to the bedroom, and that all he saw and heard afterwards, from the moving of the kit-bag to—well, to the other things this story has to tell—were caused directly by the presence of this invisible person.

And it was here, just when he most desired to keep his mind and thoughts controlled, that the vivid pictures received day after day upon the mental plates exposed in the courtroom of the Old Bailey, came strongly to light and developed themselves in the dark room of his inner vision. Unpleasant, haunting memories have a way of coming to life again just when the mind least desires them—in the silent watches of the night, on sleepless pillows, during the lonely hours spent by sick and dying beds. And so now, in the same way, Johnson saw nothing but the dreadful face of John Turk, the murderer, lowering at him from every corner of his mental field of vision; the white skin, the evil eyes, and the fringe of black hair low over the forehead. All the pictures of those ten days in court crowded back into his mind unbidden, and very vivid.

'This is all rubbish and nerves,' he exclaimed at length, springing with sudden energy from his chair. 'I shall finish my packing and go to bed. I'm overwrought, overtired. No doubt, at this rate I shall hear steps and things all night!'

But his face was deadly white all the same. He snatched up his fieldglasses and walked across to the bedroom, humming a music-hall song as he went—a trifle too loud to be natural; and the instant he crossed the threshold and stood within the room something turned cold about his heart, and he felt that every hair on his head stood up.

The kit-bag lay close in front of him, several feet nearer to the door than he had left it, and just over its crumpled top he saw a head and face slowly sinking down out of sight as though someone were crouching behind it to hide, and at the same moment a sound like a long-drawn sigh was distinctly audible in the still air about him between the gusts of the storm outside.

Johnson had more courage and will-power than the girlish indecision of his face indicated; but at first such a wave of terror came over him that for some seconds he could do nothing but stand and stare. A violent trembling ran down his back and legs, and he was conscious of a foolish, almost a hysterical, impulse to scream aloud. That sigh seemed in his very ear, and the air still quivered with it. It was unmistakably a human sigh.

'Who's there?' he said at length, finding his voice; but though he meant to speak with loud decision, the tones came out instead in a faint whisper, for he had partly lost the control of his tongue and lips.

He stepped forward, so that he could see all round and over the kit-bag. Of course there was nothing there, nothing but the faded carpet and the bulging canvas sides. He put out his hands and threw open the mouth of the sack where it had fallen over, being only three parts full, and then he saw for the first time that round the inside, some six inches from the top, there ran a broad smear of dull crimson. It was an old and faded blood stain. He uttered a scream, and drew back his hands as if they had been burnt. At the same moment the kit-bag gave a faint, but unmistakable, lurch forward towards the door.

Johnson collapsed backwards, searching with his hands for the support of something solid, and the door, being farther behind him than he realized, received his weight just in time to prevent his falling, and shut to with a resounding bang. At the same moment the swinging of his left arm accidentally touched the electric switch, and the light in the room went out.

It was an awkward and disagreeable predicament, and if Johnson had not been possessed of real pluck he might have done all manner of foolish things. As it was, however, he pulled himself together, and groped furiously for the little brass knob to turn the light on again. But the rapid closing of the door had set the coats hanging on it a-swinging, and his fingers became entangled in a confusion of sleeves and pockets, so that it was some moments before he found the switch. And in those few moments of bewilderment and terror two things happened that sent him beyond recall over the boundary into the region of genuine horror—he distinctly heard the kit-bag shuffling heavily across the floor in jerks, and close in front of his face sounded once again the sigh of a human being.

In his anguished efforts to find the brass button on the wall he nearly scraped the nails from his fingers, but even then, in those frenzied moments of alarm—so swift and alert are the impressions of a mind keyed-up by a vivid emotion—he had time to realize that he dreaded the return of the light, and that it might be better for him to stay hidden in the merciful screen of darkness. It was but the impulse of a moment, however, and before he had time to act upon it he had yielded automatically to the original desire, and the room was flooded again with light.

But the second instinct had been right. It would have been better for him to have stayed in the shelter of the kind darkness. For there, close before him, bending over the half-packed kit-bag, clear as life in the merciless glare of the electric light, stood the figure of John Turk, the murderer. Not three feet from him the man stood, the fringe of black hair marked plainly against the pallor of the forehead, the whole horrible presentment of the scoundrel, as vivid as he had seen him day after day in the Old Bailey, when he stood there in the dock, cynical and callous, under the very shadow of the gallows.

In a flash Johnson realized what it all meant: the dirty and much-used bag; the smear of crimson within the top; the dreadful stretched condition of the bulging sides. He remembered how the victim's body had been stuffed into a canvas bag for burial, the ghastly, dismembered fragments forced with lime into this very bag; and the bag itself produced as evidence—it all came back to him as clear as day...

Very softly and stealthily his hand groped behind him for the handle of the door, but before he could actually turn it the very thing that he most of all dreaded came about, and John Turk lifted his devil's face and looked at him. At the same moment that heavy sigh passed through the air of the room, formulated somehow into words: 'It's my bag. And I want it.'

Johnson just remembered clawing the door open, and then falling in a heap upon the floor of the landing, as he tried frantically to make his way into the front room.

He remained unconscious for a long time, and it was still dark when he opened his eyes and realized that he was lying, stiff and bruised, on the cold boards. Then the memory of what he had seen rushed back into his mind, and he promptly fainted again. When he woke the second time the wintry dawn was just beginning to peep in at the windows, painting the stairs a cheerless, dismal grey, and he managed to crawl into the front room, and cover himself with an overcoat in the armchair, where at length he fell asleep.

A great clamour woke him. He recognized Mrs Monks's voice, loud and voluble.

'What! You ain't been to bed, sir! Are you ill, or has anything 'appened? And there's an urgent gentleman to see you, though it ain't seven o'clock yet, and——'

'Who is it?' he stammered. 'I'm all right, thanks. Fell asleep in my chair, I suppose.'

'Someone from Mr Wilb'rim's, and he says he ought to see you quick before you go abroad, and I told him——'

'Show him up, please, at once,' said Johnson, whose head was whirling, and his mind was still full of dreadful visions.

Mr Wilbraham's man came in with many apologies, and explained briefly and quickly that an absurd mistake had been made, and that the wrong kit-bag had been sent over the night before.

'Henry somehow got hold of the one that came over from the courtroom, and Mr Wilbraham only discovered it when he saw his own lying in his room, and asked why it had not gone to you,' the man said.

'Oh!' said Johnson stupidly.

'And he must have brought you the one from the murder case instead, sir, I'm afraid,' the man continued, without the ghost of an expression on his face. 'The one John Turk packed the dead body in.

Mr Wilbraham's awful upset about it, sir, and told me to come over first thing this morning with the right one, as you were leaving by the boat.'

He pointed to a clean-looking kit-bag on the floor, which he had just brought. 'And I was to bring the other one back, sir,' he added casually.

For some minutes Johnson could not find his voice. At last he pointed in the direction of his bedroom. 'Perhaps you would kindly unpack it for me. Just empty the things out on the floor.'

The man disappeared into the other room, and was gone for five minutes. Johnson heard the shifting to and fro of the bag, and the rattle of the skates and boots being unpacked.

'Thank you, sir,' the man said, returning with the bag folded over his arm. 'And can I do anything more to help you, sir?'

'What is it?' asked Johnson, seeing that he still had something he wished to say.

The man shuffled and looked mysterious. 'Beg pardon, sir, but knowing your interest in the Turk case, I thought you'd maybe like to know what's happened——'

'Yes.'

'John Turk killed hisself last night with poison immediately on getting his release, and he left a note for Mr Wilbraham saying as he'd be much obliged if they'd have him put away, same as the woman he murdered, in the old kit-bag.'

'What time—did he do it?' asked Johnson.

'Ten o'clock last night, sir, the warder says.'

THE LAYING OF A RED-HAIRED GHOST

I stumbled across this story only recently whilst completing this collection and no reference is made to it in my *Algernon Blackwood: A Bio-Bibliography* (1987). It is one example of, I suspect, many hidden stories by Blackwood in forgotten magazines from the dawn of this century. I found it in *The Lady's Realm* for September 1909, a magazine which published several interesting but forgotten ghost stories. By this time Blackwood had investigated many seances but, as he later wrote, 'spiritualism, apart from the exciting phenomena it promised . . . left me rather unstirred'. He had encountered many false mediums and perhaps this story was written in response to their activities.

It was a strange and incredible story, Jim thought, as he sat opposite his sister in the firelight, and listened to her nervous and disjointed telling of it. They held little in common, these two, and had not met for some years; she was greatly his senior, and when she had married Captain Blundell, who combined a love of spirits with a credulous belief in spiritualism, Jim sheered off altogether. He could not stand a man who came drunk to his own table, and who, in his sober moments, could talk of nothing but the vulgar claptrap of seances and spirit-rapping.

But now, six months after the funeral, Jim found himself summoned down by a pathetic little letter; and there he was after tea, in a corner of the big drawing-room, watching his sister's pale, emotional face in the firelight, and wondering how any woman could possibly believe all she was telling him.

In spite of this 'wonder', however, he was beginning to feel conscious of a certain 'creepiness' down the back, and several times he caught himself wishing that the footman would bring the lamps, and be quick about it.

'As you know, Jim, Harry was a tremendous spiritualist,' she went on, with a little show of natural embarrassment. 'He was always having seances and what he called "experiments" in the house, up to the day of his seizure.'

'Mediums?' asked Jim, feeling the old contempt stir in him.

She nodded, with a gesture imploring his patience.

'Every professional medium in the United Kingdom has slept in this house,' she answered. 'They came down, male and female, in endless succession for weekend visits, and for two years I kept a diary of all their phenomena.'

Jim shuffled nervously, fearing a detailed account.

'But a few months before his death,' she went on, 'all this came to a sudden stop. He gave up having paid mediums——'

'You must have been glad,' said Jim, with genuine sympathy.

'Because he said he had found something better. You see, our circles were made up of people staying in the house—always devout believers—and when there were not enough of these he brought in recruits from among the servants. First the upper servants, then anybody. Gardeners, grooms, upper housemaids, and even cooks have all sat at various times with us round the table or cabinet, watching hands, faces, and sometimes full-form figures flit about the room. Oh, it was very wonderful!'

Jim poked the fire, and lit another cigarette hastily. He believed nothing; but it was foolish, he considered, for nervous persons like his sister to talk of such things after dark, especially in a lonely country house with ill-lighted corridors and ghostly staircases. Moreover, she was always peering over her shoulder as though she saw something in the great darkened room behind her.

'It was on one of these occasions,' she continued, lowering her voice, 'he discovered that one of the servants was a medium of exceptional powers. After that no professional ever entered the house again.'

'And this medium-servant—?' asked her brother impatiently.

'Was Masters.'

'What?' he cried: 'Masters, the old housekeeper?'

'Yes; she began by going into a trance at one of the seances, and my husband said she possessed most unusual powers and must sit for development.'

'And you got the same results with that old woman?'

'Even better. Oh, Masters was extraordinary!' replied his sister with enthusiasm. 'Simply extraordinary! But it's not that I want to tell you about. It's something very different.'

Jim noticed her hesitation and embarrassment, and wondered what he was going to hear next. He suggested ringing for the lights, but his sister objected that she did not want the servants to overhear a single word. Her manner became more mysterious. She drew her chair closer, and began to speak in a hushed voice, but with great earnestness.

'It's what has gone on since—that I want to tell you,' she whispered. 'Since my husband's death, I mean—what goes on now——'

'Now!' repeated Jim, feeling more and more uncomfortable.

'And I sent for you because you are the only one of the family left. I could never speak to a stranger of this.'

'Of course not,' he said hurriedly. 'You say things go on now, do you?' He glanced quickly at her face, and noted its sudden pallor and the unmistakable signs of fear in her manner. 'Do you mean in this house?'

He got up to ring the bell for the lamps, but she drew him back into the chair.

'Wait till I've finished, please, Jim. You know, this is a very large house,' she went on disconnectedly, still under her breath for fear of listeners. 'And a very lonely one; and I've been living here since my husband died.'

'Yes,' he said emphatically.

'I only use a small part of it. The rest—his part—is shut up.'

'Naturally.'

'I have fewer servants too.'

'Of course.'

'And the greatest difficulty in keeping them. They won't stay. They are always hearing noises in the unused part of the house—his part. And some of them swear they have met IT on the stairs.'

Jim looked up quickly; he was alarmed at her tone of voice.

'Met what?' he asked aloud.

'Him,' she whispered back across the firelight. 'He's been about all the time. He's always about now. He's not far from you and me at this very moment, probably.'

Her brother sprang up, and faced the darkening room with his back to the fire. Her serious manner dismayed him a good deal.

'You mean——' he began.

'Harry still lives here—still comes here.'

'Helen!' he said severely—'your nerves are unstrung. What in the world do you mean by talking in this way?'

'Exactly what I say, Jim. Harry is still in this house,' she answered quietly, in a tone that sent the shivers down his back.

'The house is h—h—aunted, you mean!'

'I mean that Harry is still about in it,' she whispered.

'But have you seen him?'

'Often,' she went on, her excitement growing as she saw her brother's interest. 'And he's always telling me to do things. He says his happiness depends on my doing them. He says this all the time. He comes at night to my room; and even when I don't see him, I hear his voice in the dark whispering at me.'

Jim straightened himself up, and drew a long, deep breath. He was slowly forming his own conclusions. He knew a splendid nerve specialist in town, who would soon know how to put the matter right. He was not subtle-minded himself, and hardly knew how to deal with such a case, but the doctor would manage all that. So, for the moment, he said nothing, and schooled himself to listen with sympathy and patience. In spite of his conclusions, however, he regretted that his sister looked to him for protection in such a matter, and almost wished he had not come.

'Then, only a month ago,' she went on, 'Masters herself came to give warning. She cried a lot, and declared she really could not stand it any longer.'

'Masters sees him too?'

'As often as I do nearly. The very night she gave notice he came into my room and said I must not let her go on any account, for she was such a wonderful medium, and he could not manifest at all without a medium. If Masters left he would be unable to come back, and he would suffer—and be very unhappy.'

'So the wretched woman is still here?'

'I was obliged to double her wages before she'd consent to stay, and even now I'm always afraid she'll go out of her mind or do something dreadful like that.'

The entrance of the footman with the much longed-for lamps put an end to their conversation for the moment, and the dressing-gong postponed it still further; but after a depressing *tête-à-tête* dinner, Jim asked to see Masters alone in the smoking-room. His sister was not there, for he did not wish her nerves to be further excited before going to bed.

He talked to Masters about family matters that interested them both, before approaching the topic of main interest. She volunteered little, but answered all his questions frankly, and he soon saw that she believed in it all even more implicitly than did his sister. She was less intelligent, and of course more credulous, and she told him some amazing bits of information about her late master which only confirmed Jim in his theory that these two hysterically inclined women were completely hypnotized into the belief that Captain Blundell had returned to the scene of his orgies and 'experiments', and still walked the rooms and passages of the old family mansion. She mentioned that even with her higher wages she did not think she could stand it much longer.

Jim asked her particularly about the first seance at which she went into a trance.

'I simply felt kind of faint,' she told him, 'and then turned of a sudden all unconscious. That's all I knew till I woke up and they told me all what had 'appened while I was asleep. "In a trance" the poor Captain called it. And after that I used to sit twice a week regular for him.'

Jim felt sure she believed every word she uttered. Her descriptions of her meeting with the Captain since his death were very vivid, and she turned pale and trembled all over while she spoke of seeing his red head and bloated face bending over her bed in the night time. And when she told how she saw him moving silently down the corridors, sometimes overtaking and passing her without a word, and vanishing in the doorway of his old room, Jim was distinctly sorry that he had not waited for her recital until the morning.

But it did not in the least shake his belief that both women were entirely deluded, and his mind was already at work on a plan to send the foolish old housekeeper off on a holiday, while he got his sister up to London, and induced her to see a specialist.

He avoided further conversation on the subject that night—for his own sake as much as for theirs, and he felt quite angry with himself to note that his nerves gave an involuntary start when his sister led him to his lofty panelled bedroom, and informed him that this was the very room her husband had died in six months previously.

'There is far more chance of your seeing him if you sleep here,' she explained, 'and then you can judge for yourself. Masters, who sleeps just across the passage so as to be near me, tried hard to prevent my putting you here; but I knew you wouldn't feel the least afraid. But, do please remember, Jim,' she added pleadingly, 'if he comes, not to speak roughly or unkindly to him.'

She was gone and the door closed behind her.

Jim's reflections for the next few minutes were very far from pleasant.

He believed none of it, but he had nerves for all that; and to be put to sleep in the death-room, with a medium servant opposite and a hysterical sister a little farther up the passage—this was more than he had bargained for. His mind and imagination were alive with all the stories of the evil apparition he had heard; and even his bedroom, he noticed, was littered with spiritualist journals and cheap occult magazines, dealing with the marvellous and terrifying side of this class of things.

No wonder, he reflected, that these women, living alone in the country, their minds still dominated by the bluster and superstition of the bibulous Blundell—no wonder they still saw him walking the floors and whispering at them in the darkness of the night. It was matter for surprise they did not see and hear a great deal more.

And, although Jim possessed a strong will, and had soon reduced his imagination to order, it required considerable effort on his part to crawl between the sheets of old Blundell's bed and blow the candles out on the table beside him. And the last picture in his mind as he finally fell asleep took the form of this man as he had seen him at his sister's wedding years ago—with his flaming red hair, his bloated cheeks, and his small, pig-like eyes.

For all that, however, he slept undisturbed, and during the following day he tried to divert his sister's thoughts as much as possible to other things than spirits. He also contrived that Masters should never once see her alone.

For three days the household moved along normal and unexciting channels of ordinary country life, but the fourth morning Helen came down to breakfast pale and trembling, and declared her husband had appeared to her in the night, and had whispered that he could not come as before so long as Jim was in the house, and that he was suffering and very unhappy. Her brother's sceptical attitude, he said, destroyed the conditions, and made it almost impossible for him to materialize.

'That explains, you see, why he has not appeared to you,' she said weepingly.

Jim did not care what the explanation might be, so long as the apparition did not actually come; and this only made him feel more than ever that his theory was correct, and that the whole story was a tissue of moonshine and hysteria.

But that very night something happened that compelled him to reconsider his theories, and, if possible, to readjust them.

It was after midnight when he came up from the smoking-room, where an interesting novel had detained him far beyond his usual hour. In order not to disturb his sister, whose room he had to pass, he took off his shoes and walked on tiptoe up the stairs. The house was dark and silent, and the great hall he had to pass through seemed unusually large. Its proportions seemed almost to have altered. To find his way he was obliged to keep his hand on the rail; but half way up he became so confused as to his exact whereabouts that he decided to return to the smoking-room and get a candle.

It was at this very moment that his nerves signalled a warning to him. His heart suddenly began to beat very fast, and as he turned to grope his way downstairs he became aware that 'something' had moved up directly in front of him out of the darkness.

Something, he felt positive, was standing within two feet, or less, of his person. In another second he would touch it. Everything was pitch-black; and at once his mind was flooded with the details of what his sister and Masters had seen. With terrible vividness the horrible stories came before him. The hair rose on his head, and he felt his knees shake. The theory about hypnotized and hysterical women, so convincing in the daylight, seemed in a second to have become inadequate and absurd. The frightened face of the housekeeper and his sister's pallor occurred to him with new meaning.

He tried hard to pull himself together, and began to fumble in his pocket for a match; but he only just had time to move a little to one side and get his back up against the wall, when the darkness before him grew faintly luminous, and he plainly saw a figure moving slowly past him down the stairs.

Jim felt the sweat trickling down his neck as he stared. Something with human shape passed him slowly, silently, with a sort of dim light of its own just sufficient to make it visible. It made absolutely no sound, but he felt the air stir on his cheek; and, just at the second when it was closest to him, it turned slowly round and showed him its face.

Jim almost screamed aloud. It was a man with bloated cheeks, small shining eyes, and red hair!

He thought every instant the figure would spring at him out of the darkness, and he almost fell forward on to it, and feared he would collapse on the floor from sheer fright. But, in the same second, it passed him and was gone; moving by with soundless feet as though his own presence had been quite unobserved.

His first thought was to rush to his sister or to Masters, and tell them what he had seen. But cooler thoughts followed quickly, when he reflected how mortified he would be to confess that he was too frightened to follow the figure and speak to it. Instead, his trembling fingers found a match, and he at once struck a light and and peered about him.

The shadows ran away on all sides, and he saw a long empty corridor, lined with pictures, but devoid of all doors or furniture, and certainly destitute of any other human figure than his own. But it was not the passage he knew! Evidently he had taken the wrong turning in the dark. He ought to have gone up another flight of stairs before turning, and he forthwith began to retrace his steps by the light of the match, and happily reached his own door before its last flicker left him in the darkness again.

And, once within his own room, he locked the door, poked the fire into a blaze, lit every candle he could find—and then sat down to think it all over.

After thinking it over for half an hour, safe from the paralysing effects of fear, Jim realized honestly enough that his theories needed readjusting. He, therefore, readjusted them to the best of his ability—and then got into bed and slept peacefully till morning.

Next day he told his sister what he had seen, but assured her at the same time that he had a plan for making the unhappy spirit return to its grave and rest quietly.

'It was Harry, you see, as I told you.'

'It gave me an awful turn,' said Jim. 'Eyes, face, hair and all. It was exactly like him.'

'And you really think you can stop it without making him unhappy?' she asked plaintively.

'I'll try. It won't make him unhappy, I promise that. Don't let Masters know I've seen him, or she'll have hysterics.'

Jim arranged with his sister that he should slip into her room late that night, unobserved, and sleep on the sofa behind the curtains. She was to wake him when the apparition came, in case he was asleep. For the rest she must have confidence in him—and wait results.

At a few minutes past eleven Jim took up his position on the sofa behind the curtains, making himself comfortable with rugs and pillows. His sister was soon asleep. But he himself lay there with every sense alert, waiting for the first signs of the apparition. The room was in complete darkness, the house silent as the grave.

It was well after one o'clock when the sound of a door-handle being turned roused him out of a light doze and made his hand seek the dark lantern ready for use. Very cautiously and quietly the door was opened—and someone moved stealthily into the room.

The darkness was too great to allow him to see a vestige of anything, but from the sound of drapery brushing against the wardrobe he knew that the intruder was standing somewhere between him and the front of the bed.

An instant later he knew that this was correct, for the faint, pale, luminous glow he had seen the night before on the stairs made itself visible just where the bed ended, and Jim was able to make out by its aid the indistinct outline of a human head and shoulders.

At the same moment his sister moved uneasily in her sleep. The bed was being gently shaken; and almost immediately afterwards the jolting awakened her, and he heard her terrified voice from the bedclothes:

'Harry, is that you, dear?'

A sepulchral whisper replied from the shape at the foot of the bed:

'It is. But I cannot come again while your brother is in the house.'

The light shifted a little, and Jim plainly saw the mass of red hair on the figure's head.

'I will tell him,' answered Helen, in a terrified whisper. 'Please do not be angry with me.'

'I am angry only because you do not obey me,' continued the hoarse whisper. 'You do not carry out what I say.'

'But what have I not done?'

'The money I want left to my faithful old housekeeper is still not arranged for. You have not altered the will as I directed.'

'But I will do so tomorrow, Harry dear—at once,' said the other with a gulp of terror.

Meanwhile Jim had stealthily left his hiding-place on tiptoe and come close up to the apparition of Captain Blundell. He was almost touching it, and as his sister uttered these last words, he encircled the figure with his arms, and clapped his handkerchief over its mouth. There was a smothered cry, and a wild rush across the room in the darkness. Helen uttered a piercing scream, and when the door slammed behind him, Jim found himself out in the passage, with a very solid apparition struggling in his arms most violently.

'If you don't keep quiet, I'll stun you, d'ye hear?' he whispered.

The figure made no reply, and he dragged and carried the still struggling 'Captain Blundell' down the passage into his own room. Once in, he produced the rope he had already provided in view of this very climax, and tied up the apparition so that it could not possibly move.

Then he ran back to his sister's room as fast as his legs could carry him, first locking his door on the outside.

He found her with every candle alight, sobbing with terror, and in a condition certainly bordering on hysteria.

'Oh, Jim, did you see him that time? But what happened, and did he try to injure you? It was all so terrible....'

'Come quickly,' cried her brother. 'Come to my room. I've laid the ghost. You never need be afraid again.'

He dragged her by the hand, clad in a dressing-gown and shaking like a leaf, down the passage to his own room. He unlocked the door and they went in together. Silence and darkness met them.

'Now, Helen,' he said, 'I'll give you a light and you shall see the spirit better than you've ever seen it before.'

There was a sound of heavy shuffling in the darkness. He turned his dark lantern on the scene at the same moment.

Helen gave a long scream and caught his arm for support. There, in front of them, leaning in a half-faint against the bed-post, just as Jim had left her, stood Masters, the old housekeeper! She had a villainous red wig on her head: her cheeks were rouged violently, and her eyes painted. And at her feet lay a faintly luminous slate, and the sheet she had used to wrap round her neck and shoulders.

Before releasing her, Jim insisted on Helen taking him at once to the woman's bedroom, where, as he suspected, they found further paraphernalia, consisting of a second red wig, grease paint, rubber hands, a couple of slates, and white sheets with loose arms carefully sewed on to them. She had learned all the tricks from the 'professionals', and had played them at their own game and beaten them clean out of the market.

But Helen Blundell was never troubled again by the apparition of her late husband, and Masters, the faithful old housekeeper, had to seek another place without a character.

THE MESSAGE OF THE CLOCK

As early as 1904 Blackwood had written a rather mystical dream-like story in 'The House of the Past'. He would return to these visionary mood stories periodically as in 'The Old Man of Visions', 'The South Wind' and 'Imagination'. But those found their way into his collections. 'The Message of the Clock', from *Nash's Magazine* for June 1910, somehow slipped through the net.

SUDDENLY, in most singular fashion, Smith, the patent agent, became aware of the clock upon his mantelpiece.

His mind was an exact one, dealing soberly with life as he saw it, and the way he saw it was as a series of hard, pellet-like facts, behind which he never divined a possible flaming glory. The artistic temperament touched him not. Religion, beauty, wonder—all that tended to make clients unreasonable or things in life seem other than they are—he loathed. Yet here he was, on the eve of Easter, still postponing his country visit, simply because the poor woman in the flat below—who painted pictures and starved in the process—lay dying. Here he was, lingering on in town almost against his will, scarcely knowing why he did so, held there by something that was not a fact, and despising himself (with a kind of curious amazement) for so doing.

For it was not the blunt fact of the woman's dying that kept him; it was something intangible connected with her dying. This much he realized: it was something queer.

And thus, as he sat pondering the matter between the hour of tea and dinner, he became suddenly aware, in this curious fashion, of the presence of the clock. It was startling.

Now, a clock was merely a piece of mechanism—clumsy mechanism—for had he not filed hundreds of specifications to improve them? His own specimen was square and ugly, with a dirty white face, and holes for two keys. Never before had he noticed how it ticked even, and it had no 'strike'. Yet now, with abrupt insistence, he became aware in the stillness that its steady little hammering note claimed attention— that it ticked, indeed, almost like a voice. For the first time he realized that it was there—busy and important—fussy! It was a Presence. He was no longer *quite* alone. So strong, indeed, was the feeling that he turned to look at it, as he might have turned to someone who stood waiting beside him with a message. And this was an extraordinary idea to enter the mind of Smith, the patent agent: a clock, ticking out a communication!

'Quarter to seven,' he observed. 'And probably wants winding.'

This last he added by way of explanation to himself. He moved forward to insert the key—then stopped short. 'Can't be that,' he murmured. 'I wound it only this morning——'

Puffing hard at his pipe, he stood and stared; he listened. By some process of the mind he did not understand—and instinctively opposed—it was borne in upon him that this ticking of the clock led up to something—to a certain moment. It was like a telegraph instrument clicking out a message, a little voice consciously drawing his attention to something—to something that was *about to happen.* Without understanding it quite, Smith experienced the imaginative truth that, if the mind dwells long enough upon an object, that object becomes invested with a personality. The voice of that clock became alive, and held intercourse with him. But why it should have led him to think something was going to happen—and happen at seven o'clock— perplexed him to the point of positive annoyance.

This was a state of mind the patent agent regarded with suspicion and dislike. He deliberately tried to think of something else; yet without success. His thoughts always turned back to the personality of the woman downstairs who lay dying, the artist whom he had seen, though never spoken with, and about whom he had gathered all kinds of intimate details owing to that curious leakage that turns a House of Flats into a huge Whispering Gallery.

Her mode of life, he always felt, in some inexplicable way challenged his own, as though character created an atmosphere that could spread mysteriously through bricks and mortar like an emanation, to affect other minds. Insensibly, often, he had found himself contrasting her life with his: his self-centred, utilitarian, highly moral existence, believing only in 'facts'; and hers, the vain fluttering of a soul after Beauty—achieving nothing, yet shedding about her an atmosphere of light, considering all she possessed as belonging to everyone in need of it. He knew, for instance, how she often kept her models when she had no work for them, and even fed them to her own want. The servants carried some rather wonderful stories about—stories that made him feel uncomfortable till he banished them.... So that when he had heard a few days before that she lay dangerously ill—lonely, perhaps dying—he contrasted his jolly Easter in the country with her own dismal prospects, and the instinct stirred in him to stay on a little in town ... perhaps to help ... perhaps only to *know* ... he scarcely understood himself ... yet he had stayed....

Again the ticking of the clock interrupted his reverie.

'Ten minutes to seven,' he read.

It was very curious; he could not keep his mind from her. On the floor below all was silent. A wind sang mournfully past the walls, carrying a million raindrops that beat their tiny hammers upon the windows. Queer new thoughts attacked his mind, showing him in swift, fugitive vision possibilities of life that a temperament like hers might hold. Perhaps the truth was that this little wave of unwonted sympathy touched into being a new corner of his own consciousness. The figure of the woman, as he had once passed her on the stairs, rose with haunting persistence before him. She had no beauty, strictly speaking, this elderly Irish woman, but her face had that touch of soul that painted it sometimes with a burning glory, and was gone, so that all who saw it experienced a sudden and inexpressible yearning for high things.

And he, Smith, had caught her once or twice with that look. It was very wonderful, very radiant. It had made him pause and ask himself whether, after all, it was she that was wasting time, or himself. Her motto, he had heard, was 'Help others, and pass on'; and she practised it, passing on without reward; she gave herself freely, not counting the cost—time, money, sympathy. Yet, here she was at this moment dying, almost in want, nothing saved, nothing put by, nothing achieved—a failure. Was it worthwhile—this life of unpractical dreaming? He had wondered about it before. He wondered about it now....

Again the voice of the clock drew his attention.

'Five minutes to seven.'

It was very haunting, this persistent calling of the clock; he began to feel unaccountably ill at ease and restless. A sensation of eeriness came over him. He wished the hour of seven were past. He drew the curtains closer to shut out the sighing of the wind. More than once he looked over his shoulder, expecting something, he knew not what.... Once he even thought of going downstairs to inquire of the nurse.... Perhaps he might be able to help.

He was still sitting, however, in his armchair opposite the mirror when the sound of the door opening softly behind him drew his attention. The curtain on the rod made it swish audibly. He instantly looked up and saw the figure of the very woman he had been thinking about reflected in the glass before him. In her eyes was that flame seen sometimes in the eyes of the mad, sometimes in those of religious enthusiasts—that lightning of the disturbed soul which seeks to reconcile an inner glory with the common light of the sun. Only, with her now, the soul was not disturbed; the flame was steady and permanent; and an expression of peace and happiness, extraordinarily beautiful, rested upon her features as the mirror gave them back to him.

She was sleep-walking—he realized that, of course—under the stress of fever or delirium. He must act promptly and get her downstairs again, or call for the nurse. Yet he found himself able to do none of these things. He could only stare, with a sense of wonder so exquisite that it was pain—stare at the radiant and beatific expression in the mirror before him.

Amazed, and yet not amazed—conscious, too, of a kind of elevating terror—he then stood bolt upright and tried to turn and face her. Finding this was somehow impossible, he tried to speak. This also failed him. He could not move his lips. The beauty of that look held him spellbound and speechless. He stood motionless, staring at her image in the glass—the image of this dying woman, silent and wonderful behind him—unbelievably glorious!

Then, with extraordinary softness, the whisper of a voice floated to his ear:

'It is more wonderful even than I dreamed. It is—and it was—worthwhile!'

Smith suddenly realized something new, and his heart gave a horrid jump. He turned sharply round, a terror of the unknown clutching him. The room was absolutely empty.

The ticking of the clock, sounding up till now like a tiny hammer in his brain, had ceased; and he saw that the hands pointed to seven. The mechanism had accountably run down.... It was only on the following day, however, he learned that the human mechanism had also run down at the same moment.

The vision he dismissed easily as a dream, but that running down of the clock puzzled him dreadfully for years....

THE SINGULAR DEATH OF MORTON

When Blackwood settled in Switzerland early in 1909 he made his home at Bôle near Neuchatel, near the border with France and the Jura Mountains. Several of his stories from this period are located there, 'The Man Who Played Upon the Leaf', 'The Occupant of the Room', 'Special Delivery' and 'The Lost Valley' amongst them. 'The Singular Death of Morton', published in the short-lived magazine *The Tramp* for December 1910, is the only time Blackwood used the traditional vampire theme in his fiction. How much of the tale was drawn from experience or from local gossip, I do not know, but in all of Blackwood's stories there is no smoke without fire.

Dusk was melting into darkness as the two men slowly made their way through the dense forest of spruce and fir that clothed the flanks of the mountain. They were weary with the long climb, for neither was in his first youth, and the July day had been a hot one. Their little inn lay further in the valley among the orchards that separated the forest from the vineyards.

Neither of them talked much. The big man led the way, carrying the knapsack, and his companion, older, shorter, evidently the more fatigued of the two, followed with small footsteps. From time to time he stumbled among the loose rocks. An exceptionally observant mind would possibly have divined that his stumbling was not entirely due to fatigue, but to an absorption of spirit that made him careless how he walked.

'All right behind?' the big man would call from time to time, half glancing back.

'Eh? What?' the other would reply, startled out of a reverie.

'Pace too fast?'

'Not a bit. I'm coming.' And once he added: 'You might hurry on and see to supper, if you feel like it. I shan't be long behind you.'

But his big friend did not adopt the suggestion. He kept the same distance between them. He called out the same question at intervals. Once or twice *he* stopped and looked back too.

In this way they came at length to the skirts of the wood. A deep hush covered all the valley; the limestone ridges they had climbed gleamed down white and ghostly upon them from the fading sky. Midway in its journeys, the evening wind dropped suddenly to watch the beauty of the moonlight—to hold the branches still so that the light might slip between and weave its silver pattern on the moss below.

And, as they stood a moment to take it in, a step sounded behind them on the soft pine-needles, and the older man, still a little in the rear, turned with a start as though he had been suddenly called by name.

'There's that girl—again!' he said, and his voice expressed a curious mingling of pleasure, surprise and—apprehension.

Into a patch of moonlight passed the figure of a young girl, looked at them as though about to stop yet thinking better of it, smiled softly, and moved on out of sight into the surrounding darkness. The moon just caught her eyes and teeth, so that they shone; the rest of her body stood in shadow; the effect was striking—almost as though head and shoulders hung alone in mid air, watching them with this shining smile, then fading away.

'Come on, for heaven's sake,' the big man cried. There was impatience in his manner, not unkindness. The other lingered a moment, peering closely into the gloom where the girl had vanished. His friend repeated his injunction, and a moment later the two had emerged upon the high road with the village lights in sight beyond, and the forest left behind them like a vast mantle that held the night within its folds.

For some minutes neither of them spoke; then the big man waited for his friend to draw up alongside.

'About all this valley of the Jura,' he said presently, 'there seems to me something—rather queer.' He shifted the knapsack vigorously on his back. It was a gesture of unconscious protest. 'Something uncanny,' he added, as he set a good pace.

'But extraordinarily beautiful——'

'It attracts you more than it does me, I think,' was the short reply.

'The picturesque superstitions still survive here,' observed the older man. 'They touch the imagination in spite of oneself.'

A pause followed, during which the other tried to increase the pace. The subject evidently made him impatient for some reason.

'Perhaps,' he said presently. 'Though I think myself it's due to the curious loneliness of the place. I mean, we're in the middle of tourist-Europe here, yet so utterly remote. It's such a neglected little corner of the world. The contradiction bewilders. Then, being so near the frontier, too, with the clock changing an hour a mile from the village, makes one think of time as unreal and imaginary.' He laughed. He produced several other reasons as well. His friend admitted their value, and agreed half-heartedly. He still turned occasionally to look back. The mountain ridge where they had climbed was clearly visible in the moonlight.

'Odd,' he said, 'but I don't see that farmhouse where we got the milk anywhere. It ought to be easily visible from here.'

'Hardly—in this light. It was a queer place rather, I thought,' he added. He did not deny the curiously suggestive atmosphere of the region, he merely wanted to find satisfactory explanations. 'A case in point, I mean. I didn't like it quite—that farmhouse—yet I'm hanged if I know why. It made me feel uncomfortable. That girl appeared so suddenly, although the place seemed deserted. And her silence was so odd. Why in the world couldn't she answer a single question? I'm glad I didn't take the milk. I spat it out. I'd like to know where she got it from, for there was no sign of a cow or a goat to be seen anywhere!'

'I swallowed mine—in spite of the taste,' said the other, half smiling at his companion's sudden volubility.

Very abruptly, then, the big man turned and faced his friend. Was it merely an effect of the moonlight, or had his skin really turned pale beneath the sunburn?

'I say, old man,' he said, his face grave and serious, 'What do you think she was? What made her seem like that, and why the devil do you think she followed us?'

'I think,' was the slow reply, 'it was *me* she was following.'

The words, and particularly the tone of conviction in which they were spoken, clearly were displeasing to the big man, who already regretted having spoken so frankly what was in his mind. With a companion so imaginative, so impressionable, so nervous, it had been foolish and unwise. He led the way home at a pace that made the other arrive five minutes in his rear, panting, limping, and perspiring as if he had been running.

'I'm rather for going on into Switzerland tomorrow, or the next day,' he ventured that night in the darkness of their two-bedded room. 'I think we've had enough of this place. Eh? What do you think?'

But there was no answer from the bed across the room, for its occupant was sound asleep and snoring.

'Dead tired, I suppose!' he muttered to himself, and then turned over to follow his friend's example. But for a long time sleep refused him. Queer, unwelcome thoughts and feelings kept him awake—of a kind he rarely knew, and thoroughly disliked. It was rubbish, yet it made him uncomfortable, so that his nerves tingled. He tossed about in the bed. 'I'm overtired,' he persuaded himself, 'that's all.'

The strange feelings that kept him thus awake were not easy to analyse, perhaps, but their origin was beyond all question: they grouped themselves about the picture of that deserted, tumble-down chalet on the mountain ridge where they had stopped for refreshment a few hours before. It was a farmhouse, dilapidated and dirty, and the name stood in big black letters against a blue background on the wall above the door: 'La Chenille'. Yet not a living soul was to be seen anywhere about it; the doors were fastened, windows shuttered; chimneys smokeless; dirt, neglect, and decay everywhere in evidence.

Then, suddenly, as they had turned to go, after much vain shouting and knocking at the door, a face appeared for an instant at a window, the shutter of which was half open. His friend saw it first, and called aloud. The face nodded in reply, and presently a young girl came round the corner of the house, apparently by a back door, and stood staring at them both from a little distance.

And from that very instant, so far as he could remember, these queer feelings had entered his heart—fear, distrust, misgiving. The thought of it now, as he lay in bed in the darkness, made his hair rise. There was something about that girl that struck cold into the soul. Yet she was a mere slip of a thing, very pretty, seductive even, with a certain serpent-like fascination about her eyes and movements; and although she only replied to their questions as to refreshment with a smile, uttering no single word, she managed to convey the impression that she was a managing little person who might make herself very disagreeable if she chose. In spite of her undeniable charm there was about her an atmosphere of something sinister. He himself did most of the questioning, but it was his older friend who had the benefit of her smile. Her eyes hardly ever left his face, and once she had slipped quite close to him and touched his arm.

The strange part of it now seemed to him that he could not remember in the least how she was dressed, or what was the colouring of her eyes and hair. It was almost as though he had *felt*, rather than seen, her presence.

The milk—she produced a jug and two wooden bowls after a brief disappearance round the corner of the house—was—well, it tasted so odd that he had been unable to swallow it, and had spat it out. His friend, on the other hand, savage with thirst, had drunk his bowl to the last drop, too quickly to taste it even, and, while he drank, had kept his eyes fixed on those of the girl, who stood close in front of him.

And from that moment his friend had somehow changed. On the way down he said things that were unusual, talking chiefly about the 'Chenille,' and the girl, and the delicious, delicate flavour of the milk, yet all phrased in such a way that it sounded singular, unfamiliar, unpleasant even. Now that he tried to recall the sentences the actual words evaded him; but the memory of the uneasiness and apprehension they caused him to feel remained. And night ever italicizes such memories!

Then, to cap it all, the girl had followed them. It was wholly foolish and absurd to feel the things he did feel; yet there the feelings were, and what was the good of arguing? That girl frightened him; the change in his friend was in some way or other a danger signal. More than this he could not tell. An explanation might come later, but for the present his chief desire was to get away from the place and to get his friend away, too.

And on this thought sleep overtook him—heavily.

The windows were wide open; outside was a garden with a rather high enclosing wall, and at the far end a gate that was kept locked because it led into private fields and so, by a back way, to the cemetery and the little church. When it was open the guests of the inn made use of it and got lost in the network of fields and vines, for there was no proper route that way to the road or the mountains. They usually ended up prematurely in the cemetery, and got back to the village by passing through the church, which was always open; or by knocking at the kitchen doors of the other houses and explaining their position. Hence the gate was locked now to save trouble.

After several hours of hot, unrefreshing sleep the big man turned in his bed and woke. He tried to stretch, but couldn't; then sat up panting with a sense of suffocation. And by the faint starlight of the summer night, he saw next that his friend was up and moving about the room. Remembering that sometimes he walked in his sleep, he called to him gently:

'Morton, old chap,' he said in a low voice, with a touch of authority in it, 'go back to bed! You've walked enough for one day!'

And the figure, obeying as sleep-walkers often will, passed across the room and disappeared among the shadows over his bed. The other plunged and burrowed himself into a comfortable position again for sleep, but the heat of the room, the shortness of the bed, and this tiresome interruption of his slumbers made it difficult to lose consciousness. He forced his eyes to keep shut, and his body to cease from fidgeting, but there was something nibbling at his mind like a spirit mouse that never permitted him to cross the frontier into actual oblivion. He slept with one eye open, as the saying is. Odours of hay and flowers and baked ground stole in through the open window; with them, too, came from time to time sounds—little sounds that disturbed him without being ever loud enough to claim definite attention.

Perhaps, after all, he did lose consciousness for a moment—when, suddenly, a thought came with a sharp rush into his mind and galvanized him once more into utter wakefulness. It amazed him that he had not grasped it before. It was this: the figure he had seen was *not the figure of his friend.*

Alarm gripped him at once before he could think or argue, and a cold perspiration broke out all over his body. He fumbled for matches, couldn't find them; then, remembering there was electric light, he scraped the wall with his fingers—and turned on the little white switch. In the sudden glare that filled the room he saw instantly that his friend's bed was no longer occupied. And his mind, then acting instinctively, without process of conscious reasoning, flew like a flash to their walk of the day—to the tumble-down 'Chenille,' the glass of milk, the odd behaviour of his friend, and—to the girl.

At the same second he noticed that the odour in the room which hitherto he had taken to be the composite odour of fields, flowers and night, was really something else: it was the odour of freshly turned earth. Immediately on the top of this discovery came another. Those slight sounds he had heard outside the window were not ordinary nightsounds, the murmur of wind and insects: they were footsteps moving softly, stealthily down the little paths of crushed granite.

He was dressed in wonderful short order, noticing as he did so that his friend's night-garments lay upon the bed, and that he, too, had therefore dressed; further—that the door had been unlocked and stood half an inch ajar. There was now no question that he *had* slept again: between the present and the moment when he had seen the figure there had been a considerable interval. A couple of minutes later he had made his way cautiously downstairs and was standing on the garden path in the moonlight. And as he stood there, his mind filled with the stories the proprietor had told a few days before of the superstitions that still lived in the popular imagination and haunted this little, remote pine-clad valley. The thought of that girl sickened him. The odour of newly turned earth remained in his nostrils and made his gorge rise. Utterly and vigorously he rejected the monstrous fictions he had heard, yet for all that, could not prevent their touching his imagination as he stood there in the early hours of the morning, alone with night and silence. The spell was undeniable; only a mind without sensibility could have ignored it.

He searched the little garden from end to end. Empty! Opposite the high gate he stopped, peering through the iron bars, wet with dew to his hands. Far across the intervening fields he fancied something moved. A second later he was sure of it. Something down there to the right beyond the trees was astir. It was in the cemetery.

And this definite discovery sent a shudder of terror and disgust through him from head to foot. He framed the name of his friend with his lips, yet the sound did not come forth. Some deeper instinct warned him to hold it back. Instead, after incredible efforts, he climbed that iron gate and dropped down into the soaking grass upon the other side. Then, taking advantage of all the cover he could find, he ran, swiftly and stealthily, towards the cemetery. On the way, without quite knowing why he did so, he picked up a heavy stick; and a moment later he stood beside the low wall that separated the fields from the churchyard—stood and stared.

There, beside the tombstones, with their hideous metal wreaths and crowns of faded flowers, he made out the figure of his friend; he was stooping, crouched down upon the ground; behind him rose a couple of bushy yew trees, against the dark of which his form was easily visible. He was not alone; in front of him, bending close over him it seemed, was another figure—a slight, shadowy, slim figure.

This time the big man found his voice and called aloud:

'Morton, Morton!' he cried. 'What, in the name of heaven, are you doing? What's the matter——?'

And the instant his deep voice broke the stillness of the night with its clamour, the little figure, half hiding his friend, turned about and faced him. He saw a white face with shining eyes and teeth as the form rose; the moonlight painted it with its own strange pallor; it was weird, unreal, horrible; and across the mouth, downwards from the lips to the chin, ran a deep stain of crimson.

The next moment the figure slid with a queer, gliding motion towards the trees, and disappeared among the yews and tombstones in the direction of the church. The heavy stick, hurled whirling after it, fell harmlessly half way, knocking a metal cross from its perch upon an upright grave; and the man who had thrown it raced full speed towards the huddled up figure of his friend, hardly noticing the thin, wailing cry that rose trembling through the night air from the vanished form. Nor did he notice more particularly that several of the graves, newly made, showed signs of recent disturbance, and that the odour of turned earth he had noticed in the room grew stronger. All his attention was concentrated upon the figure at his feet.

'Morton, man, get up! Wake for God's sake! You've been walking in——'

Then the words died upon his lips. The unnatural attitude of his friend's shoulders, and the way the head dropped back to show the neck, struck him like a blow in the face. There was no sign of movement. He lifted the body up and carried it, all limp and unresisting, by ways he never remembered afterwards, back into the inn.

It was all a dreadful nightmare—a nightmare that carried over its ghastly horror into waking life. He knew that the proprietor and his wife moved busily to and fro about the bed, and that in due course the village doctor was upon the scene, and that he was giving a muddled and feverish description of all he knew, telling how his friend was a confirmed sleep-walker and all the rest. But he did not realize the truth until he saw the face of the doctor as he straightened up from the long examination.

'Will you wake him?' he heard himself asking, 'or let him sleep it out till morning?' And the doctor's expression, even before the reply came to confirm it, told him the truth. 'Ah, monsieur, your friend will not ever wake again, I fear! It is the heart, you see; *hélas*, it is sudden failure of the heart!'

The final scenes in the little tragedy which thus brought his holiday to so abrupt and terrible a close need no description, being in no way essential to this strange story. There were one or two curious details, however, that came to light afterwards. One was, that for some weeks before there had been signs of disturbance among newly made graves in the cemetery, which the authorities had been trying to trace to the nightly wanderings of the village madman—in vain; and another, that the morning after the death a trail of blood had been found across the church floor, as though someone had passed through from the back entrance to the front. A special service was held that very week to cleanse the holy building from the evil of that stain; for the villagers, deep in their superstitions, declared that nothing human had left that trail; nothing could have made those marks but a vampire disturbed at midnight in its awful occupation among the dead.

Apart from such idle rumours, however, the bereaved carries with him to this day certain other remarkable details which cannot be so easily dismissed. For he had a brief conversation with the doctor, it appears that impressed him profoundly. And the doctor, an intelligent man, prosaic as granite into the bargain, had questioned him rather closely as to the recent life and habits of his dead friend. The account of their climb to the 'Chenille' he heard with amazement he could not conceal.

'But no such chalet exists,' he said.

'There is no "Chenille". A long time ago, fifty years or more, there was such a place, but it was destroyed by the authorities on account of the evil reputation of the people who lived there. They burnt it. Nothing remains today but a few bits of broken wall and foundation.'

'Evil reputation——?'

The doctor shrugged his shoulders 'Travellers, even peasants, disappeared,' he said. 'An old woman lived there with her daughter, and poisoned milk was supposed to be used. But the neighbourhood accused them of worse than ordinary murder——'

'In what way?'

'Said the girl was a vampire,' answered the doctor shortly.

And, after a moment's hesitation, he added, turning his face away as he spoke:

'It was a curious thing, though, that tiny hole in your friend's throat, small as a pin-prick, yet so deep. And the heart—did I tell you?—was almost completely drained of blood.'

LA MAUVAISE RICHE

On first reading, 'La Mauvaise Riche' would seem to have been written at about the same time as 'The Singular Death of Morton', because it conveys much the same mood of suspense and other-worldliness. Yet it was not published until it appeared in *The Westminster Gazette* for 30 November 1912, and that paper usually published stories soon after acceptance. Perhaps the story had been earlier sold to *The Tramp* and returned when that magazine folded, or perhaps the story had been rejected by other magazines until being sold to *The Westminster Gazette*. Or quite simply the haunting peaks of the Jura may have inspired Blackwood a further time. That is always possible because the story also bears some resemblance to 'The Attic', also set in the Jura, and published in *The Westminster Gazette* seven months earlier.

I<small>F</small> seeing is believing the story, of course, is justified, and stands four-square as a fact, for certainly both my cousin and myself saw the thing as clearly as we saw the village church and the wooded mountains beyond, which were its background. There may, however, be other explanations, and my cousin, who is something of a psychologist, availed himself volubly of the occasion to ride his pet hobby. He easily riddled the saying that seeing is believing, while I listened as patiently as possible. Although no psychologist myself, I knew that the phrase was as inadequate as most other generalizations. Indeed, there is no commoner act of magic in daily life than that of sight, by which the mind projects into the air an image, translated objectively from a sensation in the brain caused by light irritating the optic nerve. 'The picture on the retina, upside down, anyhow,' he kept telling me afterwards, 'is not the object itself that throws off the light-rays, is it? You never see the actual object, do you? You're merely playing with an image, eh? It's pure image-ination, don't you see? It's simple magic, the magic that everybody denies.'

Yet, somehow, nothing he could offer by way of explanation satisfied me. The question form of his sentences, moreover, irritated. I rather clung to 'seeing is believing,' and I think in his heart he did the same, for all his cloud of words.

It was evening, and the summer dusk was falling, as we tramped in silence up the hill towards the village where my cousin, with his wife and children, occupy the upper part of an old chalet. We had been climbing Jura cliffs all day; it had been arduous, exciting work, and we both were tired out. Conversation had long since ceased; our legs moved mechanically, and we both devoutly wished we were at home. 'Ah, there's the cemetery at last,' he sighed, as the landmark near the village came into view. 'Thank goodness!' and I was too weary even to make the obvious commentary. The relief of lying down seemed in his mind. With a grunt by way of reply I glanced carelessly at the rough stone wall surrounding the ugly patch cut squarely from the vineyards, and at the formal pines and larches that stood, plume-like, among the peasant graves. 'Old mère Corbillard is safe and snug in her last resting-place,' he added, as we passed the painted iron gate, 'and a good thing too!' There was relief in his tone, but a moment later there was vivid annoyance. 'Izzie,' he cried, stopping short, 'what are you doing again in there? You know your mother forbade you to go any more. What a naughty, disobedient child you are!' And he called to his fourteen-year-old child to come out. She came at once, but listlessly, and not one whit afraid. He scolded her a little. 'I was only putting flowers on the grave,' she said. Her face wore a puzzled, scared expression, and the eyes were very bright—she had wonderful brown eyes—but it was not her father's chiding that caused the look.

She took our arms with affectionate possession, as her way was, and we all three laboured up the hill together. No more was said; her father was too tired to find further fault. 'Please don't tell mother, Daddy, will you?' she whispered, as we reached the chalet and went in; 'I promise faithfully not to go again.' He said nothing, but I saw him give her a kiss, and I gave her one myself. The feeling was strong in me that she was frightened and needed protection. I put my arm tightly round her, giving her a good warm hug. The pleading, helpless look she gave me in return I shall not soon forget.

The memory of 'old mère Corbillard' no one cared to keep alive—

the wealthy peasant who had died a week ago. Known as 'la mauvaise riche,' because of her miserly habits, she was also credited with stealing her neighbours' cats for the purpose of devouring them—'lapin de montagne,' as the natives termed the horrid dish. Her face was sinister—steel-grey eyes, hooked nose, and prominent teeth—and had the village soul been more imaginative or superstitious, she would certainly have been called a witch. As it was, she was merely passed for 'méchante' and distinctly 'toquée'. Held in general disfavour, she was avoided and disliked, and she repaid the hatred well, thanks to her money. She lived in utter solitude, the one companion, oddly enough, to whom admittance was never denied, being—Izzie. 'Oddly enough,' because, while the old woman was half-imbecile, maliciously imbecile, the child, on her side—to put it kindly—was unusually backward for her age, if not mentally deficient. But Izzie's deficiency was of mild and gentle quality—a sweet child, if ever there was one. And the parents, while barely tolerating the strange acquaintanceship, never knew how frequent the visits were. They always meant to stop the friendship, yet had never done so. Izzie, true solitary, kept to herself too much. She loved the old woman's stories. They hesitated to say the final No. Thus, at first, they let her go to put fresh flowers, which she picked herself, upon the grave, until, feeling that her too constant journeys there were morbid, the ultimatum had gone forth that they must stop. 'It's queer that you should care to go so often,' said her father. 'It's not right,' added her mother, the parents exchanging a look that meant they scented some unholy influence at work. 'But I promised to do it every day,' said Izzie frankly. Then further explanations elicited the unwelcome addition: 'She said she would come and fetch me if I didn't'—and the influence of the old woman seemed defined. 'Ha, ha!' said mother's eyes to father; 'so the old wretch frightened her apparently into the promise,' and they congratulated themselves that the mischief had been stopped in time.

The incident was slight enough. The imagination of the backward child, perhaps a little morbidly inclined owing to her love of solitude, had been unduly stimulated. It had been gently, wisely corrected, and the matter was at an end. Yet, somehow, for me, it lingered in my memory, as though something very vital lay at the core of it.

There followed forty-eight hours of soaking rain that kept us all indoors, and after it a day of cloudless sunshine that made everybody happy. We romped and played with the children, basked in the delicious heat, and were generally full of active mischief. Mother, mending stockings and trying to write letters, had a sorry time of it. But joy and forgiveness ruled the day, and one was ashamed to feel vexation at anything with such a sun in the heavens. Only Izzie, I noticed, kept apart; she was listless and indifferent, joining in no games; her thin, pale face, in contrast to the strange brilliance of her eyes, was evidence to me of some force busily at work within. But she kept it fairly well concealed; it seemed natural for her to moon about alone; I think no one else noticed that her behaviour was more marked than usual. With the cunning of the slow-witted she avoided me in particular, guessing that I was ready to make advances. She divined that I understood. Hiding my purpose as well as possible, I kept her closely under observation, and after supper, when she strolled off alone down the road between the vineyards, I called to Daddy to come and have a pipe. We followed her. The moment we caught her up she turned and took her place as usual, an arm to each. How tall she seemed; she almost topped her father. She kept silence, merely walking in step with us, and holding us rather close I thought, as though glad of our presence though she had started off alone. At first Daddy made efforts to draw her into conversation—efforts that failed utterly. For my part, I let her be, content to keep her arm firmly in my own, for there was very strong in me the feeling that I must protect and watch, guarding her from something that she feared yet was unable to resist. We talked across her, I guiding the conversation towards fun, and she was so tall that we had to stoop and lean forward to see each other's faces.

Hot sun had dried the road up, and the evening was still and peaceful. We paced slowly to and fro, turning always at the village fountain, and again at the crest of the hill where the descent went steeply towards the cemetery. And here, at each turning, Izzie lingered a moment and looked down the hill. I felt perceptibly the dragging on my arm. Once, at the fountain, I made to follow the road through the village. 'No,' said the child, with decision I disliked intensely, 'let's go back again,' and we obeyed meekly. 'Little tyrant,' said her unobservant father.

The mountains rose in a wall of purple shadow, their ridges outlined against a fading sky of gold and crimson. Thin columns of peat smoke traced their scaffolding across it faintly, then melted out. From time to time a group of labourers from the vineyards passed us, singing the Dalcroze songs, taking their hats off, and saying 'Bon soir, bonne nuit.' We knew them all. Izzie watched them go—with almost feverish interest. I got the queer impression she was waiting till the last group had gone home. She certainly was waiting for something;

there was a covert expectancy in her manner that stirred my former uneasiness. And this uneasiness grew stronger every minute. I could hardly listen to my cousin's desultory talk. At last I brought things suddenly to a head, for it was more than my nerves could stand. Abruptly I stood still. The other two, linked arm-in-arm, stood with me.

'Daddy,' I said sharply, 'let's go in,' and was going to add peremptorily, 'take Izzie with you,' when the words died away on my lips and the tongue in my mouth went dry. My blood seemed turned to ice. For a second I stood in rigid paralysis. For the figure between us, she whose arms were linked in ours was not Izzie, but another. A gaunt, lean face peered close into my own through the dusk as I stooped to see my cousin, and the eyes were of cold steel-grey instead of brown. The skin was lined and furrowed, and projecting teeth of an aged woman gleamed faintly below the great hooked nose. It was mère Corbillard who stood between us, hanging her withered hands upon our arms, her sinister face so close that her straggling thin grey hair even touched our shoulders.

The dreadful sight was as vividly defined as the white face of my cousin which I saw at the same instant just beyond; and by his ghastly pallor, and the water in his eyes, I knew that he had seen her too. His lips were parted, his right hand was raised and clenched. I thought he was going to strike, but instead, wrenching himself violently free, he sprang to one side with an expression of horror that was more a cry than actual words. There *was* a shriek; whose I dare not say; it may have been my own for all my scattered senses can remember. To this day what I recall was the sensation of death upon my arm, and the glare of those steely eyes that peered triumphantly into my own— then a momentary darkness.

All happened in less than a second. The figure had broken loose from between us, and was racing down the road like a flying shadow— towards the cemetery. Yet the figure we watched an instant before starting in frantic pursuit was unmistakable—Izzie.

To my cousin belongs the reward of prompt action and recapture. He simply flew. And he caught the child long before she reached the forbidden gates. Weeping, white and frightened, we half carried her indoors, and explained to her alarmed mother that she had been taken suddenly ill, a *crise de nerfs*, as Daddy, with presence of mind, described it. It was not the first time; Izzie had been too often hysterical to cause undue anxiety. Mother will never know the truth unless she reads this story, which is unlikely, since her mending and darning leave her little

La Mauvaise Riche 67

leisure for newspapers. My cousin and myself have discussed the thing *ad nauseam*, and, as I have indicated, he explained it in a variety of ways. But neither of us know what Izzie thought or felt. We, of course, dared not ask her, and the child has never volunteered a word. That she was severely frightened only is clear. She never passes the cemetery alone now, and the name of old mère Corbillard has not passed her lips a single time. My cousin's discovery of the horror, however, coincided with my own. Comparing notes proved that. He had been aware of no uneasy sensations previously, as I had been. Telepathy, therefore, was the clue he finally decided on. 'It covers more ground than the word "possession," and has besides,' as he said, 'a sort of scientific sound'.

THE SOLDIER'S VISITOR

With the outbreak of the First World War Blackwood undertook writing propaganda and much of this overlapped into his fiction. Few of the stories written at this time are worthy of more than an initial inspection. Even fewer are fantasies. One, 'Cain's Atonement', was selected in 1930 by H. Cotton Minchin as one of the best short stories of the war; another, 'The Laughter of Courage', about a war cripple with an infectious laugh, is especially poignant. But most of the stories have not stood the test of time. The two included here are examples where Blackwood's style and vision shine through the lesser values of war-inspired work. 'The Soldier's Visitor' comes from *Land and Water* for 9 October 1915, a paper devoted almost entirely to the war effort, serializing Hilaire Belloc's coverage of the hostilities. When I first read the story I was reminded of Arthur Machen's 'The Bowmen' which had appeared a year earlier. That story of spectral visions on the battlefield became a literary legend. This story, which has something of the same mood, passed by unnoticed.

I SIT in my room and dream.... Autumn steals across the slanting sunlight on the lawn, for the year stands at the keen, and the smells of childhood float beneath the thinning branches. In my long chair by the open window I sit and dream.... I played upon that lawn, I took the hawks' eggs from the dizzy, topmost branches; it was on turf like that I won the hundred yards. Sure of myself, I moved swiftly, easily, a few weeks, a few months— or was it years?—ago. ... I have forgotten. It is past. I sit and dream....

The little room is narrow, but autumn, entering softly, brings in distance as of the open sky, with misty places that are immense. Once they seemed endless. The whole world enters; there are two magnificent horizons, where the sun sets and where it rises: both I could reach easily, without toil or pain, without the help of anyone. Birds pass from one horizon to the other, singing, high above all obstacles; I loved free space as they do; the sails are flashing white on blue, blue seas; there is the plash of mountain streams, the rustle of foliage ... and the autumn wind goes past my window, picking the crisp, dying leaves from every bough.

'He will recover. At least, he will not lose the other,' are the words I remember dimly, each syllable a century, each word an age. It was so long ago. And I try to rise and see the folded daisies as they take the sunset by the grey thatched summer-house. But my body stops—I cannot move without assistance.... I remember how it happened. I remember a pause, then saying aloud as quietly as if I were playing tennis, 'Now, old chap, it's your turn! Go it!' There was a blank, but no terror, and no pain. I heard no noise, the explosion was quite soundless; my last cartridge was gone, my bayonet was in ... then came the stretcher.... God bless those fellows, those brave and tireless bearers.... A dirty job! He'll bless them for me. I can't even go across the field to find them.

The sunlight dies; the leaves are down; the chill air cloaks the laurel shrubberies in white and gauze; the soaking dew begins to fall. I am in England. England! She was in danger, so they said. That's why I'm here, I suppose. She's taking care of me. I did my bit, my best. Nine months of weary training, three days of glorious fighting. Then this...

I am carried back into the bed, the lamp is lit, the figures, speaking low and with marvellous tenderness, are gone. I am alone, my pals are out there ... where there is singing, stories, action. There is no singing here, no stories. I am in a hothouse—damn...!

I glance at my little table by the pillow, at the small white jug of liquid food, at the little silver bell, the glass with the sleeping draught ... and I turn the lamp out and watch through the open window the faces of the peeping stars. A bat flies past; I hear a moth's big wings; a corncrake whirrs and rattles far away—I used to chase all three.... No other sound is in the world. The hours are asleep. Autumn sits in her lonely wood, weaving her red and yellow leaves into a net to hold me lest I fall! When I wake in the morning, I shall see her tears upon the crimson leaves, upon the grass, upon the iron railing, big, big drops as clear as crystal, holding all the sky. I shall see the few lost stitches that she dropped, floating on cobwebs in the yellow sunlight. I shall hear her cloak sweep trailing through the beech-wood on the hill. And that is the cloak I ask to cover me—below the knees. I shall also smell the perfume of her lustrous hair—but that hair, that perfume I shall take to wrap my thoughts in, and my dreams, through years to come....

For I shall recover. But I shall not—no, I shall never again in this world—I cannot say it—below both knees—I know it—I am nothing.

There came a knock quite suddenly at the door ... and I shut my eyes, because I had no liking for my night-nurse. I left my hand outside upon the coverlet, that she might take my pulse, then leave me without that meeting of the eye, that intimate gesture, that exchange of little words that were distasteful to me. It was, no doubt, a sick man's whim, and yet to me just then it was intolerable. To meet the eye is an intimacy that draws the other person near, too near, unless she be desired and desirable. I feel the soul in contact. It is only one degree more intimate than to hear the mention of my name, my little name. ... And yet, before my mind could question—it works slowly, thickly in this pain—who it was for certain my voice had answered, I had said, 'Come in....'

I closed my eyes, however, none the less. But, through my lids, I felt the searching glance that saw me—more—that met my own. And I heard my name, my little name. A strange and marvellous thrill went through me. The very intimacies I had dreaded I now claimed eagerly. I opened my eyes and looked.

No especial revelation of beauty have I ever claimed in life, but I have known ideals, I have had my dreams like other men. The figure I now saw before me was surely not of this earth. The stars, the moon, sunlight, and wild flowers had made her, perhaps.... I was speechless.

'I have come like this,' said the woman in the soft brown garment, 'because there are things that I can give you now. Before—when you could seek them—you could not find them. Now that you cannot go to them they may come to you. They are all within your reach.'

And then I saw that, while more beautiful and desirable than anyone I had ever known, she was yet strangely familiar to me. Where, how, under what conditions, I could not recall. She was some Grandeur, surely. Queens and the like, I knew, were visiting chaps like me, and yet she was not dressed as such folks dress, and her robe of russet-brown spread in some kind of imperial way behind her. It trailed, I fancied, through the open window, joining the mist above the lawn. The stars shone in it very faintly. But it was her incomparable beauty that made it difficult to speak, for my heart became suddenly so large it choked me.

'I must have dreamed of you,' I murmured at length. A feeling of endless life rose in me—the life people so glibly call eternal. It was beyond description.

'Dreamed!' she echoed gently, shaking her head and smiling. 'Oh no; not dreamed! I called you and you came.' There was a touch of sternness in her smile that stirred the blood in me. But I did not understand.

'You *called* me?' I asked faintly, for such beauty put confusion in me.

'And you came,' she answered. 'It was no dream. You gave me all you had to give.' She paused an instant; there was moisture in her eyes. 'It is now my turn to give all you desire, all you ask or dream.'

The feeling of familiarity was afflicting; but still I could not understand. As she spoke I saw burning love in the great clear eyes. But there was more than love; there was sympathy, understanding—a woman who could understand everything in the world—there was admiration, gratitude, and more than these—I swear it—there was worship.

'I have asked for nothing,' I faltered, an unbelievable happiness rising. 'I did not call—I had no thought—at least I only——'

'It is yours—all, all,' she answered, 'because of that. You did not ask, you did not think of self.'

My face, of course, betrayed me hopelessly. The strange joy found utterance in a somewhat trembling voice, humbly, perhaps a little awed.

'I meant your Beauty...!' I whispered it in my inmost heart. For there was a shyness in me I could not understand.

And then a strange thing happened, for, as she stood between me and the open window, a light air stirred her dress, and I caught the gleam of something bright beneath, almost as though she wore a breastplate of some kind—like shining armour.

'Who are you, then?' I murmured, trying to raise myself, but sinking back again before the painful effort. I had the feeling that for such love as hers, such beauty, splendour, strength, no loss, no pain was of the least account. I forgot my conditions, almost my identity. I was just—a man like other men.

'I am rich,' she answered, 'I am true, and I am faithful unto death and after it. All that you ask is mine to give. And I am here to give it you.'

'Me—?' I could not believe my ears. Something broke within me, bathing my soul in light. I repeated my astonished questions. I mentioned my name. I thought swiftly. Everything, by heaven, was worth it, if this were true.

She looked down at me for a long time without speaking. Then her lips moved a little; the wonderful eyes brimmed over; she said two perfect words as she gazed at me: 'Thank you....' It was followed by my name, my little name.

What happened exactly I cannot tell. I remember thinking it must be somewhere a miserable mistake, that it was too impossible for truth, when in the midst of my anguish she again repeated my name with such pride and gratitude in her voice, such love and admiration in her eyes, that my doubts were gone and I felt re-made in joy. 'It is written here,' she said, pointing to where her heart lay beating behind the gleaming metal.

She then bent over me and kissed me ... she took me in her comforting arms ... I fell asleep. And in my sleep I dreamed of a new and glorious movement, light as air, and easy, swift as wind. Everything in the world was mine, for everything came to me of its own accord. All space lay within my reach. I was no longer walking, running, climbing. I had wings.... But also I remembered where it was that I had seen her, and consequently why I loved her so. I understood at last, God bless her, and I loved her all the more.

Hitherto, indeed, I had asked nothing of her knowingly, yet I had taken all she had to give. I suppose, unconsciously as it were, I knew this well enough. That, apparently, was why I fought.... At any rate, I remembered clearly where I had seen her, and why she seemed so curiously familiar, yet unrealized; for her face, now stamped upon my soul, is also stamped upon every copper penny of the Realm.

THE MEMORY OF BEAUTY

The second of the war-inspired stories included here is not a fantasy, but it does show the fantastic elements that Blackwood could bring to play on the matter of a soldier's convalescence. It was also published in *Land and Water* for 3 January 1918.

IT began almost imperceptibly—about half-past three o'clock in the afternoon, to be exact—and Lennart, with his curiously sharpened faculties, noticed it at once. Before anyone else, he thinks, was aware of it, this delicate change in his surroundings made itself known to these senses of his, said now to be unreliable, yet so intensely receptive and alert for all their unreliability. No one else, at any rate, gave the smallest sign that something had begun to happen. The throng of people moving about him remained uninformed apparently.

He turned to his companion, who was also his nurse. 'Hullo!' he said to her, 'There's something up. What in the world is it?'

Obedient to her careful instructions, she made, as a hundred times before, some soothing reply, while her patient—'Jack,' she called him—aware that she had not shared his own keen observation, was disappointed, and let the matter drop. He said no more. He went back into his shell, smiling quietly to himself, peaceful in mind, and only vaguely aware that something, he knew not exactly what, was wrong with him, and that his companion humoured him for his own good. She did the humouring tenderly, and very sweetly, so that he liked it, his occasional disappointment in her rousing no shadow of resentment or impatience.

This was his first day in the open air, the first day for weeks that he had left a carefully shaded room, where the blinds seemed always down, and looked round him upon a world spread in gracious light. Physically, he had recovered health and strength; nursing and good food, rest and sleep, had made him as fit as when he first went out with his draft months ago. Only he did not know that he had gone out, nor what had happened to him when he was out, nor why he was the object now of such ceaseless care, attention, and loving tenderness. He remembered nothing; memory, temporarily, had been sponged clean as a new slate. That his nurse was also his sister was unrecognized by his mind. He had forgotten his own name, as well as hers. He had forgotten—everything.

The October day had been overcast, high, uniform clouds obscuring the sun, and moving westwards before a wind that had not come lower. No breeze now stirred the yellow foliage, as he sat with his companion upon a bench by Hampstead Heath, and took the air that helped to make him whole. In spite of the clouds, however, the day was warm, and calm, as with a touch of lingering summer. He watched the sea of roofs and spires in blue haze below him; he heard the muffled roar of countless distant streets.

'Big place, that,' he mentioned, pointing with his stick. There was an assumed carelessness that did not altogether hide a certain shyness. '*Some* town—eh?'

'London, yes. It's huge, isn't it?'

'London....' he repeated, turning to look at her quickly. He said no more. The word sounded strange; the way he said it—new. He looked away again. No, he decided she was not inventing just to humour him; that was the real name, right enough. She wasn't 'pulling his leg'. But the name amused him somehow; he rather liked it.

'Mary,' he said, 'now, that's a nice name too.'

'And so is Jack,' she answered, whereupon the shyness again descended over him, and he said no more. Besides, the change he had noticed a moment ago, was becoming more marked, he thought, and he wished to observe it closely. For in some odd way it thrilled him.

It began, so far as he could judge, somewhere in the air above him, very high indeed, while yet its effect did not stay there, but spread gently downwards, including everything about him. From the sky, at any rate, it first stole downwards; and it was his extreme sensitiveness which made him realize next that it came from a particular quarter of the sky; in the eastern heavens it had its origin. He was sure of this; and the thrill of wonder, faint but marvellously sweet, stirred through his expectant being. He waited and watched in silence for a long time. Since Mary showed no interest, he must enjoy it alone. Indeed, she had not even noticed it at all.

Yet none of these people about him had noticed it either. Some of them were walking a little faster than before, hurrying almost, but no one looked up to see what was happening; there were no signs of surprise anywhere. 'Everybody must have forgotten!' he thought to himself, when his mind gave a sudden twitch. Forgotten! Forgotten what? He moved abruptly, and the girl's hand stole into his, though she said no word. He was aware that she was watching him closely but a trifle surreptitiously he fancied.

He did not speak, but his wonder deepened. This 'something' from the eastern sky descended slowly, yet so slowly that the change from one minute to another was not measurable. It was soft as a dream and very subtle; it was full of mystery. Comfort, and a sense of peace stole over him, his sight was eased, he had mild thoughts of sleep. Like a whisper the imperceptible change came drifting through the air. It was exquisite. But it was the wonder that woke the thrill in him.

'Something *is* up, you know,' he repeated, though more to himself than to his companion. 'You can't mistake it. It's all over the place!' He drew a deeper breath, pointing again with his stick over the blue haze where tall chimneys and needle spires pierced. 'By Jove,' he added, 'it's like a veil—gauze, I mean—or something—eh?' And the light drawing itself behind the veil, grew less, while his pulses quickened as he watched it fade.

Her gentle reply that it was time to go home to tea, and something else about the cooling air, again failed to satisfy him, but he was pleased that she slipped her arm into his and made a gesture uncommonly like a caress. She was so pretty, he thought, as he glanced down at her. Only it amazed him more and more that no thrill stirred her blood as it stirred his own, that there was no surprise, and that the stream of passing people hurrying homewards showed no single sign of having noticed what *he* noticed. For his heart swelled within him as he watched, and the change was so magical that it troubled his breath a little. Hard outlines everywhere melted softly against a pale blue sea that held tints of mother-of-pearl; there was a flush of gold, subdued to amber, a haze, a glow, a burning.

This strange thing stealing out of the east brought a wonder that he could not name, a wonder that was new and fresh and sweet as though experienced for the first time. For his mind qualified the beauty that possessed him, qualified it in this way, because—this puzzled him—it was not *quite* 'experienced for the first time'. It was old, old as himself; it was familiar....

'Good Lord!' he thought, 'I've got that rummy feeling that I've been through all this before—somewhere,' and his mind gave another sudden twitch, which, again, he did not recognize as a memory. A spot was touched, a string was twanged, now here, now there, while Beauty, playing softly on his soul, communicated to his being gradually her secret rhythm, old as the world, but young ever in each heart that answers to it. Below, behind, the thrill, these deeply buried strings began to vibrate....

'The dusk is falling, see,' the girl said quietly, 'It's time we were going back.'

'Dusk,' he repeated, vaguely, 'the dusk ... falling ...' It was half a question. A new expression flashed into his eyes, then vanished instantly. Tears, he saw, were standing in her own. She had felt, had noticed, after all, then! The disappointment, and with it the shyness, left him; he was no more ashamed of the depth and strength of this feeling that thrilled through him so imperiously.

But it was after tea that the mysterious change took hold upon his being with a power that could build a throne anew, then set its rightful occupant thereon. By his special wish the lights were not turned on. Before the great windows, opened to the mild autumn air, he sat in his big overcoat and watched.

The change, meanwhile, had ripened. It lay now fullblown upon the earth and heavens. Towards the sky he turned his eyes. The change, whose first delicate advent he had noticed, sat now enthroned above the world. The tops of trees were level with his window-sill, and below lay the countless distant streets, not slumbering, he felt surely, but gazing upwards with him into this deep sea of blackness that had purple for its lining and wore ten thousand candles blazing in mid-air. *Those* lights were not turned out; and this time he wondered why he had thought they might be, ought to be, turned out. This question definitely occurred to him a moment, while he watched the great footsteps of the searchlights passing over space....

The amazing shafts of white moved liked angels lighting up one group of golden points upon another. They lit them and swerved on again. In sheer delight, he lay in his chair and watched them, these rushing footsteps, these lit groups of gold. They, the golden points, were motionless, steady; *they* did not move or change. And his eyes fastened upon one, then, that seemed to burn more brightly than the rest. Though differing from the others in size alone, he thought it more beautiful than all. Below it far, far down in the west, lay a streak of faded fire, as though a curtain with one edge upturned hung above distant furnaces. But this trail of the sunset his mind did not recognize. His eye returned to the point of light that seemed every minute increasingly familiar, and more than familiar—most kindly and well-loved. He yearned towards it, he trembled. Sitting forward in his chair, he leaned upon the window-sill, staring with an intensity as if he would rise through the purple dark and touch it. Then, suddenly, it—twinkled.

'By Jove!' he exclaimed aloud, 'I know that chap. It's—it's—Now, where the devil did I see it before? Wherever was it...?'

He sank back, as a scene rose before his inner eye. It must have been, apparently, his 'inner' eye, for both his outer eyes were tightly closed as if he slept. But he did not sleep; it was merely that he saw something that was even more familiar though not less wonderful, than these other sights.

Upon a dewy lawn at twilight two children played together, while a white-capped figure, from the window of a big house in the background, called loudly to them that it was time to come indoors and make themselves ready for bed. He saw two Lebanon cedars, the kitchen-garden wall beyond, the elms and haystacks further still, looming out of the summer dusk. He smelt pinks, sweet-william, roses. He ran full speed to catch his companion, a girl in a short tumbled frock, and knew that he was dressed as a soldier, with a wooden sword and a triangular paper hat that fell off, much to his annoyance, as he ran. But he caught his prisoner. Leading her by the hair towards the house, his GHQ, he saw the evening star 'simply shining like anything' in the pale glow of the western sky. But in the hall, when reached, the butler's long wax taper, as he slowly lit the big candles, threw a gleam upon his prisoner's laughing face, and it was, he saw, his sister's face.

He opened his eyes again and saw the point of light against the purple curtain that hung above the world. It twinkled. The wonder and the thrill coursed through his heart again, but this time another thing had come to join them, and was rising to his brain. 'By Jove, I know that chap!' he repeated. 'It's old Venus, or I'm a dug-out!'

And when, a moment later, the door opened and his companion entered, saying something about its being time for bed, because the 'night has come'—he looked into her face with a smile: 'I'm quite ready, Mary,' he said, 'but where in the world have you been to all this time?'

ONANONANON

'Onanonanon' is the last Blackwood's early group of stories collected here. It was published in *The English Review* for March 1921 and I have no idea why it was overlooked for inclusion in Blackwood's subsequent collection *Tongues of Fire*. It has an unsettling nightmarish quality about it absent from most of his other work. It was directly inspired by his activities as a secret agent, but Blackwood has drawn it close to home, even in the use of his own code name, Baker. Blackwood may well have suffered just such a delirium. For all I know everything you are about to read in this story happened exactly as described.

CERTAIN things had made a deep impression in his childhood days; among these was the incident of the barking dog.

It barked during his convalesence from something that involved scarlet and a peeling skin; his early mind associated bright colour and peeling skin with the distress of illness. The tiresome barking of a dog accompanied it. In later years this sound always brought back the childhood visualization: across his mind would flit a streak of vivid colour, a peeling skin, a noisy dog, all set against a background of emotional discomfort and physical distress.

'It's barking at *me*!' he complained to his old nurse, whose explanation that it was 'Carlo with his rheumatics in the stables' brought no relief. He spoke to his mother later: 'It never, never stops. It goes on and on and on on purpose—onanonanon!'

How queer the words sounded! He had got them wrong somewhere —onanonanon. Or was it a name, the name of the barking animal— Onan Onan Onanonanon?

His mother's words were more comforting: 'Carlo's barking because you're ill, darling; he wants you to get well.' And she added: 'Soon I'll bring him in to see you. You shall ride on his back again.'

'Would he peel if I stroked him?' he enquired, a trifle frightened. 'Is the skin shiny like mine?'

She shook her head and smiled. 'I'll explain to him,' she went on, 'and then he'll understand. He won't bark any more.' She brought the picture-book of natural history that included all creatures in Ark and Zoo and Jungle. He picked out the brightly coloured tiger.

'A *tiger* doesn't bark, does it?' he asked, and her reply added slightly to his knowledge, but much to his imagination. 'But does it ever *bark*?' he persisted. 'That's really what I asked.'

'Growls and snarls,' said a deep voice from the doorway. He started; but it was only his father, who then came in and amused him by imitating the sound a tiger makes, until Carlo's naughtiness was forgotten, and the world went on turning smoothly as before.

After that the barking ceased; the rheumatic creature sniffed the air and nosed the metal biscuit tray in silence. He understood apparently. It had been rather dreadful, this noise he made. The sharp sound had broken the morning stillness for many days; no one but the boy was awake at that early hour; the boy and the dog had the dawn entirely to themselves. He used to lie in bed, counting the number of barks. They seemed endless, they jarred, they never stopped. They came singly, then in groups of three and four at a time, then in a longer series, then singly again. These single barks often had a sound of finality about them, the creature's breath was giving out, it was tired; it was the full-stop sound. But the true full-stop, the final bark, never came—and the boy had complained.

He loved old Carlo, loved riding on his burly back that wobbled from side to side, as they moved forward very slowly; in particular he loved stroking the thick curly hair; it tickled his fingers and felt nice on his palm. He was relieved to know it would not peel. Yet he wondered impatiently why the creature he loved to play with should go on making such a dreadful noise. 'Doesn't he know? Can't he wait till I'm ready?' There were moments when he doubted if it really was Carlo, when he almost hated the beast, when he asked himself, 'Is this Carlo, or is it Onanonanon...?' The idea alarmed him rather. Onanonanon was not quite friendly, not quite safe.

At the age of fifty he found himself serving his King during the Great War—in a neutral country whose police regarded him with disfavour, and would have instantly arrested and clapped him into gaol, had he made a slip. He did not make this slip, though incessant caution had to be his watchword. He belonged to that service which runs risks yet dares claim no credit. He passed under another name than his own, and his alias sometimes did things his true self would not do. This *alter ego* developed oddly. He projected temporarily, as it were, a secondary personality—which he disliked, often despised, and sometimes even feared. His sense of humour, however, made light of the split involved. When he was followed, he used to chuckle: 'I wonder if the sleuths know which of the two they're tracking down—myself or my alias?'

It was in the melancholy season between autumn and winter, snow on the heights and fog upon the lower levels, when he was suddenly laid low by the plague that milked the world. The Spanish influenza caught him. He went to bed; he had a doctor and a nurse; no one else in the hotel came near his room; the police forgot him, and he forgot the police. His hated alias, Baker, also was forgotten, or perhaps merged back into the parent self.... Outside his quarters on the first floor the plane trees shed their heavy, rain-soaked leaves, letting them fall with an audible plop upon the gravel path; he heard the waves of the sullen lake in the distance; the crunching of passing feet he heard much closer. The heating was indifferent, the light too weak to read by. It was a lonely, dismal time. On the floor above two people died, three on the one below, the French officer next door was carried out. The hotel, like many others, became a hospital.

In due course, the fever passed, the intolerable aching ceased, he forgot the times when he had thought he was going to die. He lay, half convalescent, remembering the recent past, then the remoter past, and so slipped back to dim childhood scenes when the cross but faithful old nurse had tended him. He smelt the burning leaves in the kitchen-garden, and heard the blackbird whistle beyond the summer-house. The odour of moist earth in the toolhouse stole back, with the fragrance of sweet apples in the forbidden loft. These earliest layers of memory fluttered their ghostly pictures like a cinema before his receptive mind. There were eyes long closed, voices long silent, the touch of hands long dead and gone. The rose-garden on a sultry August afternoon was vivid, with the smell of the rain-washed petals, as the sun blazed over them after a heavy shower. The soaked lawn emitted warm little bubbles like a soft squeezed sponge, audibly; even the gravel steamed. He remembered Carlo, with his rheumatism, his awkward gambol, his squashy dog-biscuit beside the kennel and—his bark.

In the state of semi-unconsciousness he lay, weary, weak, depressed, and very lonely. The nurse, on her rare visits, afflicted him, the hotel guests did not ask after him. To the Service at home he was on the sick-list, useless. The morning newspaper and the hurried, perfunctory visits of the doctor were his only interest. It seemed a pity he had not died. The mental depression after influenza can be extremely devastating. He looked forward to nothing.

Then, suddenly, the dog began its barking.

He heard it first at six o'clock when, waking, hot and thirsty in a bed that had lost its comfort, he wondered vaguely if the day was going to be fine or wet. His window opened on to the lake. He watched the shadows melt across the dreary room. The late dawn came softly, its hint of beauty ever unfulfilled. Would it be gold or grey behind the mountains? The dog went on barking.

He dozed, counting the barks without being aware that he did so. He felt hot and uncomfortable, and turned over in bed, counting automatically as he did so: 'fifteen, sixteen, seventeen'—pause—'eighteen, nineteen'—another pause, then with great rapidity, 'twenty, twenty-one, twenty-two, twenty-three——' He opened his eyes wide and cursed aloud. The barking stopped.

The wind came softly off the lake, entering the room. He heard the last big leaf of the plane trees rattle to the gravel path. As it touched the ground the barking began again, his counting—now conscious counting—began with it.

'Curse the brute!' he muttered, and turned over once more to try and sleep. The rasping, harsh staccato sound reached his ears piercingly through sheets and blankets; not even the thick duvet could muffle it. Would no one stop it? Did no one care? He felt furious, but helpless, dreadfully helpless.

It barked, stopped, then barked again. There were solitary, isolated barks, followed by a rapid series, short and hurried. A shower of barks came next. Pauses were frequent, but they were worse than the actual sound. It continued, it went on, the dog barked without ceasing. It barked and barked. He had lost all count. It barked and barked and barked. It stopped.

'At last!' he groaned. 'My God! Another minute, and I——!'

His whole body, as he turned over, knew an immense, deep relaxation. His jangled nerves were utterly exhausted. A great sigh of relief escaped him. The silence was delicious. He rested at last. Sleep, warm and intoxicating, stole gently back. He dozed. Forgetfulness swam over him. He lay in down, in cotton-wool. Police, alias, nurse and loneliness were all obliterated, when, suddenly, across the blissful peace, cracked out that sharp, explosive sound again—the bark.

But the dog barked differently this time; the sound was much nearer. At first this puzzled him. Then he guessed the truth; the animal had come into the hotel and up the stairs; it was outside in the passage. He opened his eyes and sat up in bed. The door, to his surprise, was being cautiously pushed ajar. He was just in time to see who pushed it with such gentle, careful pressure. Standing on the landing in the early twilight was Baker, his other self, his alias, the personality he disliked and sometimes dreaded. Baker put his head round the corner, glanced at him, nodded familiarly, and withdrew, closing the door instantly, making no slightest sound. But, before it closed, and before he had time even to feel astonishment, the dog had been let in. And the dog, he saw at once was old Carlo!

Having expected a little stranger dog, this big, shaggy, familiar beast caused him to feel a sense of curious wonder and bewilderment.

'But were *you* the dog down there that barked?' he asked aloud, as the friendly creature came waddling to the bedside. 'And have you come to say you're sorry?'

It blinked its rheumy eyes and wagged its stumpy tail. He put out his hand and stroked its familiar, wobbly back. His fingers buried themselves in the stiff crinkly hair. Its dim old eyes turned affectionately up at him. It smiled its silly, happy smile. He went on rubbing. 'Carlo, good old Carlo!' he mumbled; 'well, I'm blessed! I'll get on your back in a minute and ride——'

He stopped rubbing. '*Why* did you come in?' he asked abruptly, and repeated the question, a touch of anxiety in his voice. 'How did you manage it, really? Tell me, Carlo?'

The old beast shifted its position a little, making a sideways motion that he did not like. It seemed to move its hind legs only. Its muzzle now rested on the bed. Its eyes, seen full, looked not quite so kind and friendly. They cleared a little. But its tail still wagged. Only, now that he saw it better, the tail seemed longer than it ought to have been. There was something unpleasant about the dog—a faint inexplicable shade of difference. He stared a moment straight into its face. It no longer blinked in the silly, affectionate way as at first. The rheum was less. There was a light, a gleam, in the eyes, almost a flash.

'*Are* you—Carlo?' he asked sharply, uneasily, 'or are you—Onanonanon?

It rose abruptly on its hind legs, laying the front paws on the counterpane of faded yellow. The legs made dark streaks against this yellow.

He had begun stroking the old back again. He now stopped. He withdrew his hand. The hair was coming out. It came off beneath his fingers, and each stroke he made left a line of lighter skin behind it. This skin was yellowish, with a slight tinge, he thought, of scarlet.

The dog—he could almost swear to it— had altered; it was still altering. Before his very eyes, it grew, became curiously enlarged. It now towered over him. It was longer, thinner, leaner than before, its tail came lashing round its hollow, yellowing flanks, the eyes shone brilliantly, its tongue was a horrid red. The brute straightened its front paws. It was huge. Its open mouth grinned down at him.

He was petrified with terror. He tried to scream, but the only sound that came were little innocent words of childhood days. He almost lisped them, simpering with horror: 'I'd get on your back—if I was allowed out of bed. You'd carry me. I'd ride.'

It was a desperate attempt to pacify the beast, to persuade it, even in this terrible moment, to be friendly, a feeble, hopeless attempt to convince *himself* that it was—Carlo. The Monster was twelve feet from head to tail, of dull yellow striped with black. The great jaws, wide open, dripped upon his face. He saw the pointed teeth, the stiff, quivering whiskers of white wire. He felt the hot breath upon his cheeks and lips. It was fetid. He tasted it.

He was on the point of fainting when a step sounded outside the door. Someone was coming.

'Saved!' he gasped.

The suspense and relief were almost intolerable. The touch of a hand feeling cautiously, stealthily, over the door was audible. The handle rattled faintly.

'Saved!' his heart repeated, as the great brute turned its giant head to listen.

He knew that touch. It was Baker, his hated alias, come in the nick of time to rescue him. Yet the door did not open. Instead, the monster lashed its tail, it stiffened horribly, it turned its head back from watching the door, and lowered itself appallingly. The key turned in the lock, a bolt was shot. He was locked in alone with a tiger. He closed his eyes.

His recurrent nightmare had ruined his sleep again, and outside, in the dreary autumn dawn, a little dog was yapping fiendishly on and on and on and on.

THE NOVELS

THE FIRST FLIGHT
[from *Jimbo*]

Blackwood did not graduate from the short story to the novel despite what the sequence of publication of his work might lead us to believe. Long before his first collection was published he had already written a book-length adventure which eventually became known as *Jimbo*. In fact, according to his autobiography, he had written it twice. With the success of his short fiction and the need to rely on his writing for his income, after 1908 Blackwood looked to his novels more seriously. He submitted the manuscript to Macmillan's on 16 November 1908 and his letter has fortunately survived, and I am grateful to Macmillan's for making it available to me. I reprint part of it here:

> I venture to submit for your consideration an original manuscript called 'An Imaginative Boy'. It is neither a children's story nor a novel, and though it is addressed more to caretakers of children than to general readers, I honestly do not quite know into what class of books it falls. If, however, in your judgement it has no value, I shall be glad, on hearing from you, to send stamps for its return, or to call at your office for the parcel.

I wonder how many manuscripts are submitted so gentlemanly these days. Blackwood's attempt to categorize the novel highlights his dilemma over his fiction, for *Jimbo* is a book about children as much as it is for children, and it was an area he would explore at much greater depth in *The Education of Uncle Paul* and *A Prisoner in Fairyland*. In *Jimbo* Blackwood captured most ingeniously the working of a child's mind, and the whole book is a delight. Jimbo is a young boy who, whilst playing with his friends, is tossed by a bull and knocked unconscious. The novel then slips into the boy's subconscious mind. He finds himself trapped in a big empty house but he is befriended by his governess, Miss Lake, who tries to help him. He learns that the only way he can escape from the empty house is by flying, and Miss Lake undertakes to teach him to fly. The extract presented here describes his first trial flight.

I

To enter the world of wings is to enter a new state of existence. The apparent loss of weight; the ability to attain full speed in a few seconds, and to stop suddenly in a headlong rush without fear of collapse; the power to steer instantly in any direction by merely changing the angle of the body; the altered and enormous view of the green world below—looking down upon forests, seas and clouds; the easy voluptuous rhythm of rising and falling in long, swinging undulations; and a hundred other things that simply defy description and can be appreciated only by actual experience, these are some of the delights of the new world of wings and flying. And the fearful joy of very high speed, especially when the exhilaration of escape is added to it, means a condition little short of real ecstasy.

Yet Jimbo's first flight, the governess had been careful to tell him, could not be the flight of final escape; for, even if the wings proved equal to a prolonged effort, escape was impossible until there was somewhere safe to escape to. So it was understood that the practice flights might be long, or might be short; the important thing, meanwhile, was to learn to fly as well as possible. For skilled flying is very different to mere headlong rushing, and both courage and perseverance are necessary to acquire it.

With rare common sense Miss Lake had said very little about the possibility of failure. Having warned him about the importance of not falling, she had then stopped, and the power of suggestion had been allowed to work only in the right direction of certain success. While the boy knew that the first plunge from the window would be a moment fraught with the highest danger, his mind only recognized the mere off-chance of falling and being caught. He felt confidence in himself, and by so much, therefore, were the chances of disaster lessened.

For the rest of the afternoon Jimbo saw nothing of his faithful companion; he spent the time practising and resting, and when weary of everything else, he went to the window and indulged in thrilling calculations about the exact height from the ground. A drop of three storeys into a paved courtyard with a monster waiting to catch him, and a high wall too close to allow a proper swing, was an alarming matter from any point of view. Fortunately, his mind dwelt more on the delight of prospective flight and freedom than on the chances of being caught.

The yard lay hot and naked in the afternoon glare and the enclosing wall had never looked more formidable; but from his lofty perch Jimbo could see beyond into soft hayfields and smiling meadows, yellow with cowslips and buttercups. Everything that flew he watched with absorbing interest: swift blackbirds, whistling as they went, and crows, their wings purple in the sunshine. The song of the larks, invisible in the sea of blue air sent a thrill of happiness through him—he, too, might soon know something of that glad music—and even the stately flight of the butterflies, which occasionally ventured over into the yard, stirred anticipations in him of joys to come.

The day waned slowly. The butterflies vanished; the rooks sailed homewards through the sunset; the wind dropped away, and the shadows of the high elms lengthened gradually and fell across the window.

The mysterious hour of the dusk, when the standard of reality changes and other worlds come close and listen, began to work its subtle spell upon his soul. Imperceptibly the shadows deepened as the veil of night drew silently across the sky. A gentle breathing filled the air; trees and fields were composing themselves to sleep; stars were peeping; wings were being folded.

But the boy's wings, trembling with life to the very tips of their long feathers, these were not being folded. Charged with excitement, like himself, they were gathering all their forces for the supreme effort of this first journey out into the open spaces where they might touch the secret sources of their own magical life.

For a long, long time he waited; but at last the trap-door lifted and Miss Lake appeared above the floor. The moment she stood in the room he noticed that her wings came through two little slits in her gown and folded down closely to the body. They almost touched the ground.

'Hush!' she whispered, holding up a warning finger.

She came over on tiptoe and they began to talk in low whispers.

'He's on the watch; we must speak very quietly. We couldn't have a better night for it. The wind's in the south and the moon won't be up till we're well on our way.'

Now that the actual moment was so near the boy felt something of fear steal over him. The night seemed so vast and terrible all of a sudden—like an immense black ocean with no friendly islands where they could fold their wings and rest.

'Don't waste your strength thinking,' whispered the governess. 'When the time comes, act quickly, that's all!'

She went over to the window and peered out cautiously, after a while beckoning the child to join her.

'He is there,' she murmured in his ear. Jimbo could only make out an indistinct shadowy object crouching under the wall, and he was not even positive of that.

'Does he know we're going?' he asked in an awed whisper.

'He's there on the chance,' she muttered, drawing back into the room. 'When there's a possibility of anyone getting frightened he's bound to be lurking about somewhere near. That's Fright all over. But he can't hurt you,' she added, 'because you're not going to get frightened. Besides, he can only fly when it's dark; and tonight we shall have the moon.'

'I'm not afraid,' declared the boy in spite of a rather fluttering heart.

'Are you ready?' was all she said.

At last, then, the moment had come. It was actually beside him, waiting, full of mystery and wonder, with alarm not far behind. The sun was buried below the horizon of the world, and the dusk had deepened into night. Stars were shining overhead; the leaves were motionless; not a breath stirred; the earth was silent and waiting. 'Yes, I'm ready,' he whispered, almost inaudibly.

'Then listen,' she said, 'and I'll tell you exactly what to do: Jump upwards from the window ledge as high as you can, and the moment you begin to drop, open your wings and strike with all your might. You'll rise at once. The thing to remember is to *rise as quickly as possible*, because the wall prevents a long, easy, sweeping rise; and, whatever happens, you must clear that wall!'

'I shan't touch the ground then?' asked a faint little voice.

'Of course not! You'll get near it, but the moment you use your wings you'll stop sinking, and rise up, up, up, ever so quickly.'

'And where to?'

'To me. You'll see me waiting for you above the trees. Steering will come naturally; it's quite easy.'

Jimbo was already shaking with excitement. He could not help it. And he knew, in spite of all Miss Lake's care, that Fright was waiting in the yard to catch him if he fell, or sank too near the ground.

'I'll go first,' added the governess, 'and the moment you see that I've cleared the wall you must jump after me. Only do not keep me waiting!'

The girl stood for a minute in silence, arranging her wings. Her fingers were trembling a little. Suddenly she drew the boy to her and kissed him passionately.

'Be brave!' she whispered, looking searchingly into his eyes, 'and strike hard—you can't possibly fail.'

In another minute she was climbing out of the window. For one second he saw her standing on the narrow ledge with black space at her feet; the next, without even a cry, she sprang out into the darkness, and was gone.

Jimbo caught his breath and ran up to see. She dropped like a stone, turning over sideways in the air, and then at once her wings opened on both sides and she righted. The darkness swallowed her up for a moment so that he could not see clearly, and only heard the threshing of the huge feathers; but it was easy to tell from the sound that she was rising.

Then suddenly a black form cleared the wall and rose swiftly in a magnificent sweep into the sky, and he saw her outlined darkly against the stars above the high elm tree. She was safe. Now it was his turn.

'Act quickly! Don't think!' rang in his ears. If only he could do it all as quickly as she had done it. But insidious fear had been working all the time below the surface, and his refusal to recognize it could not prevent it weakening his muscles and checking his power of decision. Fortunately something of his Older Self came to the rescue. The emotions of fear, excitement, and intense anticipation combined to call up the powers of his deeper being: the boy trembled horribly, but the old, experienced part of him sang with joy.

Cautiously he began to climb out on to the windowsill; first one foot and then the other hung over the edge. He sat there, staring down into black space beneath.

For a minute he hesitated; despair rushed over him in a wave; he could never take that awful jump into emptiness and darkness. It was impossible. Better be a prisoner for ever than risk so fearful a plunge. He felt cold, weak, frightened, and made a half-movement back into the room. The wings caught somehow between his legs and nearly flung him headlong into the yard.

'Jimbo! I'm waiting for you!' came at that moment in a faint cry from the stars, and the sound gave him just the impetus he needed before it was too late. He could not disappoint her—his faithful friend. Such a thing was impossible.

He stood upright on the ledge, his hands clutching the window-sash behind, balancing as best he could. He clenched his fists, drew a deep, long breath, and jumped upwards and forwards into the air.

Up rushed the darkness with a shriek; the air whistled in his ears; he dropped at fearful speed into nothingness.

At first everything was forgotten—wings, instructions, warnings, and all. He even forgot to open his wings at all, and in another second he would have been dashed upon the hard paving-stones of the courtyard where his great enemy lay waiting to seize him.

But just in the nick of time he remembered, and the long hours of practice bore fruit. Out flew the great red wings in a tremendous sweep on both sides of him, and he began to strike with every atom of strength he possessed. He had dropped to within six feet of the ground; but at once the strokes began to tell, and oh, magical sensation! He felt himself rising easily, lightly, swiftly.

A very slight effort of those big wings would have been sufficient to lift him out of danger, but in his terror and excitement he quite miscalculated their power, and in a single moment he was far out of reach of the dangerous yard and anything it contained. But the mad rush of it all made his head swim; he felt dizzy and confused, and, instead of clearing the wall, he landed on the top of it and clung to the crumbling coping with hands and feet, panting and breathless.

The dizziness was only momentary, however. In less than a minute he was on his feet and in the act of taking his second leap into space. This time it came more easily. He dropped, and the field swung up to meet him. Soon the powerful strokes of his wings drove him at great speed upwards, and he bounded ever higher towards the stars.

Overhead, the governess hovered like an immense bird, and as he rose up he caught the sounds of her wings beating the air, while far beneath him, he heard with a shudder a voice like the rushing of a great river. It made him increase his pace, and in another minute he found himself among the little whirlwinds that raced about from the beating of Miss Lake's great wings.

'Well done!' cried the delighted governess. 'Safe at last! Now we can fly to our heart's content!'

Jimbo flew up alongside, and together they dashed forward into the night.

II

There was not much talking at first. The stress of conflicting emotions was so fierce that the words choked themselves in his throat, and the desire for utterance found its only vent in hard breathing.

The intoxication of rapid motion carried him away headlong in more senses than one. At first he felt as if he never would be able to keep up; then it seemed as if he never would get down again. For with wings it is almost easier to rise than to fall, and a first flight is, before anything else, a series of vivid and audacious surprises.

For a long time Jimbo was so dizzy with excitement and the novelty of the sensation that he forgot his deliverer altogether.

And what a flight it was! Instead of the steady race of the carrier pigeon, or of the rooks homeward bound at evening, it was the seesaw motion of the wren's swinging journey across the lawn; only heavier, faster, and with more terrific impetus. Up and down, each time with a rise and fall of twenty feet, he careered, whistling through the summer night; at the drop of each curve, so low that the scents of dewy grass rose into his face; at the crest of it, so high that the trees and hedges often became mere blots upon the dark surface of the earth.

The fields rushed by beneath him; the white roads flashed past like streaks of snow. Sometimes he shot across sheets of water and felt the cooler air strike his cheeks; sometimes over sheltered meadows, where the sunshine had slept all day and the air was still soft and warm; on and on, as easily as rain dropping from the sky, or wind rushing earthwards from between the clouds. Everything flew past him at an astonishing rate—everything but the bright stars that gazed calmly overhead; and when he looked up and saw their steadfastness it helped to keep within bounds the fine alarm of this first excursion into the great vault of the sky.

'Gently, child!' gasped Miss Lake behind him. 'We shall never keep it up at this rate.'

'Oh! but it's so wonderful,' he cried, drawing in the air loudly between his teeth, and shaking his wings rapidly like a hawk before it drops.

The pace slackened a little and the girl drew up alongside. For some time they flew forward together in silence.

They had been skirting the edge of a wood, when suddenly the trees fell away and Jimbo gave a scream and rose fifty feet into the air with a single bound. Straight in front of him loomed an immense, glaring disc that seemed to swim suddenly up into the sky above the trees. It hung there before his eyes and dazzled him.

'It's only the moon,' cried Miss Lake from below.

Jimbo dropped through the air to her side again with a gasp.

'I thought it was a big hole in the sky with fire rushing through,' he explained breathlessly.

The boy stared, full of wonder and delight, at the huge flaming circle that seemed to fill half the heavens in front of him.

'Look out!' cried the governess, seizing his hand.

Whish! whew! whirr! A large bird whipped past them like some winged imp of darkness, vanishing among the trees far below. There would certainly have been a collision but for the girl's energetic interference.

'You must be on the look-out for these night-birds,' she said. 'They fly so unexpectedly, and, of course, they don't see us properly. Telegraph wires and church steeples are bad too, but then we shan't fly over cities much. Keep a good height, it's safer.'

They altered their course a little, flying at a different angle, so that the moon no longer dazzled them. Steering came quite easily by turning the body, and Jimbo still led the way, the governess following heavily and with a mighty business of wings and flapping.

It was something to remember, the glory of that first journey through the air. Sixty miles an hour, and scarcely an effort! Skimming the long ridges of the hills and rushing through the pure air of mountain tops; threading the star-beams; bathing themselves from head to foot in an ocean of cool, clean wind; swimming on the waves of viewless currents—currents warmed only by the magic of the stars, and kissed by the burning lips of flying meteors.

Far below them the moonlight touched the fields with silver and the murmur of the world rose faintly to their ears, trembling, as it were, with the inarticulate dreams of millions. Everywhere about them thrilled and sang the unspeakable power of the night. The mystery of its great heart seemed laid bare before them.

It was like a wonder-journey in some Eastern fairy tale. Sometimes they passed through zones of sweeter air, perfumed with the scents of hay and wild flowers; at others, the fresh, damp odour of ploughed fields rose up to them; or, again, they went spinning over leagues of forest where the tree-tops stretched beneath them like the surface of a wide, green sea, sleeping in the moonlight. And, when they crossed open water, the stars shone reflected in their faces; and all the while the wings, whirring and purring softly through the darkness, made pleasant music in their ears.

'I'm tired,' declared Jimbo presently.

'Then we'll go down and rest,' said his breathless companion with obvious relief.

She showed him how to spread his wings, sloping them towards the ground at an angle that enabled him to shoot rapidly downwards, at the same time regulating his speed by the least upward tilt. It was a glorious motion, without effort or difficulty, though the pace made it hard to keep the eyes open, and breathing became almost impossible. They dropped to within ten feet of the ground and then shot forward again.

But, while the boy was watching his companion's movements, and paying too little attention to his own, there rose suddenly before him out of the ground a huge, bulky form of something—and crash—he flew headlong into it.

Fortunately it was only a haystack; but the speed at which he was going lodged his head several inches under the thatch, whence he projected horizontally into space, feet, arms, and wings gyrating furiously. The governess, however, soon released him with much laughter, and they dropped down into the fallen hay upon the ground with no worse result than a shaking.

'Oh, what a lark!' he cried, shaking the hay out of his feathers, and rubbing his head rather ruefully.

'Except that larks are hardly night-birds,' she laughed, helping him.

They settled with folded wings in the shadow of the haystack; and the big moon, peeping over the edge at them, must have surely wondered to see such a funny couple, in such a place, and at such an hour.

'Mushrooms!' suddenly cried the governess, springing to her feet. 'There must be lots in this field. I'll go and pick some while you rest a bit.'

Off she went, trapesing over the field in the moonlight, her wings folded behind her, her body bent a little forward as she searched, and in ten minutes she came back with her hands full. That was undoubtedly the time to enjoy mushrooms at their best, with the dew still on their tight little jackets, and the sweet odour of the earth caught under their umbrellas.

Soon they were all eaten, and Jimbo was lying back on a pile of hay, his shoulders against the wall of the stack, and his wings gathered round him like a warm cloak of feathers. He felt cosy and dozy, full of mushrooms inside and covered with hay and feathers outside. The governess had once told him that a sort of open-air sleep sometimes came after a long flight. It was, of course, not a real sleep, but a state in which everything about oneself is forgotten; no dreams, no movement, no falling asleep and waking up in the ordinary sense, but a condition of deep repose in which recuperation is very great.

Jimbo would have been greatly interested, no doubt, to know that his real body on the bed had also just been receiving nourishment, and was now passing into a quieter and less feverish condition. The parallel always held true between himself and his body in the nursery, but he could not know anything about this, and only supposed that it was this open-air sleep that he felt gently stealing over him.

It brought at first strange throughts that carried him far away to other woods and other fields. While Miss Lake sat beside him eating her mushrooms, his mind was drawn off to some other little folk. But it was always stopped just short of them. He never could quite see their faces. Yet his thoughts continued their search, groping in the darkness; he felt sure he ought to be sharing his adventures with these other little persons, whoever they were; they ought to have been sitting beside him at the very moment, eating mushrooms, combing their wings, comparing the length of their feathers, and snuggling with him into the warm hay.

But they obstinately hovered just outside his memory, and refused to come in and surrender themselves. He could not remember who they were, and his yearnings went unsatisfied up to the stars, as yearnings generally do, while his thoughts returned weary from their search and he yielded to the seductions of the soothing open-air sleep.

The moon, meanwhile, rose higher and higher, drawing a silver veil over the stars. Upon the field the dews of midnight fell silently. A faint mist rose from the ground and covered the flowers in their dim seclusion under the hedgerows. The hours slipped away swiftly.

'Come on, Jimbo, boy!' cried the governess at length. 'The moon's below the hills, and we must be off!'

The boy turned and stared sleepily at her from his nest in the hay.

'We've got miles to go. Remember the speed we came at!' she explained, getting up and arranging her wings.

Jimbo got up slowly and shook himself.

'I've been miles away,' he said dreamily, 'miles and miles. But I'm ready to start at once.'

They looked about for a raised place to jump from. A ladder stood against the other side of the haystack. The governess climbed up it and Jimbo followed her drowsily. Hand in hand they sprang into the air from the edge of the thatched roof, and their wings spread out like sails to catch the wind. It smote their faces pleasantly as they plunged downwards and forwards, and the exhilarating rush of cool air banished from the boy's head the last vestige of the open-air sleep.

The First Flight

'We must keep up a good pace,' cried the governess, taking a stream and the hedge beyond in a single sweep. 'There's a light in the east already.'

As she spoke a dog howled in a farmyard beneath them, and she shot upwards as though lifted by a sudden gust of wind.

'We're too low,' she shouted from above. 'That dog felt us near. Come up higher. It's easier flying, and we've got a long way to go.'

Jimbo followed her up till they were several hundred feet above the earth and the keen air stung their cheeks. Then she led him still higher, till the meadows looked like the squares on a chess-board and the trees were like little toy shrubs. Here they rushed along at a tremendous speed, too fast to speak, their wings churning the air into little whirlwinds and eddies as they passed, whizzing, whistling, tearing through space.

The fields, however, were still dim in the shadows that precede the dawn, and the stars only just beginning to fade, when they saw the dark outline of the Empty House below them, and began carefully to descend. Soon they topped the high elms, startling the rooks into noisy cawing, and then, skimming the wall, sailed stealthily on outspread wings across the yard.

Cautiously dropping down to the level of the window, they crawled over the sill into the dark little room, and folded their wings.

THE VISION OF THE WINDS
[from *The Education of Uncle Paul*]

The breadth of Blackwood's imagination is no better seen than in this extract from *The Education of Uncle Paul*, his second novel, published nine months after *Jimbo* in November 1909. Blackwood put much of himself into the book, and in many ways it is autobiographical. Paul Rivers returns from many years in America to live with his sister, widow of his boyhood friend. He describes Paul Rivers much as he might himself. Rivers had spent much of his time alone in the vast timber forests. 'It was a life of solitude, but a life close to Nature; borne in his canoe down swift wilderness streams; meeting the wild animals in their secret haunts; becoming intimate with dawns and sunsets, great winds, the magic of storms and stars, and being initiated into the profound mysteries of the clean and haunted regions of the world.' All that Blackwood had done but unlike Blackwood, Paul Rivers can find no medium of expression for the delights within him. He muses early in the book: 'I know ... that the pine-trees hold wind in their arms as cups hold rare wine, and that when it spills I hear the exquisite trickling of its music—but I can't tell anyone *that*!' But then he meets his sister's children. The eldest was nicknamed Nixie, the second, another girl, was called Toby, and the third, a young boy of eight or nine, was nicknamed Jonah. Through the children's own imagination, Uncle Paul is able to reveal his innermost visions of wonder and he joins them in their 'aventures'. Now, at last, he can unburden himself of the vision of the winds.

IT was a hot afternoon in mid-June, and Paul was lying with his pipe upon the lawn. His sister was out driving. He was alone with the children and the smaller portion of the menagerie—smaller in size, that is, not in numbers; cats, kittens, and puppies were either asleep, or on the hunt, all about them. And from an open window a parrot was talking ridiculously in mixed French and English.

The giant cedars spread their branches; in the limes the bees hummed drowsily; the world lay a scented garden around him, and a very soft wind stole to and fro, stirring the bushes with sleepy murmurs and making the flowers nod.

China and Japan lay panting in the shade behind him, and not far off reposed the big grey Persian, Mrs Tompkyns. Regardless of the heat, Pouf, Zezette, and Dumps flitted here and there as though the whole lawn was specially made for their games; and Smoke, the black cat, dignified and mysterious, lay with eyes half-closed just near enough for Paul to stroke his sleek, hot sides when he felt so disposed. He—Smoke that is—blinked indifferently at passing butterflies, or twitched his great tail at the very tip when a bird settled in the branches overhead; but for the most part he was intent upon other matters—matters of genuine importance that concerned none but himself.

A few yards off Jonah and Toby were doing something with daisies—what it was Paul could not see; and on his other side Nixie lay flat upon the grass and gazed into the sky. The governess was—where all governesses should be out of lesson-time—elsewhere.

'Nixie, you're sleeping. Wake up.'

She rolled over towards him. 'No, Uncle Paul, I'm not. I was only thinking.'

'Thinking of what?'

'Oh, clouds and things; chiefly clouds, I think.' She pointed to the white battlements of summer that were passing very slowly over the heavens. 'It's so funny that you can see them move, yet can't see the thing that pushes them along.'

'Wind, you mean?'

'H'mmmmm.'

They lay flat on their backs and watched. Nixie made a screen of her hair and peered through it. Paul did the same with his fingers.

'You can touch it, and smell it, and hear it,' she went on, half to herself, 'but you can't *see* it.'

'I suspect there are creatures that can see the wind, though,' he remarked sleepily.

'I 'spect so too,' she said softly. 'I think I could, if I really tried hard enough. If I was very, oh very kind and gentle and polite to it, I think——'

'Come and tell me quietly,' Paul said with excitement. 'I believe you're right.'

He scented a delightful aventure. The child turned over on the grass twice, roller fashion, and landed against him, lying on her face with her chin in her hands and her heels clicking softly in the air.

She began to explain what she meant. 'You must listen properly because it's rather difficult to explain, you know'; he heard her breathing into his ear, and then her voice grew softer and fainter as she went on. Lower and lower it grew, murmuring like a distant mill-wheel, softer and softer; wonderful sentences and words all running gently into each other without pause, somewhere below ground. It began to sound far away, and it melted into the humming of the bees in the lime trees.... Once or twice it stopped altogether, Paul thought, so that he missed whole sentences.... Gaps came, gaps filled with no definite words, but only the inarticulate murmur of summer and summer life....

Then, without warning, he became conscious of a curious sinking sensation, as though the solid lawn beneath him had begun to undulate. The turf grew soft like air, and swam up over him in green waves till his head was covered. His ears became muffled; Nixie's voice no longer reached him as something outside himself; it was within—curiously running, so to speak, with his blood. He sank deeper and deeper into a delicious, soothing medium that both covered and penetrated him.

The child had him by the hand, that was all he knew, then—a long sliding motion, and forgetfulness.

'I'm off,' he remembered thinking, 'off at last into a real aventure!'

Down they sank, down, down; through soft darkness, and long, shadowy places, passing through endless scented caverns, and along dim avenues that stretched, for ever and ever it seemed, beneath the gloom of mighty trees. The air was cool and perfumed with earth. They were in some underworld, strangely muted, soundless, mysterious. It grew very dark.

'Where are we, Nixie?' He did not feel alarm; but a sense of wonder, touched delightfully by awe, had begun to send thrills along his nerves.

Her reply in his ear was like a voice in a tiny trumpet, far away, very soft. 'Come along! Follow me!'

'I'm coming. But it's so dark.'

'Hush,' she whispered. 'We're in a dream together. I'm not sure where exactly. Keep close to me.'

'I'm coming,' he repeated, blundering over the roots beside her; 'but where are we? I can't see a bit.'

'Tread softly. We're in a lost forest—just before the dawn,' he heard her voice answer faintly.

'A forest underground—? You mean a coal measure?' he asked in amazement.

She made no answer. 'I think we're going to see the wind,' she added presently.

Her words thrilled him inexplicably. It was as if—in that other world of gross values—someone had said, 'You're going to make a million!' It was all hushed and soft and subdued. Everything had a coating of plush.

'We've gone backwards somewhere—a great many years. But it's all right. There's no time in dreams.'

'It's dreadfully dark,' he whispered, tripping again.

The persuasion of her little hand led him along over roots and through places of deep moss. Great spaces, he felt, were about him. Shadows coated everything with silence. It was like the vast primeval forests of his country across the seas. The map of the world had somehow shifted, and here, in little England, he found the freedom of those splendid scenes of desolation that he craved. Millions of huge trees reared up about them through the gloom, and he felt their presence, though invisible.

'The sun isn't up yet,' she added after a bit. He held her hand tightly, as they stumbled slowly forward together side by side. He began to feel extraordinarily alive. Exhilaration seized him. He could have shouted with excitement.

'Hush!' whispered his guide, '*do* be careful. You'll upset us both.' The trembling of his hand betrayed him. 'You stumble like an om'ibus!'

'I'm all right. Go ahead!' he replied under his breath. 'I can see better now!'

'Now look,' she said, stopping in front of him and turning round.

The darkness lifted somewhat as he bent down to follow the direction of her gaze. On every side, dim and thronging, he saw the stems of immense trees rising upwards into obscurity. There were hundreds upon hundreds of them. His eyes followed their outline till the endless number bewildered him. Overhead, the stars were shining faintly through the tangled network of their branches. Odours of earth and moss and leaves, cool and delicate, rose about them; vast depths of silence stretched away in every direction. Great ferns stood motionless, with all the magic of frosted window panes, among their roots. All was still and dark and silent. It was the heart of a great forest before the dawn—prehistoric, unknown to man.

'Oh, I wonder—I wonder——' began Paul, groping about him

clumsily with his hands to feel the way.

'Oh, please don't talk so loud,' Nixie whispered, pinching his arm; 'we shall wake up if you do. Only people in dreams come to places like this.'

'You know the place?' he exclaimed with increasing excitement. 'So do I almost. I'm sure this has all happened before, only I can't remember——'

'We must keep as still as mice.'

'We are—still as mice.'

'This is where the winds sleep when they're not blowing. It's their resting-place.'

He looked about him, drawing a deep breath.

'Look out; you'll wake them if you breathe like *that*,' whispered the child.

'Are they asleep now?'

'Of course. Can't you see?'

'Not much—yet!'

'Move like a cat, and speak in whispers. We may see them when they wake.'

'How soon?'

'Dawn. The wind always wakes with the sun. It's getting closer now.'

It was very wonderful. No words can describe adequately the still splendour of that vast forest as they stood there, waiting for the sun-rise. Nothing stirred. The trees were carved out of some marvellous dream-stuff, motionless, yet conveying the impression of life. Paul knew it and recognized it. All primeval woods possess that quality—trees that know nothing of men and have never heard the ringing of the axe. The silence was of death, yet a sense of life that is far beyond death pulsed through it. Cisterns of quiet, gigantic, primitive life lay somewhere hidden in these shadowed glades. It seemed the counterpart of a man's soul before rude passion and power have stirred it into activity. Here all slept potentially, as in a human soul. The huge, sombre pines rose from their beds of golden moss to shake their crests faintly to the stars, awaiting the coming of the true passion—the great Sun of life, that should call them to splendour, to reality, and to the struggle of a bigger life than they yet knew, when they might even try to shake free from their roots in the hard, confining earth, and fly to the source of their existence—the sun.

And the sun was coming now. The dawn was at hand. The trees moved gently together, it seemed. The wood grew lighter. An almost imperceptible shudder ran through it as through a vast spider's web.

'Look!' cried Nixie. His simple, intuitive little guide was nearer, after all, to reality than he was, for all his subtle vision. 'Look, Uncle Paul!'

His attempt to analyse wonder had prevented his seeing it sooner, but as she spoke he became aware that something very unusual was going forward about them. His skin began to tickle, and a strange sense of excitement took possession of him.

A pale, semi-transparent substance he saw hung everywhere in the air about them, clinging in spirals and circles to the trunks, and hanging down from the branches in long slender ribbons that reached almost to the ground. The colour was a delicate pearl-grey. It covered everything as with the softest of filtered light, and hung motionless in the air in painted streamers of thinnest possible vapour.

The silken threads of these gossamer ribbons dropped from the sky in millions upon millions. They wrapped themselves round the very starbeams, and lay in sheets upon the ground; they curled themselves round the stones and crept in among the tiniest crevices of moss and bark; they clothed the ferns with their fairy gauze. Paul could even feel them coiling about his hair and beard and eyelashes. They pervaded the entire scene as light does. The colour was uniform; whether in sheets or ribbons, it did not vary in shade or in degree of transparency. The entire atmosphere was pervaded by it, frozen into absolute stillness.

'That's the winds—all that stuff,' Nixie whispered, her voice trembling with excitement. 'They're asleep still. Aren't they awful and wonderful?'

As she spoke a faint vibration ran everywhere through the ribbons. Involuntarily he tightened his grasp on the child's hand.

'That's their beginning to wake,' she said, drawing closer to him, 'like people moving in sleep.'

The vibration ran through the air again. It quivered as reflections in the surface of a pool quiver to a ghost of passing wind. They seated themselves on a fallen trunk and waited. The trees waited too; as gigantic notes in a set piece, Paul thought, that the coming sun would presently play upon like a hand upon a vast instrument. Then something moved a few feet away, and he jumped in spite of himself.

'Only Jonah,' explained his guide. 'He's asleep like us. Don't wake him; he's having a dream too.'

It was indeed Jonah, wandering vaguely this way and that, disappearing and reappearing, wholly unaware, it seemed, of their presence.

He looked like a gnome. His feet made no sound as he moved about, and after a few minutes he lost himself behind a big trunk and they saw him no more. But almost at once behind him the round figures of China and Japan emerged into view. They came, moving fast and busily, blundering against the trees, tumbling down, and butting into everything that came in their path as though they could not see properly. Paul watched them with astonishment.

'They're only half asleep, and that's why they see so badly,' Nixie told him. 'Aren't they silly and happy?'

Before he could answer, something else moved into their limited field of vision, and he was aware that a silent grey shadow was stalking solemnly by. All dignity and self-confidence it was; stately, proud, sure of itself, in a region where it was at home, conscious of its power to see and move better than anyone else. Two wide-open and brilliant eyes, shining like dropped stars, were turned for a moment towards them where they sat on the log and watched. Then, silent and beautiful, it passed on into the darkness beyond, and vanished from their sight.

'Mrs Tompkyns!' whispered Nixie. '*She* saw us all right!'

'Splendid!' he exclaimed under his breath, full of admiration.

Nixie pinched his arm. A change had come about in the last few minutes, and into this dense forest the light of approaching dawn began to steal most wonderfully. A universal murmuring filled the air.

'The sun's coming. They're going to wake now!' The child gave a little shiver of delight. Paul sat up. A general, indefinable motion, he saw, was beginning everywhere to run to and fro among the hanging streamers. More light penetrated every minute, and the tree stems began to turn from black to purple, and then from purple to faint grey. Vistas of shadowy glades began to open up on all sides; every instant the trees stood out more distinctly. The myriad threads and ribbons were astir.

'Look!' cried the child aloud; 'they're uncurling as they wake.'

He looked. The sense of wonder and beauty moved profoundly in his heart. Where, oh where, in all the dreams of his solitary years had he seen anything to equal this unearthly vision of the awakening winds?

The winds moved in their sleep, and awoke.

In loops, folds, and spirals of indescribable grace they slowly began to unwrap themselves from the tree stems with a million little delicate undulations; like thin mist trembling, and then smoothing out the ruffled surface of their thousand serpentine eddies, they slid swiftly upwards from the moss and ferns, disentangled themselves without effort from roots and stones and bark, and then, reinforced by countless thousands from the lower branches, they rose up slowly in vast coloured sheets towards the region of the tree tops.

And, as they rose, the silence of the forest passed into sound—trembling and murmuring at first, and then rapidly increasing in volume as the distant glades sent their voices to swell it, and the note of every hollow and dell joined in with its contributory note. From all the shadowy recesses of the wood they heard it come, louder and louder, leaping to the centre like running great arpeggios, and finally merging all lesser notes in the wave of a single dominant chord—the song of the awakened winds to the dawn.

'They're singing to the sun,' Nixie whispered. Her voice caught in her throat a little and she tightened her grasp on his big hand.

'They're changing colour too,' he answered breathlessly. They stood up on their log to see.

'It's the rate they go does that,' she tried to explain. She stood on tiptoe.

He understood what she meant, for he now saw that as the wind rose in ribbons, streams and spirals, the original pearl-grey changed chromatically into every shade of colour under the sun.

'Same as metals getting hot,' she said. 'Their colour comes 'cording to their speed.'

Many of the tints he found it impossible to name, for they were such as he had never dreamed of. Crimsons, purples, soft yellows, exquisite greens and pinks ran to and fro in a perfect deluge of colour, as though a hundred sunsets had been let loose and were hunting wildly for the West to set in. And there were shades of opal and mother-of-pearl so delicate that he could only perceive them in his bewildered mind by translating them into the world of sound, and imagining it was the colour of their own singing.

Far too rapidly for description they changed their protean dress, moving faster and faster, glowing fiercely one minute and fading away the next, passing swiftly into new and dazzling brilliancies as the distant winds came to join them, and at length rushing upwards in one huge central draught through the trees, shouting their song with a roar like the sea.

Suddenly they swept up into the sky—sound, colour and all—and silence once more descended upon the forest. The winds were off and about their business of the day. The woods were empty. And the sun was at the very edge of the world.

'Watch the tops of the trees now,' cried Nixie, still trembling from the strange wonder of the scene. 'The Little Winds will wake the moment the sun touches them—the little winds in the tops of the trees.'

As she spoke, the sun came up and his first rays touched the pointed crests above them with gold; and Paul noticed that there were thousands of tiny, slender ribbons streaming out like elastic threads from the tips of all the pines, and that these had only just begun to move. As at a word of command they trooped out to meet the sunshine, undulating like wee coloured serpents, and uttering their weird and gentle music at the same time. And Paul, as he listened, understood at last why the wind in the tree-tops is always more delicately sweet than any other kind, and why it touches so poignantly the heart of him who hears, and calls wonder from her deepest lair.

'The young winds, you see,' Nixie said, peering up beneath her joined hands and finding it difficult to keep her balance as she did so. 'They sleep longer than the others. And they're not loose either; they're fastened on, and can only go out and come back.'

And, as he watched, he saw these young winds fly out miles into the brightening sky, making lines of flashing colour, and then tear back with a whirring rush of music to curl up again round the twigs and pine needles.

'Though sometimes they *do* manage to get loose, and make funny storms and hurricanes and things that no one expects at all in the sky.'

Paul was on the point of replying to this explanation when something struck against his legs, and he only just saved himself from falling by seizing Nixie and risking a flying leap with her from the log.

'It's that wicked Japan again,' she laughed, clambering back on to the tree.

The puppy was vigorously chasing its own tail, bumping as it did so into everything within reach. Paul stooped to catch it. At the same instant it rose up past his very nose, and floated off through the trees and was lost to view in the sky.

Nixie laughed merrily. 'It woke in the middle of its silly little dream,' she said. 'It was only half-asleep really, and playing. It won't come back now.'

'All puppies are absurd like that——'

But he did not finish his profound observation about puppies, for his voice at that moment was drowned in a new and terrible noise that seemed to come from the heart of the wood. It happened just as in a children's fairy-tale. It bore no resemblance to the roar the winds made; there was no music in it; it was crude in quality—angry; a sound from another place.

It came swiftly nearer and nearer, increasing in volume as it came. A veil seemed to spread suddenly over the scene; the trees grew shadowy and dim; the glades melted off into mistiness; and ever the mass of sound came pouring up towards them. Paul realized that the frontiers of consciousness were shifting again in a most extraordinary fashion, so that the whole forest slipped off into the background and became a dim map in his memory, faint and unreal—and, with it, went both Nixie and himself. The ground rose and fell under their feet. Her hand melted into something fluid and slippery as he tried to keep his hold upon it. The child whispered words he could not catch. Then, like the puppy, they both began to rise.

The roar came out to meet them and enveloped them furiously in mid-air.

'At any rate, we've seen the wind!' he heard the child's voice murmuring in his beard. She rose away from him, being lighter, and vanished through the tops of the trees.

And then the roar drowned him and swept him away in a whirling tempest, so that he lost all consciousness of self and forgot everything he had ever known....

The noise resolved itself gradually into the crunching sounds of the carriage wheels and the clatter of horses' hoofs coming up the gravel drive.

Paul looked about him with a sigh that was half a yawn. China and Japan were still romping on the lawn, Mrs Tompkyns and Smoke were curled up in hot, soft circles precisely where they had been before, Toby and Jonah were still busily engaged doing 'something with daisies' in the full blaze of the sunshine, and Nixie lay beside him, all innocence and peace, still gazing through the tangle of her yellow hair at the slow-sailing clouds overhead.

And the clouds, he noticed, had hardly altered a line of their shape and position since he saw them last.

He turned with a jump of excitement.

'Nixie,' he exclaimed, 'I've seen the wind!'

She rolled over lazily on her side and fixed her great blue eyes on his own, between two strands of her hair. From the expression of her brown face it was possible to surmise that she knew nothing—and everything.

'Have you?' she said very quietly. 'I thought you might.'

'Yes, but did I dream it, or imagine it, or just think it and make it up?' He still felt a little bewildered; the memory of that strangely beautiful picture gallery still haunted him. Yonder, before the porch, the steaming horses and the smart coachman on the box, and his sister coming across the lawn from the carriage all belonged to another world, while he himself and Nixie and the other children still stayed with him, floating in a golden atmosphere where Wind was singing and alive.

'That doesn't matter a bit,' she replied, peering at him gravely before she pulled her hair over both eyes. 'The point is that it's really true! Now,' she added, her face completely hidden by the yellow web, 'all you have to do is to write it for our next Meeting—write the record of your Aventure——'

'And read it out?' he said, beginning to understand.

The yellow head nodded. He felt utterly and delightfully bewitched.

'All right,' he said; 'I will.'

'And make it a verywonderfulindeed Aventure,' she added, springing to her feet. 'Hush! Here's mother!'

Paul rose dizzily to greet his sister, while the children ran off with their animals to other things.

'You've had a pleasant afternoon, Paul, dear?' she asked.

'Oh, very nice indeed——' His thoughts were still entangled with the wind and with the story he meant to write about it for the next Meeting.

She opened her parasol and held it over her head.

'Now, come indoors,' he went on, collecting himself with an effort, 'or into the shade. This heat is not good for you, Margaret.' He looked at her pale, delicate face. 'You're tired too.'

'I enjoyed the drive,' she replied, letting him take her arm and lead her towards the house. 'I met the Burdons in their motor. They're coming over to luncheon one day, they said. You'll like *him*, I think.'

'That's very nice,' he remarked again, 'very nice. Margaret,' he exclaimed suddenly, ashamed of his utter want of interest in all she was planning for him, 'I think you ought to have a motor too. I'm going to give you one.'

'That is sweet of you, Paul,' she smiled at him. 'But really, you know, one likes horses best. They're much quieter. Motors do shake one so.'

'I don't think that matters; the point is that it's really true,' he muttered to himself, thinking of Nixie's judgement of his Aventure.

His sister looked at him with her expression of faint amusement.

'You mustn't mind me,' he laughed, planting her in a deck-chair by the shade of the house; 'but the truth is, my mind is full just now of some work I've got to do—a report, in fact, I've got to write.'

He went off into the house, humming a song. She followed him with her eyes.

'He is so strange. I do wish he would see more people and be a little more normal.'

And in Paul's mind, as he raced along the passage to his private study in search of pen and paper, there ran a thought of very different kind in the shape of a sentence from the favourite of all his books:

'Everything possible to be believed is an image of truth.'

THE CALL OF THE URWELT
[from *The Centaur*]

During May, June, and July of 1910 Blackwood travelled into the depths of the Caucasian Mountains. 'The stupendous grandeur of those almost legendary mountains made a profound impression upon a young and sensitive mind,' he later wrote. 'After an extended tour I came home charged with a thousand storms of beauty and wonder, only to find that I could not write a line about it all. Stunned and bewildered by what I had seen, the mind was speechless, incapable of expressing anything...' It took Blackwood a year to conquer this block, but in the end the flood-gates were released when Blackwood heard a penny whistle being played in the streets. 'It all stormed up out of the subconscious, and I began a book that, good or bad, released the dramatized emotions of my journey a year before through the Caucasus.' Perhaps because of the intensity of writing that followed, *The Centaur* must rank as Blackwood's most powerful work. It is a novel that in many ways defies description. Again Blackwood features in the novel, this time as Terence O'Malley, a writer of 'curious tales' and foreign correspondent for a London newspaper. Like Blackwood, O'Malley has an ardent passion for nature, and he believes man should turn to nature for his salvation. O'Malley finds himself on a roving commission to the Caucasus. On the steamer out across the Mediterranean he makes the acquaintance of the ship's doctor, a German, Heinrich Stahl. O'Malley finds he is sharing his cabin with a Russian and his son, the former an especially large, bear-like man, although his hugeness was more a mental impression than a direct inspection: 'It was upon the corner of the eye that the bulk and hugeness dawned.' In discussion with Stahl, O'Malley comes to believe that this huge stranger and his son are throwbacks from the Earth's past, beings brought into existence by the projection of the Earth's own consciousness. *Urmenschen,* Stahl called them. He explains further: 'Beings . . . not men. The prefix *ur-* I use in a deeper sense than is usually attached to it as in *urwald, urwelt* and the like. An *Urmensch* in the world today must suggest a survival of an almost incredible kind—a kind, too, utterly inadmissable and inexplicable to the materialist——'

Later Stahl clarifies further. 'He is a Cosmic Being—a direct expression of cosmic life. A little bit, a fragment, of the Soul of the World, and in that sense a survival—a survival of her youth.'

Stahl expresses concern that O'Malley is sharing a cabin with them and trusts to caution. He offers O'Malley a bed in his own cabin. O'Malley, however, feels excitement over the prospect of contact with these beings and feels less need to exercise caution.

I

THE offer of the cabin remained open. In the solitude that O'Malley found necessary that evening he toyed with it, though knowing that he would never really accept.

Like a true Celt his imagination took the main body of Stahl's words and ensouled them with his own vivid temperament. There stirred in him this nameless and disquieting joy that wrought for itself a Body from material just beyond his thoughts—that region of enormous experience that ever fringes the consciousness of imaginative men. He took the picture at its face value, took it inside with his own thoughts, delighted in it, raised it, of course, very soon to a still higher scale. If he criticized at all it was with phrases like 'The man's a poet after all! Why, he's got creative imagination!' To find his own intuitions endorsed, even half explained, by a mind of opposite type was a new experience. It emphasized amazingly the reality of that inner world he lived in.

This explanation of the big Russian's effect upon himself was terrific, and that a 'doctor' should have conceived it, glorious. That some portion of a man's spirit might assume the shape of his thoughts and project itself visibly seemed likely enough. Indeed, to him, it seemed already a 'fact', and his temperament did not linger over it. But that other suggestion fairly savaged him with its strange grandeur. He played lovingly with it.

That the Earth was a living being was a conception divine in size as in simplicity, and that the Gods and mythological figures had been projections of her consciousness—this thought ran with a magnificent new thunder about his mind. It was overwhelming, beautiful as Heaven and as gracious. He saw the ancient shapes of myth and legend still alive in some gorgeous garden of the primal world, a corner too remote for humanity to have yet stained it with their trail of uglier life. He understood in quite a new way, at last, those deep primitive longings that hitherto had vainly craved their full acknowledgment. It meant that he lay so close to the Earth that he felt her pulses as his own. The idea stormed his belief.

It was the Soul of the Earth herself that all these years had been calling to him.

And while he let his imagination play with the soaring beauty of the idea, he remembered certain odd little facts. He marshalled them before him in a row and questioned them: the picture he had seen with the Captain's glasses—those speeding shapes of beauty; the new aspect of a living Nature that the Russian's presence stirred in him; the man's broken words as they had leaned above the sea in the dusk; the curious passion that leaped to his eyes when certain chance words had touched him at the dinner-table. And, lastly, the singular impression of giant bulk he produced sometimes upon the mind, almost as though a portion of him—this detachable portion moulded by the quality of his spirit as he *felt* himself to be—emerged visibly to cause it.

Vaguely, in this way, O'Malley divined how inevitable was the apparent isolation of these two, and why others instinctively avoided them. They seemed by themselves in an enclosure where the parent lumberingly, and the boy defiantly, disported themselves with a kind of lonely majesty that forbade approach.

And it was later that same night, as the steamer approached the Lipari Islands, that the drive forward he had received from the doctor's words was increased by a succession of singular occurrences. At the same time, Stahl's deliberate and as he deemed it unjustifiable interference, helped him to make up his mind decisively on certain other points.

The first 'occurrence' was of the same order as the 'bigness'—extraordinarily difficult, that is, to confirm by actual measurement.

It was ten o'clock, Stahl still apparently in his cabin by himself, and most of the passengers below at an impromptu concert, when the Irishman, coming down from his long solitude, caught sight of the Russian and his boy moving about the dark afterdeck with a speed and vigour that instantly arrested his attention. The suggestion of size, and of rapidity of movement, had never been more marked. It was as though a cloud of the summer darkness moved beside them.

Then, going cautiously nearer, he saw that they were neither walking quickly, nor running, as he had first supposed, but—to his amazement—were standing side by side upon the deck—stock still. The appearance of motion, however, was not entirely a delusion, for he next saw that, while standing there steady as the mast and lifeboats behind them, something emanated shadow-like from both their persons and seemed to hover and play about them—something that was only approximately of their own outer shapes, and very considerably larger. Now it veiled them, now left them clear. He thought of smoke-clouds moving to and fro about dark statues.

So far as he could focus his sight upon them, these 'shadows', without any light to cast them, moved in distorted guise there on the deck with a motion that was somehow rhythmical—a great movement as of dance or gambol.

As with the appearance of 'bigness', he perceived it first out of the corner of his eye. When he looked again he saw only two dark figures, motionless.

He experienced the sensation a man sometimes knows on entering a deserted chamber in the night time, and is aware that the things in it have just that instant—stopped. His arrival puts abrupt end to some busy activity they were engaged in, which begins again the moment he goes. Chairs, tables, cupboards, the very spots and patterns of the wall have just flown back to their usual places whence they watch impatiently for his departure—with the candle.

This time, on a deck instead of in a room, O'Malley with his candle had surprised them in the act: people, moreover, not furniture. And this shadowy gambol, this silent Dance of the Emanations, immense yet graceful, made him think of Winds flying, visible and uncloaked, somewhere across long hills, or of Clouds passing to a stately, elemental measure over the blue dancing-halls of an open sky. His imagery was confused and gigantic, yet very splendid. Again he recalled the pictured shapes seen with his mind's eye through the captain's glasses. And as he watched, he felt in himself what he called 'the wild, tearing instinct to run and join them,' more even—that by rights he ought to have been there from the beginning—dancing with them—indulging a natural and instinctive and rhythmical movement that he had somehow forgotten.

The passion in him was very strong, very urgent, it seems, for he took a step forward, a call of some kind rose in his throat, and in another second he would have been similarly cavorting upon the deck, when he felt his arm clutched suddenly with vigour from behind. Someone seized him and held him back. A German voice spoke with a guttural whisper in his ear.

Dr Stahl, crouching and visibly excited, drew him forward a little.

'Hold up!' he heard whispered—for their india-rubber soles slithered on the wet decks. 'We shall see from here, eh? See something at last?' He still whispered. O'Malley's sudden anger died down. He could not give vent to it without making noise, for one thing, and above all else he wished to—see. He merely felt a vague wonder how long Stahl had been watching.

They crouched behind the lee of a boat. The outline of the ship rose, distinctly visible against the starry sky, masts, spars, and cordage. A faint gleam came through the glass below the compass-box. The wheel and the heaps of coiled rope beyond rose and fell with the motion of the vessel, now against the stars, now black against the phosphorescent foam that trailed along the sea like shining lace. But the human figures, he next saw, were now doing nothing, not even pacing the deck; they were no longer of unusual size either. Quietly leaning over the rail, father and son side by side, they were guiltless of anything more uncommon than gazing into the sea. Like the furniture, they had just—stopped!

Dr Stahl and his companion waited motionless for several minutes in silence. There was no sound but the dull thunder of the screws, and a faint windy whistle the ship's speed made in the rigging. The passengers were all below. Then, suddenly, a burst of music came up as someone opened a saloon porthole and as quickly closed it again—a tenor voice singing to the piano some trivial modern song with a trashy sentimental lilt. It was—in this setting of sea and sky—painful; O'Malley caught himself thinking of a barrel-organ in a Greek temple.

The same instant father and son, as though startled, moved slowly away down the deck into the further darkness, and Dr Stahl tightened his grip of the Irishman's arm with a force that almost made him cry out. A gleam of light from the opened porthole had fallen about them before they moved. Quite clearly it revealed them bending busily over, heads close together, necks and shoulders thrust forward and down a little.

'Look, by God!' whispered Stahl hoarsely as they moved off. 'There's a third!'

He pointed. Where the two had been standing something, indeed, still remained. Concealed hitherto by their bulk, this other figure had been left. They saw its large, dim outline. It moved. Apparently it began to climb over the rails, or to move in some way just outside them, hanging half above the sea. There was a free, swaying movement about it, not ungainly so much as big—very big.

'Now, quick!' whispered the doctor excited, in English; 'this time I find out, sure!'

He made a violent movement forward, a pocket electric lamp in his hand, then turned angrily, furiously, to find that O'Malley held him fast. There was a most unseemly struggle—for a minute, and it was caused by the younger man's sudden passionate instinct to protect his own from discovery, if not from actual capture and destruction.

Stahl fought in vain, being easily overmatched; he swore vehement German oaths under his breath; and the pocket-lamp, of course unlighted, fell and rattled over the deck, sliding with the gentle roll of the steamer to leeward. But O'Malley's eyes, even while he struggled, never for one instant left the spot where the figure and the 'movement' had been; and it seemed to him that when the bulwarks dipped against the dark of the sea, the moving thing completed its efforts and passed into the waves with a swift leap. When the vessel righted herself again the outline of the rail was clear.

Dr Stahl, he then saw, had picked up the lamp and was bending over some mark upon the deck, examining a wide splash of wet upon which he directed the electric flash. The sense of revived antagonism between the men for the moment was strong, too strong for speech. O'Malley feeling half ashamed, yet realized that his action had been instinctive, and that another time he would do just the same. He would fight to the death any too close inspection, since such inspection included also now—himself.

The doctor presently looked up. His eyes shone keenly in the gleam of the lamp, but he was no longer agitated.

'There is too much water,' he said calmly, as though diagnosing a case; 'too much to permit of definite traces.' he glanced round, flashing the beam about the decks. The other two had disappeared. They were alone. 'It was outside the rail all the time, you see,' he added 'and never quite reached the decks.' He stooped down and examined the splash once more. It looked as though a wave had topped the scuppers and left a running line of foam and water. 'Nothing to indicate its exact nature,' he said in a whisper that conveyed something between uneasiness and awe, again turning the light sharply in every direction and peering about him. 'It came to them—er—from the sea, though; it came from the sea right enough. That, at least, is positive.' And in his manner was perhaps just a touch to indicate relief.

'And it returned into the sea,' exclaimed O'Malley triumphantly. It was as though he related his own escape.

The two men were now standing upright, facing one another. Dr Stahl, betraying no sign of resentment, looked him steadily in the eye. He put the lamp back into his pocket. When he spoke at length in the darkness, the words were not precisely what the Irishman had expected. Under them his own vexation and excitement faded instantly. He felt almost sheepish when he remembered his violence.

'I forgive your behaviour, of course,' Stahl said, 'for it is consistent—splendidly consistent—with my theory of you; and of value, therefore. I only now urge you again'—he moved closer, speaking almost solemnly—'to accept the offer of a berth in my cabin. Take it, my friend, take it—tonight.'

'Because you wish to watch me at close quarters.'

'No,' was the reply, and there was sympathy in the voice, 'but because you are in danger—especially in sleep.'

There was a moment's pause before O'Malley said anything.

'It is kind of you, Dr Stahl, very kind,' he answered slowly, and this time with grave politeness; 'but I am not afraid, and I see no reason to make the change. And as it's now late,' he added somewhat abruptly, almost as though he feared he might be persuaded to alter his mind, 'I will say goodnight and turn in—if you will forgive me—at once.'

Dr Stahl said no further word. He watched him, the other was aware, as he moved down the deck towards the saloon staircase, and then turned once more with his lamp to stoop over the splashed portion of the boards. He examined the place apparently for a long time.

But O'Malley, as he went slowly down the hot and stuffy stairs, realized with a wild and rushing tumult of joy that the 'third' he had seen was of a splendour surpassing the little figures of men, and that something deep within his own soul was most gloriously akin with it. A link with the Universe had been subconsciously established, tightened up, adjusted. From all this living Nature breathing about him in the night, a message had reached the strangers and himself—a message shaped in beauty and in power. Nature had become at last aware of his presence close against her ancient face. Henceforth would every sight of Beauty take him direct to the place where Beauty comes from. No middleman, no Art was necessary. The gates were opening. Already he had caught a glimpse.

II

In the state-room he found, without surprise somehow, that his new companions had already retired for the night. The curtain of the upper berth was drawn, and on the sofa-bed below the opened porthole the boy already slept. Standing a moment in the little room with these two close, he felt that he had come into a new existence almost. Deep within him this sense of new life thrilled and glowed. He was shaking a little all over, not with the mere tremor of excitement, however, but with the tide of a vast and rising exultation he could scarce contain. For his normal self was too small to hold it. It demanded expansion, and the expansion it claimed had already begun. The boundaries of his personality were enormously extending.

In words this change escaped him wholly. He only knew that something in him of an old unrest lay down at length and slept. Less acute grew those pangs of starvation his life had ever felt—the ache of that inappeasable hunger for the beauty and innocence of some primal state before thick human crowds had stained the world with all their strife and clamour. The glory of it burned white within him.

And the way he described it to himself was significant of its true nature. For it was the analogy of childhood. The passion of a boy's longing swept over him. He knew again the feelings of those early days when

> A boy's will is the wind's will,
> And the thoughts of youth are long, long thoughts,

when all the world smells sweet and golden as a summer's day, and a village street is endless as the sky....

This it was, raised to its highest power, that dropped a hint of explanation into that queer heart of his wherein had ever burned the strange desire for primitive existence. It was the Call, though, not of his own youth alone, but of the youth of the world. A mood of the Earth's consciousness—some giant expression of her cosmic emotion—caught him. And it was the big Russian who acted as channel and interpreter.

Before getting into bed, he drew aside the little red curtain that screened his companion, and peered cautiously through the narrow slit. The big occupant of the bunk also slept, his mane-like hair spread about him over the pillow, and on his great, placid face a look of peace that seemed to deepen with every day the steamer neared her destination. O'Malley gazed for a full minute and more. Then the sleeper felt the gaze, for suddenly the eyelids quivered, moved, and lifted. The large brown eyes peered straight into his own. The Irishman, unable to turn away in time, stood fixed and staring in return. The gentleness and power of the look passed straight down into his heart, filled him to the brim with things their owner knew, and confirmed that appeasement of his own hunger, already begun.

'I tried—to prevent the—interference,' he stammered in a low voice. 'I held him back. You saw me?'

A huge hand stretched forth from the bunk to stop him. Impulsively he seized it with both his own. At the first contact he started—a little frightened. It felt so wonderful, so mighty. Thus might a gust of wind or a billow of the sea have thrust against him.

'A messenger—came,' said the man with that laborious slow utterance, and deep as thunder, 'from—the—sea.'

'From—the—sea, yes,' repeated O'Malley beneath his breath, yet conscious rather that he wanted to shout and sing it. He saw the big man smile. His own small hands were crushed in the grasp of power. 'I—understand,' he added, in a whisper. He found himself speaking with a similar clogged utterance. Somehow, it seemed, the language they ought to have used was either forgotten or unborn. Yet whereas his friend was inarticulate perhaps, he himself was—dumb. These little modern words were all wrong and inadequate. Modern speech could only deal with modern smaller things.

The giant half rose in his bed, as though at first to leap forward and away from it. He tightened an instant the grasp upon his companion's hands, then suddenly released them and pointed across the cabin. That smile of happiness spread upon his face. O'Malley turned. There the boy lay, deeply slumbering, the clothes flung back so that the air from the porthole played over the bare neck and chest; upon his face, too, shone the look of peace and rest his father wore, the hunted expression all gone, as though the spirit had escaped in sleep. The parent pointed, first to the boy, then to himself, then to this new friend standing beside his bed. The gesture including the three of them was of singular authority—invitation, welcome, and command lay in it. More—in some incomprehensible way it was majestic. O'Malley's thought flashed upon him the limb of some great oak tree, swaying in the wind.

Next, placing a finger on his lips, his eyes once more swept O'Malley and the boy, and he turned again into the little bunk that so difficultly held him, and lay back. The hair flowed down and mingled with the beard, over pillow and neck, almost to the shoulders. And something that was enormous and magnificent lay back with him, carrying with it again that sudden atmosphere of greater bulk. With a deep sound in his throat that was certainly no actual word and yet more expressive than any speech, he turned hugely over among the little, scanty sheets, drew the curtain again before his face, and returned into the world of—sleep.

III

But O'Malley rolled into his own berth below without undressing, sleep far from his eyes. He had heard the Gates of ivory and horn swing softly upon their opening hinges, and the glimpse he caught of the garden beyond made any question of slumber impossible. Again he saw those shapes of cloud and wind flying over the long hills, while the name that should describe them ran, hauntingly splendid, along the mysterious passages of his being, though never coming quite to the surface for capture.

Perhaps, too, he was glad that the revelation was only partial. The size of the vision thus invoked awed him a little, so that he lay there half wondering at the complete surrender he had made to this guidance of another soul.

Stahl's warnings ran far away and laughed. The idea even came to him that Stahl was playing with him: that his portentous words had been carefully chosen for their heightening effect upon his own imagination so that the doctor might study an uncommon and extreme 'case.' The notion passed through him merely, without lingering.

In any event it was idle to put the brakes on now. He was internally committed and must go wherever it might lead. And the thought rejoiced him. He had climbed upon a pendulum that swung into an immense past; but its return swing would bring him safely back. It was rushing now into that nameless place of freedom that the primitive portion of his being had hitherto sought in vain, and a fundamental, starved craving of his life would know satisfaction at last. Already life had grown all glorious without. It was not steel engines but a speeding sense of beauty that drove the ship over the sea with feet of winged blue darkness. The stars fled with them across the sky, dropping golden leashes to draw him faster and faster forwards—yet *within*—to the dim days when this old world yet was young. He took his fire of youth and spread it, as it were, all over life till it covered the entire world, far, far away. Then he stepped back into it, and the world herself, he found, stepped with him.

He lay listening to the noises of the ship, the thump and bumble of the engines, the distant droning of the screws under water. From time to time stewards moved down the corridor outside, and the footsteps of some late passenger still paced the decks overhead. He heard voices, too, and occasionally the clattering of doors. Once or twice he fancied someone moved stealthily to the cabin door and lingered there, but the matter never drew him to investigate, for the sound each time resolved itself naturally into the music of the ship's noises.

And everything, meanwhile, heard or thought, fed the central concern upon which his mind was busy. These superficial sounds, for instance, had nothing to do with the real business of the ship; *that* lay below with the buried engines and the invisible screws that worked like demons to bring her into port. And with himself and his slumbering companions the case was similar. Their respective power-stations, working in the subconscious, had urged them towards one another inevitably. How long, he wondered, had the spirit of that lonely, alien 'being' flashed messages into the void that reached no receiving-station tuned to their acceptance? Their accumulated power was great, the currents they generated immense. He knew. For had they not charged full into himself the instant he came on board, bringing an intimacy that was immediate and full-fledged?

The untamed longings that always tore him when he felt the great winds, moved through forests, or found himself in desolate places, were at last on the high road to satisfaction—to some 'state' where all that they represented would be explained and fulfilled. And whether such 'state' should prove to be upon the solid surface of the earth, objective; or in the fluid regions of his inner being, subjective—was of no account whatever. It would be true. The great figure that filled the berth above him, now deeply slumbering, had in him subterraneans that gave access not only to Greece, but far beyond that haunted land, to a state of existence symbolized in the legends of the early world by Eden and the Golden Age....

'You are in danger,' that wise old speculative doctor had whispered, 'and especially in sleep!' But he did not sleep. He lay there thinking, thinking, a rising exaltation of desire paving busily the path along which eventually he might escape.

As the night advanced and the lesser noises retired, leaving only the deep sound of the steamer talking to the sea, he became aware, too, that a change, at first imperceptibly, then swiftly, was stealing over the cabin. It came with a riot of silent Beauty. At a loss to describe it with precision, he nevertheless divined that it proceeded from the sleeping figure overhead and in a lesser measure, too, from the boy upon the sofa opposite. It emanated from these two, he felt, in proportion as their bodies passed into deeper and deeper slumber, as though what occurred sometimes upon the decks by an act of direct volition, took place now automatically and with a fuller measure of release. Their spirits, free of that other world in sleep, were alert and potently discharging. Unconsciously, their vital, underlying essence escaped into activity.

Growing about his own person, next, it softly folded him in, casing his inner being with glory and this crowding sense of beauty. This increased manifestation of psychic activity reached down into the very core of himself, like invisible fingers playing upon an instrument. Notes—powers—in his soul, hitherto silent because none had known how to sound them, rose singing to the surface. For it seemed at length that forms of some intenser life, busily operating, moved to and fro within the painted white walls of that little cabin, working subtly to bring about a transformation of himself. A singular change was fast and cleverly at work in his own being. It was, he puts it, a silent and irresistible Evocation.

No one of his senses was directly affected; certainly he neither saw, felt, nor heard anything in the usual acceptance of the terms; but any instant surely, it seemed that *all* his senses must awake and report to the mind things that were splendid beyond the common order. In the crudest aspect of it, he felt as though he extended and grew large—that he dreaded to see himself in the mirror lest he might witness an external appearance of bigness which corresponded to this interior expansion.

For a long time he lay unresisting, letting the currents of this subjective tempest play through and round him. Entrancing sensations of beauty and rapture came with it. The outer world seemed remote and trivial, the passengers unreal—the priest, the voluble merchant, the jovial captain, all spun like dead things at the periphery of life; whereas *he* was moving toward the Centre. Stahl——! the thought of Dr Stahl, alone intruded with a certain unwelcome air of hindrance, almost as though he sought to end it, or call a halt. But Stahl, too, himself presently spun off like a leaf before the rising wind....

And then it was that an external sense was tapped, and he did hear something. From the berth overhead came a faint sound that made his heart stand still, though not with common fear. He listened intently. The blood tearing through his ears at first concealed its actual nature. It was far, far away; then came closer, as a waft of wind brings near and carries off again a sound of bells in mountains. It fled over vales and hills, to return a moment after with suddenness—a little louder, a little nearer. And with it came an increase of this sense of beauty that stretched his heart, as it were, to some deep ancient scale of joy once known, but long forgotten....

Across the cabin, the boy moved uneasily in his sleep.

'Oh, that I could be with him where he now is!' he cried, 'in that place of eternal youth and eternal companionship!' The cry was instinctive utterly; his whole being, condensed in the single yearning, pressed through it—drove behind it. The place, the companionship, the youth—all, he knew, would prove in some strange way enormous, vast, ultimately satisfying for ever and ever, far out of this little modern world that imprisoned him....

Again, most unwelcome and unexplained, the face of Stahl flashed suddenly before him to hinder and interrupt. He banished it with an effort, for it brought a smaller comprehension that somehow involved—fear.

'Curse the man!' flamed in anger across his world of beauty, and the violence of the contrast broke something in his mind like a globe of coloured glass that had focused the exquisiteness of the vision.... The sound continued as before, but its power of evocation lessened. The thought of Stahl—Stahl in his denying aspect—dimmed it.

Glancing up at the frosted electric light, O'Malley felt vaguely that if he turned it out he would somehow yet see better, hear better, understand more; and it was this practical consideration, introduced indirectly by the thought of Stahl, that made him realize now for the first time that he actually and definitely was—afraid. For, to leave his bunk with its comparative, protective dark, and step into the middle of a cabin he knew to be alive with a seethe of invisible charging forces made him realize that distinct effort was necessary—effort of will. If he yielded he would be caught up and away, swept from his known moorings, borne through high space out of himself. And Stahl with his cowardly warnings and belittlements set fear, thus, in the place of free acceptance. Otherwise he might even have come to these long blue hills where danced and raced the giant shapes of cloud, singing while...

'Singing'! Ah! There was the clue! The sound he heard was singing—faint, low singing; close beside him too. It was the big man, singing softly in his sleep.

This ordinary explanation of the 'wonder-sound' brought him down to earth, and so to a more normal feeling of security again. He stepped cautiously from the bed, careful not to let the rings rattle on the rod of brass, and slowly raised himself upright. And then, through a slit of the curtain, he—saw. The lips of the big sleeper moved gently, the beard rising and falling very slightly with them, and this murmur that he had thought so far away, came out and sang deliciously and faint before his very face. It most curiously—flowed. Easily, naturally, almost automatically, it poured softly forth, and the Irishman at once understood why he had first mistaken it for an echo of wind from distant hills. The imagery was entirely accurate. For it was precisely the singing cry that wind makes in a keyhole, in a chimney, or passing idly over the sweep of grassy hills. Exactly thus had he often listened to it swishing through the crannies of high rocks, tuneless yet searching. In it, too, there lay some accent of a secret, dim sublimity, deeper far than any other human sound could touch. The terror of a great freedom caught him, a freedom most awfully remote from the smaller personal existence he knew Today ... for it suggested, with awe and wonder, the kind of primitive utterance that was before speech or the development of language; when emotions were still too vague and mighty to be caught by little words, but when beings, close to the heart of their great Mother, expressed the feelings, enormous and uncomplex, of the greater life they shared as portions of her,—projections of the Earth herself.

With a crash in his brain, O'Malley stopped. These thoughts, he suddenly realized, were not his own. An attack of unwonted sensations stung and scattered his mind with a rush of giant splendour that threatened to overwhelm him. He was in the very act of being carried away; his sense of personal identity menaced; surrender wellnigh already complete.

Another moment, especially if those eyes opened and caught him, he would be beyond recall in the region of these other two. The narrow space of that little cabin was charged already to the brim, filled with some overpowering loveliness of wild and simple things, the beauty of stars and winds and flowers, the terror of seas and mountains; strange radiant forms of gods and heroes, nymphs, fauns, and satyrs; the fierce sunshine of some Golden Age unspoilt, of a stainless region now long forgotten and denied—that world of splendour his heart had ever craved in vain, and beside which the life of Today faded to a wretched dream.

It was the *Urwelt* calling....

With a violent internal effort, he tore his gaze from those eyelids that fortunately opened not. At the same moment, though he did not hear them, steps came close in the corridor, and there was a rattling of the knob. Behind him, a movement from the berth below the porthole warned him that he was but just in time. The Vision he was afraid as yet to acknowledge drew with such awful speed towards the climax.

Quickly he turned away, lifted the hook of the cabin door, and passed into the passage, strangely faint. A great commotion followed him out: father and son both, it seemed, suddenly upon their feet. And at the same time the sound of 'singing' rolled into the body of a great hushed chorus, as it were of galloping winds that filled big valleys far away with a gust of splendour, faintly roaring in some incredible distance where no cities were, nor habitations of men; with a freedom, too, that was majestic and sublime. Oh! the terrific gait of that life in an open world!—Golden to the winds!—uncrowded!—The cosmic life——!

O'Malley shivered as he heard. For an instant, the true grain of his inner life, picked out in flame and silver, flashed clear. Almost—he knew himself caught back.

And there, in the dimly lighted corridor, against the panelling of the cabin wall, crouched Dr Stahl—listening. The pain of the contrast was vivid beyond words. It seemed as if he had passed from the thunder of organs to hear the rattling of tin cans. Instantly he understood the force that all along had held him back: the positive, denying aspect of this man's mind—afraid.

'*You*!' he exclaimed in a high whisper. 'What are *you* doing here?' He hardly remembers what he said. The doctor straightened up and came on tip-toe to his side. He moved hurriedly.

'Come away,' he said vehemently under his breath. 'Come with me to my cabin—to the decks—anywhere away from this—before it's too late.'

And the Irishman then realized that his face was white and that his voice shook. The hand that gripped him by the arm shook too.

They went quickly along the deserted corridor and up the stairs, O'Malley making no resistance, moving in a kind of dream. He had a fleeting recollection of an odour, sweet and slightly pungent as of horses, in his nostrils. The wind of the open decks revived him, and he saw to his amazement that the East was brightening. In that cabin, then, hours had been compressed into minutes.

The steamer had already slipped by the Straits of Messina. To the right he saw the cones of Etna, shadowy in the sky, calling across the dawn to Stromboli their smoking brother of the Lipari. To the left over the blue Ionian Sea the lights of a cloudless sunrise rose softly above the world.

And the hour of enchantment seized and shook him anew. Somewhere, across those faint blue waves, lay the things that he so passionately sought. It was the very essence of their loveliness and wonder that had charged down between the walls of that stuffy cabin below. For every morning still, at dawn, the tired world knows again the splendours of her youth; and the Irishman, shuddering a little in his sacred joy, felt that he must burst his bonds and fly to join the sunrise and the sea. The yearning, he was aware, had now increased a thousandfold: its fulfilment was merely delayed.

He passed along the decks all slippery with dew into Dr Stahl's cabin, and flung himself on the broad sofa to sleep. Sleep, too, came at once; he was profoundly exhausted; and, while he slept, Stahl watched over him, covering his body with a thick blanket.

THE SUMMONING
[from *Julius LeVallon*]

Although *Julius LeVallon* was not published until May 1916 Blackwood had completed the novel in February 1911 when he was still striving for inspiration on *The Centaur*. At that time Blackwood regarded it as the first half of a much bigger novel, but he found it difficult to continue the theme and in the end he treated it as a single work. It would be nine more years before he was able to complete the sequel, *The Bright Messenger*.

To have the creative gift to write both *Julius LeVallon* and *The Centaur* at the same time is only to demonstrate the peak of productive power Blackwood had reached in 1911. It is a deep and moving novel about two school friends, John Mason and young Julius. LeVallon can remember his past incarnations, in particular one, many aeons past, when he, along with the former incarnations of Mason and another, took part in an illegal experiment which failed. LeVallon plans to atone for that sin and to conquer anew but to do that he must find the other two souls from that past day and awaken in them the memory of the past.

The novel has two climaxes, the first being set in the days when Mason and LeVallon are at Edinburgh University. Again one is tempted to wonder how much in the novel is based on actual incidents in Blackwood's life. Some of the character of LeVallon was drawn from the Hindu medical student whom we encountered in 'A Mysterious House'. Remember the 'curious and interesting experiments' Blackwood and he conducted. How much might they be related to the following extract wherein LeVallon, whose meetings with Mason have been temporarily interrupted by the arrival of Mason's fiancée, sets out to prove his powers to Mason, the first-person narrator.

For some weeks our talks and walks were interrupted; I devoted myself to work, to intercourse with those I loved, and led generally the normal existence of a university student who was reading for examinations that were of importance to his future career in life.

Yet, though we rarely met, and certainly held no converse for some time, interruption actually there was none at all. To pretend it were a farce. The inner relationship continued as before. Physical separation meant absolutely nothing in those ties that so strangely and so intimately knit our deeper lives together. There was no more question of break between us than there is question of a break in time when light is extinguished and the clock becomes invisible. His presence always stood beside me; the beauty of his pale, un-English face kept ever in my thoughts; I heard his whisper in my dreams at night, and the ideas his curious language watered continued growing with a strength I could not question.

There were two selves in me then as in our schooldays: one that resisted, and one that yearned. When together, it was the former that asserted its rights, but when apart, oddly enough, it was the latter. There is little question, however, that the latter was the stronger of the two. Thus, the moment I found myself alone again, my father and my fiancée both gone, we rushed together like two ends of an elastic that had been stretched too long apart.

And almost immediately, as though the opportunity must not be lost, he spoke to me of an experiment he had in view.

By what network of persuasiveness he induced me to witness, if not actually to co-operate in, this experiment, I cannot pretend at this distance to remember. I think it is true that he used no persuasion at all, but that at the first mention of it my deeper being met the proposal with curious sympathy. At the horror and audacity my upper self shrank back aghast; the thing seemed wholly unpermissible and dreadful; something unholy, as of blasphemy, lay in it too. But, as usual, when this mysterious question of 'Other Places' was involved, in the end I followed blindly where he led. My older being held the casting vote. And the reason—I admit it frankly—was that somewhere behind the amazing glamour of it all lay—truth. While reason scoffed, my heart remembered and believed.

Moreover, in this particular instance, a biting curiosity had its influence too. I was wholly sceptical of results. The thing was mad, incredible, even wicked. It could never happen. Yet, while I said these words, and more besides, there ran a haunting terror in me underground that, after all ... that possibly ... I cannot even set down in words the nature of my doubt. I can merely affirm that something in me was not absolutely sure.

'The essential thing,' he told me, 'is to find an empty "instrument" that is in perfect order—young, vigorous, the tissues unwasted by decay or illness. There must have been no serious deterioration of the organs, muscles, and so forth.'

I knew then that this new experiment was akin to that other I had already witnessed. The experience on the Pentlands had also been deliberately brought about. The only difference was that this second one he announced beforehand. Further, it was of a higher grade. The channel of evocation, instead of being in the vegetable kingdom, was in the human.

I understood his meaning, and suggested that someone in deep trance might meet the conditions, for in trance he held that the occupant, or soul, was gone elsewhere, the tenement of flesh deserted.

But he shook his head. That was not, he said, legitimate. The owner would return. He watched me with a curious smile as he said this. I knew then that he referred to the final emptiness of a vacated body.

'Sudden death,' I said, while his eyes flashed back the answer. 'And the Elemental Powers?' I asked quickly.

'Wind and fire,' he replied. And in order to carry his plan into execution he proposed to avail himself of his free access to the students' Dissecting Room.

During the longish interval between the conception and carrying out of this preposterous experiment I shifted like a weathercock between acceptance and refusal. My doubts were torturing. There were times when I treated it as the proposal of a lunatic that at worst could work no injury to anyone concerned. But there were also times when a certain familiar reality clothed it with a portentous actuality. I was reminded faintly of something similar I had been connected with before. Dim figures of this lost familiarity stalked occasionally across the field of inner sight. Julius and I had done this thing together long, long ago, 'when the sun was younger,' and when we were 'nearer to the primitive beauty,' as he phrased it. In reverie, in dreams, in moments when thinking was in abeyance, this odd conviction asserted itself. It had to do with a Memory of some worship that once was mighty and effective; when august Presences walked the earth in stupendous images of power; and traffic with them had been useful, possible. The barrier between the human and the non-human, between Man and Nature, was not built. Wind and fire! It was always wind and fire that he spoke of. And I remember one vivid and terrific dream in particular in which I heard again a voice pronounce that curious name of 'Concerighé', and, though the details were blurred on waking, I clearly grasped that certain elemental powers had been evoked, by us for purposes of our own and had not been suffered to return to their appointed places; further, that concerned with us in the awful and solemn traffic was—another. We had been three.

This dream, of course, I easily explained as due directly to my talks with Julius, but my dread was not so easily dismissed, and that I overcame it finally and consented to attend was due partly to the extraordinary curiosity I felt, and partly to this inexplicable attraction in my deeper self which urged me to see the matter through. Something inevitable about it forced me. Yet, but for the settled conviction that behind the abhorrent proposal lay some earnest purpose of LeVallon's, not ignoble in itself, I should certainly have refused. For, though saying little, and not taking me fully into his confidence, he did manage to convey the assurance that this thing was not to be carried out as an end, but as a means to an end, in itself both legitimate and necessary. It was, I gathered, a kind of preliminary trial—an attempt that *might* possibly succeed, even without the presence of the third.

'Sooner or later,' he said, aware that I hesitated, 'it must be faced. Here is an opportunity for us, at least. If we succeed, there is no need to wait for—another. It is a question. We can but try.'

And try accordingly we did.

The occasion I shall never forget—a still, cold winter's night towards the middle of December, most of the students already gone down for Christmas, and small chance of the room being occupied. For even in the busiest time before examinations there were few men who cared to avail themselves of the gruesome privilege of night-work, for which special permission, too, was necessary. Julius, in any case, made his preparations well, and the janitor of the grey-stone building on the hill, whose top floor was consecrated to this grisly study of life in death, had surrendered the keys even before we separated earlier in the evening for supper at the door of the post-mortem theatre.

'Upstairs at eleven o'clock,' he whispered, 'and if I'm late—the preparations may detain me—go inside and wait. Your presence is necessary to success.' He laid his hand on my shoulder; he looked at me searchingly a moment, almost beseechingly, as though he detected the strain of opposition in me. 'And be as sympathetic as you can,' he begged. 'At least, do not actively oppose.' Then, as he turned away, 'I'll try to be punctual,' he added, smiling, 'but—well, you know as well as I do—!' He shrugged his shoulders and was gone.

You know! Somehow or other it was true: I did know. The interval of several hours he would spend in his inner chamber concentrated upon the process of feeling-with—evoking. He would have no food, no rest, no moment's pause. At the appointed hour he would arrive, charged with the essential qualities of these two elemental powers which in dim past ages, summoned by another audacious 'experiment' from their rightful homes, he now sought to 'restore'. He would seek to return what had been 'borrowed'. He would attempt to banish them again. For they could only be thus banished, as they had been summoned—through the channel of a human organism. They were of a loftier order, then, than the Powers for whose return the animal organisms of the sheep had served.

I went my way down Frederick Street with a heart, I swear, already palpitating.

Of the many thrilling experiences that grew out of my acquaintance with this extraordinary being, I think that night remains supreme—certainly, until our paths met again in the Jura Mountains. But, strangest of all, is the fact that throughout the ghastly horror of what occurred was—beauty! To convey this beauty is beyond any power that I possess, yet it was there, a superb and awful beauty that informed the meanest detail of what I witnessed. The experiment failed, of course; in the accomplishment of LeVallon's ultimate purpose, that is, it failed; but the failure was due, apparently, to one cause alone: that the woman was not present.

It is most difficult to describe, and my pen, indeed, shrinks from setting down so revolting a performance. Yet this curious high beauty redeems it in my memory as I now recall the adventure through the haze of years, and I believe the beauty was due to a deeper fact impossible to convey in words. Behind the little 'modern' experiment, and parallel to it, ran another, older Memory that was fraught with some significance of eternity. This parent memory penetrated and overshadowed the smaller copy of it; it exalted what was ugly, uplifted what seemed abominable, sublimated the distressing failure into an image of what might have been magnificent. I mean, in a word, that this experiment was a poor attempt to reconstruct an older ritual of spiritual significance whereby those natural forces, once worshipped as the gods, might combine with qualities similar to their own in human beings. The memory of a more august and effective ceremony moved all the time behind the little reconstruction. The beauty was derived from my dim recollection of some transcendent but now forgotten worship.

At the appointed hour I made my way across the Bridge and towards the Old Town where the University buildings stood. It was, as I said, a bitter night. The Castle Rock and St Giles' Cathedral swam in a flood of silvery moonlight; frost sparkled on the roofs; the spires of Edinburgh shone in the crystal wintry atmosphere. The air, so keen, was windless. Few people were about at this late hour, and I had the feeling that the occasional pedestrians, hurrying homewards in tightly buttoned overcoats, eyed me askance. No one of them was going in the same direction as myself. They questioned my purpose, looked sharply over their shoulders, then quickened their pace away from me towards the houses where the fires burned in cosy human sitting-rooms.

At the door of the great square building itself I hesitated a moment, hiding in the shadow of the overhanging roof. It was easy to pretend that moral disapproval warned me to turn back, but the simpler truth is that I was afraid. At the best of times the Dissecting Room, with its silent cargo of dreadful forms and faces, was a chamber of horrors I could never become hardened to as the majority of students did; but on this occasion, when a theory concerning life alien to humanity was to be put to so strange a test, I confess that the prospect set my nerves a-quivering and made the muscles of my legs turn weak. A cold sensation ran down my spine, and it was not the wintry night alone that caused it.

Opening the heavy door with an effort, I went in and waited a moment till the clanging echo had subsided through the deserted building. My imagination figured the footsteps of a crowd hurrying away behind the sound down the long stone corridors. In the silence that followed I slowly began climbing the steps of granite, hoping devoutly that Julius would be waiting for me at the top. I was a little late; he might possibly have arrived before me. Up the four flights of stairs I went stealthily, trying to muffle my footsteps, putting my weight heavily upon the balustrade, and doing all I could to make no sound at all. For it seemed to me that my movements were both watched and heard, and that those motionless, silent forms above were listening for my approach, and knew that I was coming.

On the landings at each turn lay a broad sweet patch of moonlight that fell through the lofty windows, and but for these the darkness would have been complete. No light, it seemed to me, had ever looked more clean and pure and welcome. I thought of the lone Pentland ridges, and of the sea, lying calm and still outside beneath the same sheet of silver, the air of night all keen and fragrant. The heather slopes came back to me, the larches and the flock of nibbling sheep. I thought of these in detail, of my fire-lit rooms in Frederick Street, of the vicarage garden at home in Kent where my boyhood had been spent; I thought of a good many things, truth to tell, all of them as remote as possible from my present surroundings; but when I eventually reached the topmost landing and found LeVallon was not there, I thought of one thing only—that I was alone. Just beyond me, through that door of frosted glass, lay in its most loathsome form the remnant of humanity left behind by death.

In the daytime, when noisy students, callous and unimaginative, thronged the room, the horror of it retreated, modified by the vigorous vitality of these doctors of the future; but now at night, amid the ominous silence, with darkness over the town and the cold of outer space dropping down upon the world, as though linking forces with that other final cold within the solemn chamber, it seemed quite otherwise. I stood shivering and afraid upon the landing, angry that I could have lent myself to so preposterous and abominable a scheme, yet determined, so long as my will held firm, to go through with it to the end.

He had asked me to wait for him—inside.

Knowing that every minute of hesitation must weaken my powers of resolve, I moved at once towards the door, then paused again. The comforting roar of the traffic floated to my ears; I heard the distant tinkle of a tramcar bell, the boom of Edinburgh, a confused noise of feet and wheels and voices, far away, it is true, but distinctly reassuring.

Outside, the life of humanity rolled upon its accustomed way, recking little of the trembling figure that stood on the top floor of this silent building, one hand on the door upon whose further side so many must one day come to final rest. For one hand already touched the freezing knob, and I was in the act of turning it when another sound, that was certainly not the murmur of the town, struck sharply through the stillness and brought all movement in me to a sudden halt.

It came from within, I thought at first; and it was like a wave of sighs that rose and fell, sweeping against the glass door a moment, then passing away as abruptly as it came. Yet it was more like wind than sighs through human lips, and immediately, then, I understood that it *was* wind. I caught my breath again with keen relief. Wind was rising from the hills, and this was its first messenger running down among the roofs and chimney-pots. I heard its wailing echoes long after it had died away.

But a moment later it returned, louder and stronger than before, and this time, hearing it so close, I know not what secret embassies of wonder touched me from the night outside, deposited their undecipherable messages, and were gone again. I can only say that the key of my emotions changed, changed, moreover, with a swelling rush as when the heavier stops are pulled out upon an organ-board. For, on entering the building, the sky had been serenely calm, and keen frost locked the currents of the air; whereas now that wind went wailing round the walls as though it sought an entrance, almost as though its crying voice veiled purpose. There seemed a note of menace, eager and peremptory, in its sudden rush and drop. It knocked upon the stones and upon the roof above my head with curious and repeated buffets of sound that resembled the 'clap' I had heard that October afternoon among the larches, only a hundred times repeated and a hundred-fold increased. The change in myself, moreover, was similar to the change then experienced—the flow and drive of bigger consciousness that helped to banish fear. I seemed to know about that wind, to feel its life and being, indeed, to share it. No longer was I merely John Mason, a student in Edinburgh, separate and distinct from all about me, but was—I realized it amazingly—a bit of life in the universe, not isolated even from the wind.

The beauty of the sensation did not last; it passed through me linked to that insistent roar; but the fact that I had felt it gave me courage. The stops were instantly pushed in again ... and the same minute the swing-door closed behind me with a sullen thud.

I stood within the chamber; Julius, I saw in a moment, was not there. I moved through the long, narrow room, keeping close beside the wall, taking up my position finally about half-way down, where I could command the six tall windows and the door. The moon was already too high to send her rays directly through the panes, but from the extensive sky-lights she shed a diffused, pale glow upon the scene, and my eyes, soon accustomed to the semi-darkness, saw everything quite as clearly as I cared about.

In front of me stretched the silent, crowded room, patchy in the moonshine, but with shadows deeply gathered in the corners; and, row after row upon the white marble slabs, lay the tenantless forms in the grotesque, unnatural positions as the students had left them a few hours before. The picture does not invite detailed description, but I at once experienced the peculiar illusion that attacks new students even in the daytime. It seemed that the sightless eyes turned slowly round to stare at me, that the shrunken lips half opened as in soundless speech, and that the heads with one accord shifted to an angle whence they could observe and watch me better. There went a rustling through that valley of dry bones as though life returned for a moment to drive the broken machinery afresh.

This sensible illusion was, of course, one I could easily dismiss. More difficult, however, was the subtler attack that came upon me from behind the sensory impressions. For, while I stood with my back against the wall, listening intently for LeVallon's step upon the stairs, I could not keep from my mind the terror of those huddled sheep upon the Pentland ridges; the whole weird force of his theories about 'life' in Nature came beating against my mind, aided, moreover, by some sympathy in myself that could never wholly ridicule their possible truth.

I gazed round me at the motionless, discarded forms, used for one brief 'section', then cast aside, and as I did so my mind naturally focused itself upon a point of dreadful and absorbing interest—which one was to be the subject of the experiment? So short a time ago had each been a nest of keenest activity and emotion, enabling its occupant to reap its harvest of past actions while sowing that which it must reap later again in its new body, already perhaps now a-forming. And of these discarded vehicles, one was to be the channel through which two elemental Powers, evoked in vanished ages, might return to their appointed place. I heard that clamouring wind against the outer walls; I felt within me the warmth of a strange enthusiasm rise and glow; and it seemed to me just then that the whole proposal was as true and simple and in the natural order of things as birth or death, or any normal phenomenon to the terror and glory of which mankind has grown accustomed through prolonged familiarity. To this point, apparently had the change in my feelings brought me. The dreadful novelty had largely gone. Something would happen, nor would it be entirely unfamiliar.

Then, on a marble slab beside the door, the body of a boy, fresh, white and sweet, and obviously brought in that very day, since it was as yet untouched by knife or scalpel, 'drew' my attention of its own accord—and I knew at once that I had found it.

Oddly enough, the discovery brought no increase of fearful thrill; it was as natural as though I had helped to place it there myself. And, again, for some reason, that delightful sense of power swept me; my diminutive modern self slipped off to hide; I remembered that a million suns surrounded me; that the earth was but an insignificant member of one of the lesser systems; that man's vaunted Reason was as naught compared to the oceans of what might be known and possible; and that this body I wore and used, like that white, empty one upon the slab, was but a transient vehicle through which *I*, as a living part of the stupendous cosmos, acted out my little piece of development in the course of an eternal journey. This wind, this fire, that Julius spoke of, were equally the vehicles of other energies, alive as myself, only less tamed and cabined, yet similarly obedient, again, to the laws of their own beings. The extraordinary mood poured through me like a flood—and once more passed away. And the wind fled singing round the building with a shout.

I looked steadily at the beautiful but vacated framework that the soul had used—used well or ill I knew not—lying there so quietly, so calmly, the smooth skin as yet untouched by knife, unmarred by needle, surrounded on all sides by the ugly and misshapen crew of older death; and as I looked, I thought of some fair shell the tide had left among the seaweed wrack, a flower of beauty shining 'mid decay. In the moonlight I could plainly see the thin and wasted ribs, the fixed blue eyes still staring as in life, the lank and tangled hair, the listless fingers that a few hours before must have been active in the flush of health, and passionately loved by more than one assuredly. For, though I knew not the manner of the soul's out-passing, this boy must have suddenly met death that very day. And I found it odd that he should now be lying here, since usually the students' work is concerned to study the processes of illness and decay. It confirmed my certainty that here was the channel LeVallon meant to use.

Time for longer reflection, however, there was none, for just then another gust of this newly risen wind fell against the building with a breaking roar, and at the same moment the swing-door opened and Julius LeVallon stood within the room.

Whether windows had burst, or the great skylights overhead been left unfastened, I had no time, nor inclination either, to discover, but I remember that the wind tore past him down the entire length of the high-ceilinged chamber, tossing the hair uncannily upon a dozen heads in front of me and even stirring the dust about my feet. It was almost as though we stood upon an open plain and met the unobstructed tempest in our teeth.

Yet the rush and vehemence with which he entered startled me, for I found myself glad of the support which a high student's stool afforded.

I leaned against it heavily, while Julius, after standing by the door a moment, turned immediately then to the left. He knew exactly where to look. Simultaneously, he saw me too.

Our eyes, in that atmosphere of shadow and soft moonlight, met also across centuries. He spoke my name; but it was no name I answered to Today.

'Come, Silvatela,' he said, 'lend me your will and sympathy. Feel now with Wind and Fire. For both are here, and the time is favourable. At last, I shall perhaps return what has been borrowed.' He beckoned me with a gesture of strange dignity. 'It is not that time of balanced forces we most desire—the Equinox—but it is the winter solstice,' he went on, 'when the sun is nearest. That, too, is favourable. We *may* transcend the appointed boundaries. Across the desert comes the leaping wind. Both heat and air are with us. Come!'

And, having vaguely looked for some kind of elaborate preparation or parade, this sudden summons took me by surprise a little, though the language somehow did not startle me. I sprang up; the stool fell sideways, then clattered noisily upon the concrete floor. I made my way quickly between the peering faces. It seemed no longer strange, this abrupt disturbance of two familiar elements, nor did I remark with unusual curiosity that the wind went rushing and crying about the room, while the heat grew steadily within me so that my actual skin was drenched with perspiration. All came about, indeed, quickly, naturally, and without any pomp of dreadful ceremonial as I had expected. Julius had come with power in his hands; and preparation, if any, had already taken place elsewhere. He spoke no further word as I approached, but bent low over the thin, white form, his face pale, stern and beautiful as I had never seen it before. I thought of a star that entered the roof of those Temple Memories, falling beneficently upon the great concave mirrors where the incense rose in a column of blue smoke. His entire personality, when at length I stood beside him, radiated an atmosphere of force as though charged with some kind of elemental activity that was intense and inexhaustible. The wonder and beauty of it swept me from head to foot. The air grew marvellously heated. It rose in beating waves that accompanied the rushing wind, like a furnace driven by some powerful, artificial draught; in his immediate neighbourhood it whirled and roared. It drew me closer. I, too, found myself bending down above the motionless, stretched form, oblivious of the other crowded slabs about us.

So familiar it all seemed suddenly. Some such scene I had witnessed surely many a time elsewhere. I knew it all before. Upon success hung issues of paramount importance to his soul, to mine, to the soul of another who, for some reason unexplained, was not present with us, and, somehow, also, to the entire universe of which we formed, with these two elements, a living, integral portion. A weight of solemn drama lay behind our little show. It seemed to me the universe looked on and waited. The issue was of cosmic meaning.

Then, as I entered the sphere of LeVallon's personality, a touch of dizziness caught me for an instant, as though this running wind, this accumulating heat, emanated directly from his very being; and, before I quite recovered myself, the moonlight was extinguished like a lamp blown out. Across the sky, apparently, rushed clouds that changed the spreading skylights into thick curtains, while into the room of death came a blast of storm that I thought must tear the windows from their very sockets in the stone. And with the wind came also a yet further increase of heat that was like a touch of naked fire on some inner membrane.

I dare not assert that I was wholly master of myself throughout the swift, dramatic scene that followed in darkness and in tumult, nor can I claim that what I witnessed in the gloom, shot with occasional gleams of moonlight here and there, was more than the intense visualization of an over-wrought imagination. It well may be that what I expected to happen dramatized itself as though it actually did occur. I can merely state that, at the moment, it seemed real and natural, and that what I saw was the opening scene in a ceremony as familiar to me as the Litany in my father's church.

For, with the pouring through the room of these twin energies of wind and fire, I saw, sketched in the dim obscurity, one definite movement—as the body of the boy rose up into a sitting posture close before our faces. It instantly then sank back again, recumbent as before upon the marble slab. The upright movement was repeated the same second, and once more there came the sinking back. There were several successive efforts before the upright position was maintained; and each time it rose slowly, gradually, all of one piece and rigidly, until finally these tentative movements achieved their object—and the boy sat up as though about to stand. Erect before us, the head slightly hanging on one side, the shoulders squared, the chest expanded as with lung-drawn air, he rose steadily above his motionless companions all round.

And Julius drew back a pace. He made certain gestures with his arms and hands that in some incalculable manner laid control upon the movements. I saw his face an instant as the moon fell on it, pale, glorious and stately, wearing a glow that was *not* moonlight, the lips compressed with effort, the eyes ablaze. He looked to me unearthly and magnificent. His stature seemed increased. There was an air of power, of majesty about him that made his presence beautiful beyond words; and yet, most strange of all, it was familiar to me, even this. I had seen it all before. I knew well what was about to happen.

His gesture changed. No word was spoken. It was a Ceremony in which gesture was more significant than speech. There was evidence of intense internal struggle that yet did not include the ugliness of strain. He put forth all his power merely—and the body rose by jerks. Spasmodically, this time, as though pulled by wires, yet with a kind of terrible violence, it floated from that marble slab into the air. With a series of quick, curious movements, half plunge, half jerk, it touched the floor. It stood stiffly upright on its feet. It rose again, it turned, it twisted, moving arms and legs and head, passing me unsupported through the atmosphere some four feet from the ground. The wind rushed round it with a roar; the fire, though invisible, scorched my eyes. This way and that, now up, now down, the body of this boy danced to and fro before me, silent always, the blue eyes fixed, the lips half parted, more with the semblance of some awful marionette than with human movement, yet charged with a colossal potency that drove it hither and thither. Like some fair Ariel, laughing at death, it flitted above the yellow Calibans of horror that lay strewn below.

Yet, from the very nature of these incompleted movements, I was aware that the experiment was unsuccessful, and that the power was insufficient. Instead of spasmodic, the movements should have been rhythmical and easy; there should have been purpose and intention in the performance of that driven body; there should have been commanding gestures, significant direction; there should have been spontaneous breathing and—a voice—the voice of Life.

And instead—I witnessed an unmeaning pantomime, and heard the wailing of the dying wind....

A voice, indeed, there was, but it was the voice of Julius LeVallon that eventually came to me across the length of the room. I saw him slowly approaching through the patches of unequal moonlight, carrying over his shoulder the frail, white burden that had collapsed against the further wall. And his words were very few, spoken more to himself apparently than to me. I heard them; they struck chill and ominous upon my heart:

'The conditions were imperfect, the power insufficient. Alone we cannot do it. We must wait for *her*.... And the channel must be another's—as before.'

The strain of high excitement passed. I knew once again that small and pitiful sensation of returning to my normal consciousness. The exhilaration all was gone. There came a dwindling of the heart. I was 'myself' again, John Mason, student at Edinburgh University. It produced a kind of shock, the abruptness of the alteration took my strength away. I experienced a climax of sensation, disappointment, distress, fear, and revolt as well, that proved too much for me. I ran. I reeled. I heard the sound of my own falling.

No recollection of what immediately followed remains with me ... for when I opened my eyes much later, I found myself prone upon the landing several floors below, with Julius bending solicitously over me, helping me to rise. The moonlight fell in a flood through a window on the stairs. My recovery was speedy, though not complete. I accompanied him down the remaining flight, leaning upon his arm; and in the street my senses, though still dazed, took in that the night was calm and cloudless, that the moonlight veiled the stars by its serene brightness, and that the clock above the University building pointed to the hour of two in the morning.

The cold was bitter. There was no wind!

Julius came with me to my door in Frederick Street, but the entire distance of a mile neither of us spoke a word.

At the door of my lodging-house, however, he turned. I drew back instinctively, hesitating, for my desire was to get upstairs into my own room with the door locked safely behind me. But he caught my hand.

'We failed tonight,' he whispered, 'but when the real time comes we shall succeed. *You* will not—fail me then?'

In the stillness of very early morning, the moon sinking towards the long dip of Queensferry Road, and the shadows lying deep upon the deserted streets, I heard his voice once more come travelling down the centuries to where I stood. The atmosphere of those other days and other places came back with incredible appeal upon me.

He drew me within the chilly hallway, the sound of our feet echoing up the spiral staircase of stone. Night lay silently over everything, sunrise still many hours away.

I turned and looked into his eager, passionate face, into his eyes that still shone with the radiance of the two great powers, at the mouth and lips which now betrayed the exhaustion that had followed the huge effort. And something appealing and personal in his entire expression made it impossible to refuse. I shook my head, I shrank away, but a voice I scarcely recognized as my own gave the required answer. My upper and my under selves conflicted; yet the latter gave the inevitable pledge: 'Julius ... I promise you.'

He gazed into my eyes. An inexpressible tenderness stole into his manner. He took my hand and held it. The die was cast.

'She is now upon the earth with us,' he said. 'I soon shall find her. We three shall inevitably be drawn together, for we are linked by indestructible ties. There is this debt we must repay—we three who first together incurred it.'

There was a pause. Far away I heard a cart rumbling over the cobbles of George Street. In another world it seemed, for the gods were still about us where we stood. Julius moved from me. Once more I saw his eyes fixed pleadingly, almost yearningly upon my own. Then the street door closed upon him and he was gone.

RADIO TALKS

THE BLACKMAILERS

Blackwood had first been approached by the BBC to broadcast one of his stories as early as 1926. Blackwood replied that the idea 'interested' him but as he was abroad the opportunity was not possible. In fact it was not until 1934 that Blackwood was cornered, first on *In Town Tonight*, where he told a story as part of his interview (alas the title and text of that story have not survived) and then by pioneer producer Cecil Madden who secured Blackwood a storytelling spot for live transmission on 15 June 1934. Come the day, Blackwood was suffering from a cold and the broadcast was postponed until 11 July. The story Blackwood told was 'The Blackmailers'. It was one of two Blackwood had written specially for radio, the other being 'Lock Your Door'. The Director of Talks was a little alarmed as to the subject matter of both stories. He favoured 'The Blackmailers', though he commented 'I don't doubt that we shall have a good many letters from listeners saying that we are corrupting the youth of England with morbid fancies and distasteful subjects.' Blackwood understood the alarms but did not think them serious. 'My own public, whatever that may mean, expect a queer sort of grim story from me and would be disappointed with an ordinary tale.' And so the story went ahead, the first of over sixty radio broadcasts Blackwood would make over the next seventeen years.

The success of the story caused Cecil Madden to start a series of horror stories on the BBC Empire Programme, called *Nightmare*. Blackwood adapted two of his stories for the series, 'A Haunted Island' and 'By Water'. Publishers Allen & Unwin showed interest in the series and agreed to publish an anthology of the stories under the title *My Grimmest Nightmare* (1935). Blackwood's 'A Haunted Island' was in print from another publisher and was not available, so to fill the gap 'The Blackmailers' was used, its first appearance in print.

A̲LEXANDER'S experience with the blackmailer was unique—it happened once only.

He had been happily married for some years, with two children, and was doing well enough in his insurance business. Life, indeed, was quite rosy, when one day a stranger called at the office and asked to see him alone. This stranger was an elderly man of perhaps rather shabby appearance, but his face and manner were quite engaging, and he had a really pleasant smile. His voice was cultured. He was obviously a gentleman, a university man probably. At the same time, there was something about him that hesitated; he seemed shy, a trifle nervous even. In spite of the worn, cheap clothing, however, he made the best impression, and Alexander believed that a bit of good business was coming his way.

They went into the inner private room. The interview began in the bluntest possible way. Something very determined had come into the stranger's manner, almost as though he had screwed himself to say what he came to say and meant to see it through.

'My name is Lawson,' he announced, 'and I need money badly.'

He spoke rapidly, yet with a curious reluctance, as though he said something he had learned by heart and rather hated saying. 'Some letters of yours,' he went on—'it doesn't matter how—have come into my possession. If you will give me £20, they're yours.' And he drew from his pocket a small packet, fluttering them before the other's eyes so that the handwriting was plainly visible. The hand that held the letters shook.

The shock to Alexander, instead of the pleasant surprise he had rather expected, was overwhelming. With one look he had recognized the paper and the handwriting. He blenched. A cold sweat broke out on him. He was not naturally a man of much nerve and he realized that a bluff of any sort was useless. He *had* written those letters. He was frightened to the bone. All he could do in that first instant was to stagger to a chair, for his legs were too weak to support him. He just sat down. The other man remained standing, keeping a certain distance.

'T-twenty pounds,' stammered Alexander, half to himself, trying vainly to collect his thoughts. He was shivering visibly. Hot and cold he was. He knew he was quite helpless. This was blackmail.

'And I'll hand them over,' Lawson was saying. Then he added, as though relieved to say it: 'And you'll never set eyes on me again.'

'But—I—I haven't got it,' went on Alexander in a panic, his mind flooding with pictures of his wife, his children, his happy home. 'It's impossible—utterly impossible.'

'But you can get it,' suggested Lawson quietly. And though his voice sounded determined, merciless even, there was that odd touch of reluctance again in his manner, as though he was ashamed to say the words. He stood there on the office carpet, watching his victim's face, giving him time apparently. Putting the letters back into his pocket, he waited in silence. A hint of contempt, it may be, lay in this silence, contempt for the other's craven attitude and lack of fight. And Alexander somehow was aware of this, even while he tried frantically to think out ways and means. He would have paid £1,000, let alone £20, to have those letters back and see them burn. But where could he find £20 at a moment's notice? Though recovering a little from the first awful shock, his mind worked badly. He *did* think once of the law which allowed a plaintiff in a blackmail case to conceal his name. He also thought of threatening to go to the police at once. Only the pluck to carry the bluff through failed him—and he knew it. He was so terrified, so painfully anxious to get those letters back that he kept his mind chiefly on the £20 and where in the devil he could find it. The name of a pal who might lend it crossed his bewildered mind at last.

'If you will come back in an hour, in half an hour even,' he said at last in a low, stammering voice, 'I—I think I can have it for you.' Without knowing exactly why, he suddenly added then: 'You're a— gentleman, I see.' The words came on their own accord. Lawson lowered his eyes. He didn't answer. 'If you go out,' he said then quietly, 'I'm afraid I must come with you. I'm sorry—but—you understand.'

'Oh, yes, I understand—of course,' said the other.

In the end this is what happened. They went out together. Alexander, greatly to his surprise, got his £20. They came back together, always side by side. Alexander handed over the money and took the letters in his hand. He counted them. He was shaking so violently that he had to count them a second time. One, two, three! The cold sweat broke out on him afresh.

'Three,' he whispered. 'Is that *all* you've got?'

Lawson, he saw, actually blushed. He was already at the door on his way out. 'I think so,' he replied, forcing the pleasant smile on to his face as he told the deliberate lie. 'I'll look again when I get home, and if there is another you shall have it.'

The expression on the face startled Alexander, for behind the forced smile, behind the sudden blush, was misery—abject misery. The hideous shame was clear to see, but the grim determination too.

'Another...?' repeated Alexander. 'But you've got a lot more—a dozen at least...' he cried.

But Lawson was gone.

Alexander sat motionless for some minutes, clutching the letters feverishly as though they might be snatched away. He had gone to pieces badly. How the man had come into possession of the horrible letters puzzled him utterly. But that did not matter: he *had* got them, and he, Alexander, *had* written them—oh, a dozen at least, perhaps two dozen. Twenty pounds for three! With more to follow! He thought of his wife, his children, his happy home.... He thought of Lawson— his voice, his manner, his whole attitude. A gentleman, yes, a man of education and refinement. That sudden blush, the nervous, deprecating air, the reluctance, the look of shame. A man ashamed of yielding to the temptation chance has put in his way, eager to get away the moment the hideous deal was over and the money in his pocket. Yet a man, Alexander now began too late to realize, he might have bargained and pleaded with. The fellow's better nature was plain to see— underneath.

Alexander cursed himself for his collapse and lack of pluck. A bold front, a threat of the police, and Lawson in his turn would have weakened, possibly collapsed himself. A good bluff and Alexander might have got those letters—all of them, not merely three—for nothing.

The telephone rang. He realized he still sat clutching his three letters, and that it was office hours and he had much to do. But the instant he was free again, he quickly locked the door and lit a match. He burnt the letters—without reading them—and smudged the black ashes into dust in his waste-paper basket.

Still trembling with the shock and horror of it all, he could not work. He took the afternoon off, walking feverishly round and round the parks, thinking feverishly, but without result. The night at home was the most miserable he had ever known, the children on his knee, the wife he loved beside him. If he slept at all, he hardly knew it. He had come, however, to a decision—to two in fact. And the next day he went to a solicitor, putting a hypothetical case before him. But the strong advice to go straight to the police was beyond his powers. Even as 'Mr X', he could not face a trial. His second decision was to plead with Lawson, plead for time at any rate. The man had a better nature he felt he could appeal to. He would do this—the next time. For he knew, of course, there would be a next time. Lawson before long would call again.

But Lawson did not call again. After weeks of unspeakable terror and anguish, a letter came, to his home address this time. It was very brief, the handwriting rather suggesting the scholar.

I *have* come across another letter. Perhaps you would prefer to call for it yourself. A fiver would meet the case. I do not wish to cause unnecessary pain. It is, apparently, the only one.

The address was in Kilburn, and Alexander took five Treasury notes and went, one thing comforting him a little—the obvious fact, namely that Lawson was not a thoroughgoing and experienced blackmailer, or he would never have taken risks and laid himself open to such an easy trap. In his mind he had already rehearsed what he meant to say. His plea would be as moving as only truth could make it. But he planned a threat as well, a bluff of course, but a bluff that would sound genuine—that if driven to kill himself, he would leave the evidence behind him and Lawson would be at once arrested.

He could be firm this time, with the firmness of a desperate man. Desperate indeed he was, but firmness did not belong to his weak, impulsive, rather nerveless type.

Expecting a block of cheap flats, or a single room in a mean lodging-house, he found instead a small detached building, quite a decent little place, and a deaf old woman admitted him, announcing him by name, into a room that looked half study, half library. For it held numerous books, and a writing-table was covered with papers. Lawson, at the far end of it, stood to receive him. But the interview hardly went according to plan, for as Alexander handed over the Treasury notes and received the letter in exchange, the other again took the cash as with a kind of shrinking, horrible reluctance. He was trembling, his face was very white, his voice, as he said 'Thank you,' trembled too. And before Alexander could recover from his moment's surprise and bring out either his plea or his threat, Lawson was speaking.

'I'm in a terrible position myself,' he said in a very low voice, '*Terrible*.' His face expressed real anguish. 'With any luck,' he went on in a whisper, his eyes on the floor, 'I would repay you—one day.'

He placed the notes in a drawer of his desk, while Alexander's eye, watching the movement, read the titles of some books above: a volume of Matthew Arnold's poems, a Greek lexicon, Gibbon's *Decline and Fall*.

But it was Lawson's sign of weakness that then helped the other to find some, at least, of the words he had meant to use. It was the bluff that rose first to the surface of his bewildered mind.

'You know—that I can go to the police,' he heard himself saying.

The other looked sideways towards the window, so that Alexander caught the face at a new angle. He noticed the ravaged expression. Lawson was suffering intensely.

'I know,' came the reply calmly, without turning the head. 'But you wouldn't—any more than *I* would.'

The conviction in the words, their truth as well, confused and bewildered the wretched victim still more. His thoughts scattered hopelessly. He said the first thing that came into his head. All idea of a plea for mercy had vanished.

'If you drive me to kill myself—and I'm near it now—you'd be arrested at once. I could leave the proofs.'

It was the way Lawson shrugged his shoulders that completed his feeling of utter hopelessness. It had dawned upon him suddenly that Lawson's position was somehow similar to his own, his desperation as dreadful. Lawson himself was at the last gasp.

'You've got a lot more, of course?' he heard himself asking in a faint voice.

Lawson now turned and faced him. His expression was awful, itiful at the same time.

'I'm afraid so,' he whispered, and his manner again showed that deep reluctance, with a sort of shame and horror against himself. 'One or two—I'm afraid,' he repeated. He drew a heavy sigh and put up his hand to hide his eyes. 'I'm . . . frightfully sorry,' he muttered, half to himself. He was trembling from head to foot.

The interview was over. Alexander left the house an utterly hopeless man. The situation was now clear to him, of course. Lawson, normally a decent fellow probably, was being blackmailed himself. Alexander understood, he even sympathized, but with this understanding vanished the last vestige also of any hope. He realized now *precisely* how desperate Lawson was.

The ghastly suffering and anguish of the weeks and months that followed need no description—his sleeplessness, his frantic resorts to finding cash, the moneylenders, his wife's discovery that something very serious was wrong, the way he fobbed her off with a story of bad business. The visits to Kilburn were repeated and repeated, though the interview usually took place in silence now. Money was paid, letters were handed over—without a word, both men, indeed, seemed approaching the last gasp. As for Alexander, he found it difficult to believe that he had written so many letters. But he had.

The cumulative effect at last broke his life to pieces. His health was gone, his mind became queer. Turning frantically to one desperate plan after another, all of them useless, he was driven finally into that dreadful, final corner where an Emergency Exit seemed inevitable. And this was not nerve, it was merely the ultimate decision of an utterly ruined, ordinary man. He bought a pistol. In his mind came the mad suggestion that it was as easy to end two lives as one. He went to the little Kilburn house for the last time. This was definitely to be his last visit. He took no money with him, but in his hip-pocket lay the Browning with three cartridges in the chamber—the third in case of mischance.

Exactly how he intended to act was far from clear to him. He had rehearsed no plan. That time was past. The loaded pistol lay in his pocket. He left the rest to impulse.

It was an evening in late October, summertime now over, and dusk spread over the dreary Kilburn streets. He came straight from the office by Tube. After leaving the train he walked very rapidly. Then he broke into a run, with the feeling that the faster he went the sooner the awful thing would be over. He arrived panting, reaching the house almost before he knew it. He was utterly distraught, his mind, even his senses, behaving wildly, inaccurately.

There was no answer to the violent pull he gave the bell, the deaf old woman did not appear, and then he noticed for the first time that the front door stood ajar. And he just walked in. The tiny hall was empty too. He closed the door behind him and walked across to the library. Only too well he knew it. There was no need to be shown in. He was expected. And he was punctual. Six was striking.

The house, it then occurred to him, was exceptionally quiet. There was an extraordinary stillness about it—a stillness he didn't like. There was also—though he only recalled this afterwards—a faint odour of a peculiar kind. Giving a loud knock without waiting for an answer, he opened it the same instant and walked straight in without further ado.

He saw Lawson at once. He was not standing as usual, but sitting facing him in the leather armchair with its patches of untidy horsehair sticking out. And he declares that the moment his eyes rested on him a disagreeable shudder ran down his spine. It was not the shudder of loathsome anxiety he knew so well, but something he had never felt before. Distracted, half crazy though his mind undoubtedly was at the time, it took in one thing at least quite clearly. Lawson looked different. He had changed. Wherein this alteration lay exactly Alexander could not say. He only knew that it frightened him in a new way and that his back had goose-flesh. An awful fear crawled over him.

Lawson not only looked different—he behaved differently. He did not get up, but sat in the chair staring into his visitor's face. There was something wrong, not merely different. And Alexander stopped dead just inside the door, forgetting even to close it behind him. He stood there spellbound, returning the stare. His first instinct was to turn tail and run, only his legs felt suddenly weak, his control of the muscles gone. He held his breath. What amazed him more than anything else was the expression on his enemy's face. For it wore a happy, kindly smile; the ravaged, suffering look had left it, there lay a curious soft pity on it. Unaccountably, he felt his heart beginning to swell. He could not take his eyes from that happy, pitiful face, that motionless figure in the chair. It was perhaps two minutes, perhaps only two seconds, before he heard the voice.

For Lawson spoke—in a scarcely audible whisper. There was obviously a tremendous strain and effort behind the whisper, as though he could only just manage it: yet Alexander heard every syllable distinctly.

'You won't need that pistol, either for me or for yourself. I have posted the others to you—with what—money I had. . . .' and the whisper died away into silence. The lips still moved, but no sound came from them. Lawson himself had not moved at all—he had not made even the smallest movement—once.

There was a sound in the hall, and Alexander involuntarily turned his head an instant. He recognized the deaf woman's shuffling tread. Turning back to the room again almost the same moment, Lawson the blackmailer was no longer staring at him from the leather chair. He was not in the chair at all. He was not even in the room. The room was empty. The only visible living person in it was himself, Alexander.

It flashed across him, as the deaf servant came stumbling through the door behind him, that he had gone crazy, that his mind was gone. There was icy persipiration all over him. He was shaking violently. He heard the old woman's words in a confused jumble only, but their meaning was plain enough. Lawson, she was trying to tell him, had shot himself several hours ago . . . but had not killed himself . . . the police . . . doctors had come . . . there had been an anaesthetic . . .

he had been taken away ... but had died in the ambulance.

Alexander does not remember how he got out of the house. All he remembers is walking the streets furiously, for hours even, and somewhere or other telephoning to his wife that he was detained and would not be home till after dinner. He knows he did that. He knows also that on reaching the house very late, he talked incoherently to his frightened wife, that the children were long since in bed and asleep, and that his wife put a registered packet into his trembling hands in due course. He knows too that it contained several letters he had written years before to another woman—dreadful, damaging letters—that a couple of twenty-pound notes fell at his feet, and that the postmark on the label was 11.30 Kilburn that very morning.

THE WIG

During 1935 Blackwood became a regular guest on the early evening programme *Young Ideas* aimed at teenage listeners. Each week he told of some experience that had happened to him or to someone he knew. Amongst the stories related were his days in New York when he reported on an escaped lion from a touring circus, moose-hunting in the Canadian backwoods and one tantalizingly entitled 'The Train Ghost', record of which hasn't survived. Only one of the broadcasts sounded more like a story than a personal experience and that was 'The Wig', a typical five-minute tongue-in-cheek tale which I imagine Blackwood told behind the microphone with a rather roguish smile.

THERE'S a delightful story of a spirited old lady—as plucky as she was old, it seems—who was told on a country visit that she was in a haunted room, and asked if she minded.

'Mind?' she repeated scornfully. 'Not a scrap. Why should I?'

She was assured that while the ghost was harmless enough, it took the unusual form of a very tiny man, a little fellow, hardly bigger than a gnome.

'But it very rarely shows itself,' her hostess explained. 'I've never seen it myself, though I've lived here many years. It's always my friends who have the luck.'

'Well,' snorted the plucky old lady, 'I'm one of your friends, so I hope I shall be lucky.'

She was. She locked her door, as against any possible tricks, and in due course climbed into bed and began to read. As she read, a movement caught her eye. At the far end of the room, out of the panelled wall, emerged a figure—an extremely diminutive little man. He came out into the middle of the room, plain as a leg of mutton. He skipped about a bit, as though dancing, hopping to and fro like a bird, but looking at her as he did so. His bright eyes never left her face. He watched; he seemed to study her. Then, abruptly, with a sudden rush, he darted across the room, took a springing leap upon her bed, reached out a tiny hand, snatched the wig off her head, shot down again, scuttled over the floor, and rushed up the face of the big cupboard like a shadow. Between the top of this cupboard and the ceiling there was a space of two feet. He perched himself there, sitting cross-legged, waving the wig to and fro in the air with a smile of great glee. And, as he did so, repeating over and over again in a high, thin, squeaky voice: 'Here we are! Here we are! All alone till morning!'

The plucky, high-spirited lady watched and listened for a few minutes and then turned out the light and fell asleep. Next morning she tried to persuade herself that she had dreamt the whole little episode but against this explanation was the fact that her wig still lay on the top of that high cupboard and that she had a rare old job climbing up with a chair to get it down again.

KING'S EVIDENCE

In order to meet the demand for his broadcasts, Blackwood turned to adapting his stories for radio rather than writing new ones. In some cases he hardly had to change a word, the story fortuitously fitting in to the ten- or fifteen-minute slot available. Occasionally though there was a need for major revision and sometimes he completely rewrote a story using only the basic idea. The most drastic changes he made were to the story 'Confession' originally published in *The Wolves of God* in 1921. His new version, 'King's Evidence', is to all intents a new story. It was first broadcast in the BBC National Programme on 27 June 1936 with a second live reading on the BBC Home Service on Christmas Eve 1940. It was from that broadcast that the story saw its first publication in the BBC's European Service programme guide *London Calling* for 9 January 1941. Its success was demonstrated by its subsequent selection for Hilton Browne's volume of *Best Broadcast Stories* in 1944.

WHEN Flanagan left his nursing home that November afternoon the last rays of the red sunset lay over Regent's Park. It was very still. The air was raw, but the sky was clear, if with a hint of possible fog to come.

Flanagan was on his way to South Kensington by the Underground. He was in high spirits. His fear of open spaces—agorophobia so-called—at last was really cured. He no longer dreaded to cross a square, a lawn, a field. This terrible affliction, inherited from shell-shock, was a thing of the past, thank heaven. For months he had been unable even to cross the open garden of the home. Gradually the specialists had weaned him from that awful terror. Already he had made smaller journeys alone. Now he was fit for a longer effort.

'It'll do you good,' said the matron, seeing him off. 'Go and have tea with your pal. An open space won't bother you a bit, and anyhow there are no open spaces on the Underground. Be back for dinner at 7.0.'

And Tim Flanagan, young Canadian soldier, who knew nothing of London beyond the precincts of his nursing home, started off full of confidence. Exact directions—first right, second left, etc.—lay in his pocket. To a man of the backwoods it was child's play. He took the Underground at Regent's Park and reached South Kensington easily, of course. Then, leaving the train twenty minutes later and coming up to street level, he entered a world of blackness he had never known before, though he had read about it—a genuine London pea-soup fog.

'Gosh!' he said to himself. 'This is the real thing!'

The station hall itself was darkened with all its lights. He faced a wall of opaque, raw, stifling gloom that stung his eyes and bit into his throat. The change was so sudden, it amazed him. But the novelty at first stimulated him, accustomed as he was to the clear Canadian air. It seemed unbelievable, but it was true. He watched the people grope their way out into the street—and vanish. He hesitated. A slight shiver ran over him.

'Come on now, Tim Flanagan!' he said, 'you know the directions by heart'—and he plunged down into the filthy blackness of the open street. First to the right, second to the left—and within five minutes he was completely lost.

He stood still, aware suddenly that he must keep himself in hand. He repeated calmly the directions he knew so well. But got them mixed. How many turns had he made so far? He wasn't sure. Memory was already out of gear a little. Too dark to read the paper in his pocket. Nothing to help him—no stars, wind, scent, sound of running water, moss on the north side of the trees.

Groping figures emerged, vanished, reappeared, dissolved. He heard shuffling feet, sticks tapping. Saw an occasional taxi crawling by the curb, the passenger walking. They loomed, faded, were gone. A swirl in the fog showed a faint light, and he staggered towards it and recognized an island. Thank heaven for that refuge! A figure or two arrived and left as he stood there, clutching the lamp-post. They asked the way, choking; he asked the way, coughing. They lurched off and the murk covered them. Like blind fish, he thought, on the ocean bed. But his confusion and bewilderment became serious, with unpleasant symptoms he thought done with for ever. There were no carts, no taxis now, no figures either. He was alone, an empty space about him—the two things he dreaded most. He waved his stick. It struck nothing solid. In spite of the cold, he was sweating. And panic slowly raised its ugly head.

'I must get across to a pavement. I must cross that open space. I must...!'

It took him fifteen minutes, most of the way on his hands and knees, but the moment of collapse was close as he crawled along pluckily by the pavement railings. Then he saw a slight thickening of the fog beneath the next lamp, grotesquely magnified. Was it real? It moved. It moved towards him. It was a human being. If it was a human being he could speak to—be with—he would be saved. It came up close against his face. It was a woman.

He gasped out at it, pulling himself up by the railing.

'Lost your way like me, Ma'am? D'you know where you are? Morley Place I'm looking for. For heaven's sake...!'

His voice stopped dead. The woman was peering down at him. He saw her face quite clearly—the brilliant, frightened eyes, the skin white like linen. She was young, wrapped in a dark fur coat. She had beauty—beauty of a sort. He didn't care who or what she was. To him she meant safety only.

There was no answer to his questions. She whispered, as though speech were difficult: 'Where am I? I came out so suddenly. I can't find the way back...'—and was gone from his side into the swirling fog.

And Flanagan, without an instant's hesitation, went after her. He must be with a human being. She moved swiftly, seemed sure of her way, she never faltered. Terrified he might lose her, he kept breathlessly at her heels. She uttered no sound, no cry, not once did she turn her head. But her unfaltering speed helped to restore his own confidence. She knew her way now beyond all question. But two things struck him as odd: first, that she made no sound—he heard no footsteps—second, that she left a curious faint perfume in the air, a perfume that made him uneasy—connecting it somehow with misery and pain.

Abruptly then she swerved, so abruptly that he almost touched her, and passed through an iron gate across a tiny garden to a house.

She did not turn her head, but he heard her queer whispering voice again: 'I've found it. Now I can get back.'

'May I come in, too?' he cried, exhausted. 'Don't leave me!

If I'm left alone I shall go mad!'

There was no answer. She passed like a feather up the stone steps and vanished into the house. The front door, he noticed, was ajar already. Nor did she close it behind her. He followed her into a pitch-black hall, then collapsed in a heap on the stone floor. But he was safe. The open spaces of the street were behind him. He heard a door open and close upstairs. Complete silence followed.

A couple of minutes later he struggled to his feet, switched on his electric torch, and realized at once that the house was untenanted. Dust-sheets covered the hall furniture. Through a door, half open, he saw pictures screened on the walls, brackets draped. But companionship, human companionship was what he wanted, and must have, or his mind would go. He was shaking like a leaf. So he crept upstairs on tiptoe and reached the landing. Then stood still. His knees felt like blotting-paper.

He saw a long corridor with closed doors. And he cautiously tried three in succession—empty rooms, furniture under dust-sheets, blinds drawn, mattresses rolled up. At the fourth door he knew he was right, for the strange, unpleasant odour caught his nostrils. And this time he knew instantly why it brought pain and misery—anaesthetic, ether, or chloroform.

His next glance showed him the young woman lying in her fur coat on the bed. The body lay at full length. Motionless. He had seen death too often to be mistaken, much less afraid. He stole up, felt her cheek, still warm. An hour or so ago she was alive. He gently raised a closed eyelid, but hurriedly let it fall again, and in the presence of death instinctively he took his hat off, laying it on the bed. His hand then, moving towards the heart, encountered a hard knob—the head of a long steel hat-pin driven up to its hilt. But his own private terror was now lost in something greater. He drew the pin out slowly and placed it on her breast. And in doing so he noticed a blood stain on his finger. At which instant there was a loud clanging noise downstairs—the front door being closed. A frenzied realization of his position blazed into his mind—a dead woman, alone together in an empty house, blood on his hand, fingerprints on the door handle and pin, body still warm, police!

The sinister combination cleared his brain. Heart racing madly, he switched out his light, and darted across the landing to the room opposite, seeing as he ran the flicker of an electric torch on banisters and ceiling, as the man holding it rapidly climbed the stairs. He managed it just in time. Through the crack of his own door he saw the outline of the man slip into the room where the dead—the murdered—woman lay, and close the door carefully behind him. Only his outline had been visible, blurred in the deep shadow behind the torch he carried.

The one thing Flanagan knew was that he must get away instantly. He crept out, stole along the landing on tiptoe, and began the perilous descent with the utmost caution. Each time a board creaked his heart missed a beat. He tested each step. Half way down, to his horror, his foot tripped in a rod—with an uproar like a hand-grenade in his forgotten trenches. Concealment was now impossible. He took the last flight in a leap, shot across the hall, tore open the front door, just as his pursuer, with torch in hand, had reached the top of the stairs. The light flashed down on to him for a second. He wasn't sure. He banged the door, and plunged headlong into the welcome, all-obscuring fog outside.

He ran wildly, fast as he could, across the little garden, out into the street. The fog held no terrors for him now. His one object was to put distance between him and that house of death. Sense of direction he had none. There was no sound of steps behind him. For ten, fifteen minutes, he raced along. He must have gone a long way—a mile at least—when his legs failed him, his mind went blank, his strength was gone, and the terror of open spaces rose over him like ice. He dropped in his tracks, clinging to the cold, wet area railing, one thought only hideously clear in his brain before it stopped functioning—he had left his hat beside the body on the bed.

Unconsciousness followed. He had no recollection exactly till a voice sounded, a man's voice, kindly.

'Can I be of any assistance? Come, let me help you. Take my arm. I'm a physician. Luckily, too, you're just outside my house....'

And Flanagan felt himself half dragged, half pushed into a warm, well-lit hall, the stranger having opened the door with a latchkey. A few minutes later, he was sipping whisky before a blazing fire, trying to stammer his thanks and gratitude. 'Got lost,' he managed to say, 'agor—agorophobia, sir, you know ... shell shock ... You've saved me...'

And some fifteen minutes later, whisky, warmth, and experienced human sympathy had worked wonders.

The doctor's handling of the terrified youth was masterly. Flanagan found fuller control came back. He even smoked a cigarette with pleasure.

'You know,' the doctor was saying in his pleasant gentle voice, 'I rather guessed it might be shell shock. I've seen so many cases...' as Flanagan now began to take him in more fully; elderly, with a very determined, implacable look sometimes behind what was a good, almost a benevolent face. A man not to be trifled with, he felt. 'And I'm encouraged,' the doctor went on smilingly, 'to hazard a second guess—that you've had another violent shock, too—quite recently,' He looked hard into Flanagan's eyes: 'Am I not right—eh? Yes, I felt sure of it.' There came a little pause. 'Now, why not tell me about it,' came the suggestion, soothingly, yet with more authority in the tone. 'It will help you—relieve your mind. Suppression is bad, remember. And we're complete strangers to one another. I don't know your name. You don't known mine. Tell me about it. Confession,' he laughed, 'is good for the soul, they say.'

Flanagan hesitated. 'It's too incredible,' he mumbled, though burning to get it out of him. 'You just couldn't believe it, sir.'

In the end he told it, all of it, faithfully.

'Pretty tall story, isn't it, sir?'

'Tall, yes,' came the quiet reply, 'but not incredible—as I know from many a strange experience.' He paused and sipped his drink. 'In fact as one confidence deserves another,' he went on, 'I might now tell you of an oddly similar case that came my way. It may make you feel more comfortable,' he added with skilful tact, 'to hear my story. I won't give names, of course. It's about an officer at the front—great friend of mine—middle-aged, rich, just married to a young girl—a cheap, pleasure-loving sort, utterly worthless, I'm afraid. While he was fighting for his country, she took a lover. Planned to run away. Only somehow the husband got wind of it out in France. He got leave, too, just in the nick of time....'

'Well rid of her,' Flanagan put it.

'Perhaps,' said the doctor. 'Only he determined to make that riddance final.'

Flanagan gasped, but not audibly. And that implacable look on the other's face had hardened him a little. He listened more closely, he watched more closely, too. He was thinking hard. Reflecting. A touch of uneasiness stirred in him.

'Go on, please,' he said.

The doctor went on; in a lowered tone. 'They met, he found out, this guilty pair, in an empty house, a house belonging to the husband. And the woman, using her latchkey, slipped in. She left the door ajar for the lover. She found death waiting for her. It was a painless death. Her lover, for some reason, was late. The fog possibly. It must have been a night rather like this, I gather...'

'The lover,' Flanagan whispered, for his voice failed him somehow, 'the lover didn't come, you mean?'

'A man did come in,' was the doctor's quiet answer, 'but he hardly tallied with the description the husband had. A stranger, apparently. Saw the door ajar and came in for shelter perhaps—just as you might have done.'

Flanagan felt a shiver run down his spine. 'And the husband,' he asked under his breath, 'where was he all this time?'

'Oh,' came the answer at once, 'waiting outside—concealed in the fog. Watching. He saw the man go in, of course. Five minutes later he went in after him.'

Flanagan stood straight up with a sudden jerk. 'I'll be going,' he said abruptly, and added some words of mumbled thanks. The doctor said nothing. He, too, rose to his feet. They passed into the hall.

'But you can't go out in the fog like that,' said the doctor, quietly enough. 'Why, you've got no hat. Here, I'll lend you one.' And he casually took a hat from a row on the rack and Flanagan mechanically put it on his head. He didn't shake the offered hand. Perhaps he hadn't seen it. He went out.

The fog had lifted a bit. He found his station easily. Open spaces did not bother him.

In the bright light of the train he took off the borrowed hat and looked it over. It was his own hat.

LOCK YOUR DOOR

As previously mentioned, 'Lock Your Door' had been submitted by Blackwood along with 'The Blackmailers' in 1934. It failed to score with the Director of Talks even though Blackwood told him that 'I have often told it among friends when story-telling comes on the tap, and it never fails to thrill.' The typescript stayed with Blackwood, miraculously surviving the bombing of his lodgings in the Blitz (probably because he had his scripts with him down in the air raid shelter) and when it was finally resubmitted to the BBC in 1946 there were no qualms over its use. It was broadcast in the Home Service's *Stories Old and New* series on 6 May 1946. So far as I can tell it was never set into print although Blackwood did tell it on television in March 1948 and it was also one of six short films Blackwood made in 1950 for Rayant Pictures. This is its first publication.

MISS JENKINS, an elderly spinster, was certainly a courageous woman; she had been known to stand up to savage dogs, even to a bull in a field. At the same time, she took her precautions. She liked to know where she stood when danger was about. Chief among these precautions was the habit of locking her bedroom door. It was ingrained in her deepest being.

When teased about it and asked if the habit had ever justified itself, she said frankly: 'No—not yet, I admit. But you never know. Some day....'

And at last that 'some day' came. Her account of what happened is very circumstantial, but I think honest too. Explanation, however, she had none—none whatever.

This is her account: she got mixed up in a minor railway accident when a coach ran off the lines at a little wayside station on the way to the Scottish border. It was not serious; no one was injured beyond a severe shaking; but all had to bundle out—at about one o'clock in the morning. It was an isolated spot and help was out of the question before daylight. Not even a house was in sight. So it meant that the handful of travellers would have to make-do till morning in the tiny waiting-room.

This didn't suit Miss Jenkins. For one thing, of course, she couldn't lock the door; but, more than that, she couldn't face sitting on a hard bench with a bunch of strangers, some of whom were distinctly hysterical. So outside, on the dim-lit platform, she got the ear of the only porter, a little old man with a face scarred by smallpox, and learned that there was a house in a hamlet about a mile away where she might find a room, if she explained the situation. Miss Jenkins didn't hesitate. It was a warm summer night. She started off, carrying her precious bag firmly. Yes, she had a little bag, though its contents were not what you or I should call precious, even if of sentimental value to herself.

Off she trudged under the bright stars, using her umbrella as a walking stick, losing her way once on the bit of moorland, but in due course finding the tiny hamlet. It was easy to recognize the two-storey house. It stood isolated. And she was about to knock when she saw, to her surprise, that the door was ajar and that a man stood waiting for her—a little old man, also with a pockmarked face, who might indeed have been the porter's twin brother. And stranger still, he seemed to expect her. Evidently, the porter must have somehow got word to him. Anyhow, after listening in silence to her rambling story, he produced a candlestick and led her up the creaky, carpetless stairs to a small, dingy room on the first floor. He didn't suggest refreshment; nor, indeed, she remembered later, did he say much of anything. He just left the candle with her and went off upstairs to finish his own night's sleep no doubt. And, though glad to get the room, Miss Jenkins was also glad to see his back, for his odd silence was definitely of the surly kind.

Miss Jenkins, in very much of a flutter at her own boldness, waited till she heard his door bang, and then examined the room. There was little to examine. A small empty cupboard, a washstand that couldn't have concealed a cat, and a bed so high off the floor that she could look right through to the other side. Then she walked over the door— and locked it, the big key turning rather noisily.

This done, she fell to what she described as 'composing herself'. She reviewed the accident and thanked heaven she wasn't in that station waiting-room. She also realized that, while wholly uninjured, she was badly shaken, her nerves not quite as steady as they might have been. Natural enough, she decided. Some women would have fainted. She further noted an unusual feeling of cold, though the summer night was warm. And then, while engaged in this review of the immediate past, sitting quietly on the edge of the dirty-looking bed, she heard a voice saying 'Lock your door', a voice apparently in the room. And this startled her so much that for a moment she didn't move. She just sat there rigidly holding her bag tight.

Frightened? Yes, of course, she was frightened, but for some reason not unduly so. She sat there motionless, while her mind kept repeating 'I did lock it, I have locked it,' and waiting to hear if the voice would speak again. It did not. But only after several minutes did she make a great effort and got on to her feet and repeated her search of the room. She carried the candle with her, dropping tallow everywhere, and of course she found no one. She was the only person in that room.

It was strange, it was even alarming; but Miss Jenkins faced the situation just as before she had faced a savage dog and a bull in a field— finally persuading herself that her nerves were more disordered than she had realized, and this nonsense was their way of proclaiming the fact. 'Maybe it's suppressed shock,' she told herself. 'I'd better lie down a bit. I'll be calmer that way,'— and then the voice came again 'Lock your door.' Louder than before.

It came this time before she had actually climbed up on to the high bed. It caught her between sitting up and lying down, and she held breathless in that position, her heart thumping violently, the candle dripping its tallow all over the dirty counterpane. Her thoughts flew in all directions like scattered hens. And this time she was more than frightened, for here was something utterly beyond her. How could a voice sound in an empty room? Was the balance of her mind so disturbed that she was suffering the delusion of hearing voices where none existed? It was a dreadful thought.

And it was then that help came, though not in very convincing form: she noticed for the first time the window was open. It was open at the bottom. She had been trying to persuade herself that the voice both times had come from her own lips without her realizing it. The open window provided a better clue. There had been a voice outside, a noise at least that she had twisted to sound like syllables. And her courage revived like a compressed spring released. She walked boldly across and stuck her head out into the night. Darkness, total darkness, and silence, utter silence. She didn't call out. She just waited, waited several minutes. But nothing stirred. There was not a breath of wind.

She drew back into the nasty little room and crossed it shakily, the candle, she noticed, trembling in her hand. She was trembling all over now. The sensation of cold had increased. But her native courage came to help her. She made up her mind: the best, the only, thing to do was to lie as quietly as might be on the top of the dirty bed and wait for the morning. Yes, that was the sensible thing to do. She might even fall asleep, for she felt tired in her very bones. Shivering too with that curious cold. Only ... was it better to put the candle out, or leave it burning? Sleep was more likely to come if the room was in darkness. On the other hand, wasn't it wiser to be able to see...? Then she made her decision: darkness was best; and she leaned over to blow out the candle. She blew it out.

LOCK YOUR DOOR!

It seemed to her like a thunder clap. And this time she didn't argue with herself, didn't reflect, didn't even think. She obeyed. Automatically, she half sprang, half slithered off the bed and reached the door in two strides. Automatically, too, she seized hold of the big key and turned it. She suffered then a further shock. The door was NOT locked. Though she had turned the key before, she hadn't turned it far enough. All this time the door had been unlocked. She now turned the key frantically round once more, a bit further, and heard the extra click. Now it WAS locked. It made a loud, rattling noise.

But there was another noise as well; a quite different sound reached her ears. She listened intently, standing there in the dark room close against the door. It rose in the deep silence of the still night—the creaking of boards, the sound of soft footsteps coming slowly, cautiously, down the stairs from the floor above. She knew exactly what it was: someone was sneaking down the stairs on stockinged feet.

Standing there close to the door, her bag in one hand, the extinguished candle in the other, she listened with her heart in her mouth. The steps came nearer. Then the sound ceased. The steps had left the creaking stairs and were moving along the carpet of the passage leading past her door. She stood motionless, for what seemed minutes. She was holding the bag and candlestick so tight that her fingers went numb. The owner of the steps, she knew, had stopped just outside the door. Only the thin panels of wood stood between her and this other person.

The brass handle turned. She heard the sound of it turning. Heard, too, the slight creaking, straining noise as the door was pushed and the person standing outside tried to enter. She was so close that barely six inches lay between her own face and the face outside. But the door held. And again it seemed that minutes passed, though no doubt it was only seconds—and she caught the faint sound of muffled footsteps moving along the passage, then dying away as they went down into the well of the house.

Miss Jenkins could now heave a deep breath of relief.

She straightened up, her body had been bent over with her ears against the thin panels. The first thing she did was, not to scream, or anything of that sort, but to toss the candlestick on to the bed behind her. She knew the relief was temporary and the steps would come back. They did. She caught their sound first when they reached the top of the stairs and passed on to the passage carpet and were no longer audible. A moment later the doorknob rattled faintly, the door wheezed a little as it was pushed. But it held. This time she thought she caught the sound of someone breathing, but she admits this may have been imagination only. Then the stairs creaked as the steps left the passage and returned to the floor above.

She stepped slowly back then, the tension of immediate danger lifted. She breathed freely, deeply, once more. Her whole body relaxed. Only that curious sensation of cold remained. She is not quite clear about what happened next, but evidently she climbed back on to the top of the bed because she remembers feeling the hard candlestick beneath her body as she lay down. 'Soon the light will come,' she remembers muttering to herself as she stretched out. 'And he won't come back. He won't come down and try again. Thank heaven I locked the door and the key held.'

... And she opened her eyes to see the sunshine streaming in through the open window. Actually she had dropped off to sleep. The shock of the accident and the tension at the door had resulted in utter exhaustion and the reaction of sleep.

'At any rate,' she told her friends later, 'it's always wiser to lock your door, as I've so often said to you.'

What she didn't tell her friends, because she didn't know it, was that the house had been unoccupied the whole time. It had been empty for years, because it was so dreadfully haunted that no one would use it. Some thirty years earlier murder had been committed there, by a railway porter from the little wayside station, a little old man with a face scarred by smallpox, a murderer who had in due course been executed. The little railway station had no porter. A woman filled that job.

FIVE STRANGE STORIES

By 1948 Blackwood was at the height of his radio and television popularity. The BBC asked him to tell a series of five-minute strange stories to be broadcast on the Home Service last thing at night, round about half-past eleven. Blackwood picked on five brief tales that he frequently told at gatherings. Apart from 'Japanese Literary Cocktail', which was new to radio, the other four had all been narrated live in some previous talk or interview. 'The Texas Farm Disappearance' he had narrated in his spot on *The World and His Wife* series in October 1946. Both 'Pistol Against a Ghost' and 'The Holy Man' had been in an early broadcast of 'Queer Stories' in August 1934 whilst 'The Curate and the Stockbroker', probably Blackwood's most related narration, had been used in the *Young Ideas* series in October 1935 and, more significantly, was the story Blackwood told on the very first television broadcast on 2 November 1936. The full set of five was broadcast during the week beginning 10 May 1948. 'The Texas Farm Disappearance' was picked up by the BBC's audience magazine *The Listener* and published in its issue for 13 May 1948, though the others have never previously been published. The publication of 'The Texas Farm Disappearance' brought forward an interesting letter from a reader who noticed its similarity to Ambrose Bierce's story 'Charles Ashmore's Trail' published in *Can Such Things Be?* in 1893, the writer tantamount to accusing Blackwood of plagiarism. Blackwood's response is of interest. 'The facts are simple. It was in 1892 that the Texas farmer, coming out to see my herd of pedigree Jerseys, told me the story. How close it comes to a tale by Ambrose Bierce I cannot judge as I have never read it... My own guess would be that Bierce possibly heard about the disappearance the farmer told me and used it in print later.' If nothing else it attests to the authenticity of the incident.

I. THE TEXAS FARM DISAPPEARANCE

I'VE ALWAYS been interested in disappearances—total disappearances, I mean—where a human being just vanishes from the face of the earth without any explanation. And here is perhaps the strangest that ever came my way, for this one involves a different kind of space to the ordinary space we are familiar with. It was told to me by a farmer from Texas, a fellow I met and knew when I had a farm myself in Ontario, Canada.

With his mother and a younger brother he ran a farm in a rather isolated part of the State. One evening in winter, after a snowfall that had lasted all day, the wind suddenly shifted, the clouds vanished, and a full moon blazed down on the carpet of fresh snow. In that clear, dry air, it was almost bright enough to read; and the mercury shot right down below zero quickly. It was while preparing supper that the mother, needing water, asked Jim, the younger of the two brothers, to go out and fetch some from the well. This was a daily commonplace job. The well, their only house supply, never ran dry. And Jim, putting on his fur mitts and cap, sallied out with a couple of pails as usual. The distance to the well must have been perhaps one hundred and fifty yards. But the lad didn't come back, and his brother, who told me the story, went out himself to see what was the matter. No question of danger anywhere; none was possible. There on the otherwise untrodden snow were Jim's footmarks, clear as daylight, the only tracks visible. And there, also, about half way to the well, lay the two pails on the ground. Well, he followed the footsteps to the two pails and stopped just beside them. No track of any kind was visible along the further fifty yards to the well.

It was mysterious to say the least. The snow lay quite smooth with no sign of flurry or disturbance. He shouted his brother's name again and again. No answer came. Then he became a little frightened, for no conceivable explanation came to him. For the first time in his life, he told me, he really had what we call 'goose-flesh'. Then he hurried back to the house to consult with his mother. As he went, before he reached the house, he heard a voice: 'Help me! Help me!' It was Jim's voice beyond all question. It seemed to come from the air. His mother, when she rushed out, heard it too. But though they both stood there shouting and shouting, and Jim's voice, now fainter, now louder, now far away, now close, answered each time, they could never decide exactly the direction it came from. Indeed, it seemed to come from all directions, though always from the empty air about them, and never from below.

The neighbours heard it too next day when the older brother had ridden out to fetch them. All came from several miles away, so isolated was the farm. No explanation was forthcoming. Jim never came back. He was never seen again. As the winter passed the voice grew fainter, but hardly a day went by without the cry for help being heard. It was an event of the first, even of shattering, importance, to the whole country. With the warming up of the spring days, though still audible, the cry seemed fainter and fainter, more and more distant, till finally in the great heat of that Texan summer, it died away completely and was never heard again.

II. THE HOLY MAN

SOME very queer stories indeed come out of countries like India and Africa, countries whose high temperatures perhaps stimulate imagination. Those from India seem on a higher level than the African, and a number deal with remarkable exploits claimed for Holy Men, men who by following a rigorous training have developed abnormal powers in themselves: powers, for instance, that enable them to produce internal bodily heat so that they can sit practically naked and meditate in an atmosphere below zero; or cover great distances at incredible speed; prolong life fabulously; even be buried alive for long periods. One such story that came my way is, I think, out of the ordinary run.

A middle-aged English official, who told it to me, was enjoying a couple of days' hunting on his leave, and arrived one evening at the edge of a broad and stately river. He told his servant to pitch the tent for the night, and then walked to the edge of the low mud cliff and began cleaning his gun. Some thirty feet below him the river ran slowly by. Rather thick bushes came close to the water's brink. It was an utterly deserted spot. Looking out over the flood of water, golden in the sunset blaze, a moving object caught his eye, floating along with the sluggish current. It was a body, yet with something about it that puzzled him—something about the face as the body turned. His field glasses showed on examination that there was coarse grass stuffed into the open mouth. The body seemed to be that of a strapping young native with no sign of violence about it anywhere. He felt sure death had been very recent. His servant, after using the glasses, explained that by stuffing the mouth with grass evil spirits were prevented from taking possession.

There was nothing particularly unusual or startling in this, and the Englishman went on cleaning his gun when the odd behaviour of his servant drew his attention sharply. The man was trembling all over; his face wore an expression of awe, of veneration, of worship almost, yet he showed no sign of fear. Rather he seemed lost in devout wonder as, by way of answer, he interrupted his prayer, whispered, 'See, a Holy Man,' and pointed down to the narrow strip of foreshore below. And the Englishman, looking down, saw an old native dressed in a loincloth, emerging from the bushes and approaching the water.

'Watch,' whispered the servant, now on his knees.

They watched together. The native was very old, and very emaciated. At the water's edge he stopped and began making slow, sweeping gestures with his hands and arms in the direction of the young body floating past in mid-stream.

'Watch,' repeated the servant in an awestruck whisper. 'He needs it.'

Whether due to natural currents and eddies of the slow-moving river or not, the young body came nearer and nearer, till at last it lay on the sand at the old man's feet, whereupon they saw him stoop, draw it from the river and drag it after him a dozen yards till he disappeared with it behind the bushes. The field glasses showed that it was a young man's body in perfect preservation.

'Wait now,' whispered the servant, 'we see more yet.'

They waited, the Englishman with his field-glasses glued to his eyes, and about ten minutes later there was a movement in the clump of bushes, and out walked the young man. He walked away till he disappeared in the distance, vigorous, strong, moving easily and naturally into the sunset haze. A little later the Englishman scrambled down the mud cliff and there, behind the bushes, lay the worn-out, cast-off body of the old man in the loincloth.

III. PISTOL AGAINST A GHOST

IN THIS matter of ghost-hunting, there's no good using lethal weapons—swords, guns, pistols, and the like. If you do have the luck to see an apparition, and it scares you, your best weapon is keen observation and a healthy scepticism. A bold front, anyhow, and then just go for it.

But McCallister thought otherwise. He was a keen ghost-hunter, having passed the night in several haunted houses, but never once had he been lucky and seen anything. A hard-boiled investigator, he always took a pistol with him, telling all and sundry that if he saw anything, he would shoot. He meant it too. He was a good shot. Oh, yes, he would give fair notice, but then he would shoot.

He always went with two friends, both equally keen. They derided his pistol-packing habit, but couldn't change him.

On this particular occasion they were established for a night of watching in an isolated Norfolk farmhouse, so badly haunted—what with figures, footsteps, noises, and other unaccountable phenomena—that the farmer had moved with his family to another building about half a mile away. It had been too much for them.

Each of the three friends used a separate room to wait in. Outside doors and windows were securely locked. Their careful advance search of the old rambling building was over. Night fell. They dined frugally on provisions brought with them. The night was still as the grave. No wind stirred. A late October evening, it was. The stars were out. Each man had chosen his particular room. And, as usual, the two companions had urged McCallister to leave his pistol out of it if anything happened. He remained adamant. 'If I see anything,' he said obstinately, 'I shall give full warning, then shoot.' At about ten o'clock they separated for bed. Each took his candle and matches, for in this farmhouse there was no electricity.

McCallister lay down on his bed in his clothes. He hoped devoutly for some manifestation during the night. He felt neither scared nor creepy, just eaten alive with curiosity to see something. His nerves were quite steady; indeed, he had no nerves at all. By the light of his candle he tried to read. The pistol lay under his pillow. He gradually felt drowsy, blew out the candle, and went sound asleep.

The next thing he knew was that he was suddenly awake, and had been disturbed by a noise or something. He opened his eyes. He looked about him. From the uncurtained windows it was just light enough for him to see quite plainly, though without detail, a big figure standing at the end of his bed. It was unmistakable—a long, grey figure, its outline beyond question. Any doubt was put out of court by the fact that it moved. It swayed a little from side to side, a strange movement. Automatically McCallister's hand had reached for the pistol beneath his pillow. He sat up on the bed, the pistol in his hand. Then he spoke:

'I've got a pistol aimed at you. I shall count three. Then I'm going to fire, and I mean it.' And his voice sounded as though he did mean it.

The figure stopped swaying. McCallister began to count, 'One, two, three,' then he fired, aiming low below the knees. And almost before he was ready for a second shot, something hard struck him on the chest, and fell into his lap. The figure had stretched a long arm out almost as though to make a low catch. McCallister, picking up the hard object that struck him, found a bullet in his hand.

Well, something happened to McCallister's mind then. It was in complete confusion. Possibly terror was an ingredient in this confusion. He just didn't know. With a man of his type action was his one resource. He aimed the pistol again, this time higher up, and fired at the heart. Again came that amazing gesture of the figure as though it stretched an arm, a hand, as if to make a catch, and again a bullet fell back as though flung against his chest.

And then once more he fired, but this time his hand trembled so badly that his aim was hopelessly wild. Yet a third time, with the same gesture, a bullet struck his coat and fell into his lap.

I think McCallister then lost control of mind and nerves. In other words, he was scared to death, he passed out. A merciful blackness followed.

It was at breakfast next morning that some light was thrown on the horrible episode of the night. The three friends exchanged experiences. Nothing had happened, it seems, to the other two. McCallister didn't say much. He remained silent, maintaining he had slept like a top.

'Oh yeah,' laughed the man who had unpacked their luggage the night before, 'but I thought you'd have guessed from the weight of the pistol, with the bullets taken out, that you fired only blank cartridges—*at me*, old man. You had only three. I had 'em in my pocket and tossed them back at you.'

IV. JAPANESE LITERARY COCKTAIL

I REMEMBER once coming across a trick used by a Japanese author to interest a reader in his book. Instead of a preface or introduction he described some brief incident intended to whet the appetite for what was to follow: a sort of literary cocktail. It was calculated to predispose the reader favourably, to put him in the right mood. Usually it was an episode of fantastic character with a startling climax.

Let me give you an instance. A foreigner in a small Japanese city, a painter, wanted to find an old woman he could use as a model for some picture or other—an old woman with a humped back. Her face didn't matter; it was the aged figure with a humped back he was looking for.

And one evening, as dusk was falling, he chanced to see the very thing he wanted in the crowded street. He followed her, but somehow could never quite overtake her. Like some people she had the gift of slipping so fast and cleverly through the throng. He followed as quickly as he could, yet she was always a bit ahead of him. The shadows were falling and night was coming on. Finally, however, he did gain on her, just where the city ended. The houses fell away abruptly and a clear stretch of empty road began. It was the road to the cemetery. Doubtless the old woman was on her way to visit a grave.

Feeling a little embarrassed about accosting her and explaining his purpose, his knowledge of the language being slight, he seized his chance. It was now or never, he felt. So, in a few rapid strides, he overtook her and began to speak. Whereupon she turned and looked at him, though without stopping. It was the first time he had seen her face, but what he saw appalled him, for she had no face, no face at all. Just a disc of yellow flesh without eyes or mouth or nose. It was ghastly beyond words.

He was rooted to the spot with terror, for there flashed across his mind stories he had heard of a kind of ghost that made its abode in a cemetery and had no face, stories he had laughed at. And now one of those dreadful creatures stood just in front of him, silent, hideous, terrifying.

The power of movement then came back to him. He turned and raced back towards the city. His one desire was to see a normal human being, to speak with a man like himself, anyone he could find.

And there, to his great relief, he saw the Guardian coming to meet him, waving his lantern in the prescribed manner, and calling out the time in a loud voice. 'This is the Hour of the Fox', he was calling as the terrified artist joined him, breathless and shaking. He told the man what had happened, what he had just seen, and the Guardian listened with horror growing in his eyes.

'You've seen one of *those?*' he whispered, shuddering, then placed his lantern on the ground. 'Like this, you mean?' Then quietly he passed his free hand across his own face, moving it slowly downwards from his forehead to his mouth. And he, too, had no face...

V. THE CURATE AND THE STOCKBROKER

A GOOD many years ago, when Barrie's play *Mary Rose* was the talk of the town—a girl disappears in that play, you might remember, she just vanishes from the face of the Earth—London was full of talk about theories of disappearance. I remember them well. I think the most popular one was the question of higher space—that is that there is another dimension of space, at right angles to the three we know, and you slip into it, well, you just vanish, you disappear.

Well now, this is what happened to the curate and the stockbroker. It happened at a country house in Kent. There was a large weekend party of some kind, a lot of people. It rained a great deal on Friday and Saturday, but Sunday it got better, and the clouds lifting a bit, the stockbroker and the curate thought they'd get some exercise, so they went out for a tramp. I don't think they had much in common to talk about, but they got their exercise, and on the way back a short-cut tempted them. It was across a great turnip field, but it would save half a mile. Well, they started off in single file. In the distance they could see the lights in the windows of the house—and tea!

It was a misty autumn evening and dusk was falling. They started ploughing across the heavy wet turnip leaves, and a third of the way over somebody called out behind them, 'Come with me!', but when the curate, who was walking behind, turned to see who had spoken, there wasn't anybody there—no one, and there wasn't cover enough even to hide a dog. His companion, oddly enough, hadn't heard the voice. They stomped on together.

But the curate was puzzled—he was more than puzzled. He was an ardent, sincere type of chap, and felt uneasy. No echo could explain the sound. Why hadn't his companion heard the call? That 'Come with me' disturbed him. It seemed addressed to himself, he thought. He didn't like it. Nor did he like a curious cold that was creeping through the atmosphere, in spite of the heat of his body from the exercise. And he knew that voice would come again. It did, louder than before: 'Come with me.'

He stopped dead. And again his companion hadn't heard it. He wanted his tea and dry clothes. He was tired, too. 'It's the noise of our boots against the leaves—the heavy wet leaves. Come along, damn it man, let's get home.' They went on in silence. The curate's uneasiness had deepened. A dreadful fear was growing over him. He was scared in his bones; he couldn't explain it, and that made it worse, but he felt that when the voice came again, and he was sure it would, something awful, something appalling, would happen. He was ready, listening attentively, ready to turn on the instant. And just fifty yards later it came—close against the back of his head, against his very neck, much louder, like a command—a summons—a dreadful note of authority in it: 'Come with me!'

He was round on the instant, staring over the great turnip field. No one was visible. Then he turned back to his companion, and his heart missed a beat. His companion wasn't beside him, he wasn't there. His pipe, with smoke still curling up, lay quietly on a big turnip leaf. But the man who had been puffing it a moment ago had disappeared. No trace of that unfortunate stockbroker was ever seen again from that day to this.

I have been reminded of the similarity between 'Japanese Literary Cocktail' and E.F. Benson's story 'The Step' from *More Spook Stories* (1934). As with the Bierce story it may be that both writers drew their inspiration from a common source or perhaps Blackwood heard of Benson's story but forgot the provenance. I certainly do not suspect any attempt at plagiarism.

LATER STORIES

AT A MAYFAIR LUNCHEON

Following his 1924 collection *Tongues of Fire* Blackwood wrote very few stories for adult readers, although he maintained a fairly healthy output of children's stories and magazine articles and reviews. What stories he did write were eventually collected in a 1935 volume called *Shocks* which is one of the hardest of Blackwood's collections to find. Blackwood would not have bothered to assemble even that volume had it not been a contractual requirement with his publisher.

In 1945 the American author and publisher August Derleth corresponded with Blackwood with a view to assembling a volume of hitherto unreprinted material. Blackwood submitted two stories, 'The Doll' and 'The Trod' but when pushed for more responded 'Here I am not very hopeful; I think all my volumes of short stories or long-short stories have already been issued in the United States; and, alas, I have no new unpublished ones ready or in view.'

That was rather an odd statement. As we have seen 'Lock Your Door' was already in typescript form, and there had been a number of stories published in the magazines during the preceding decade. Derleth eventually published the two stories as *The Doll and One Other* in 1946, Blackwood's last original collection, and with no idea that at least eight other stories by Blackwood existed and had never been reprinted.

The first of these, written just after the publication of *Shocks* was 'At a Mayfair Luncheon'. Blackwood had written it in July 1935 while staying with Captain Boylan at Drogheda in the Irish Republic. It was published in the prestigious *Windsor Magazine* for March 1936.

ON looking back, it seemed incredible to young Monson that this could have come out of such commonplace conditions. For it started while he was reading poetic stuff about the Pæstum Temples, and then about the temples of Baalbec and the worship of Jupiter Ammon, and his thoughts had run off waywardly towards Christ and Buddha, and he had been wondering vaguely—Man in the Street that he was—how such vital and terrific forms of belief and worship could ever die—when, abruptly, someone came into his study with a tiresome interruption:

'This note come by 'and, please, sir, and would you please answer immedshately, thank you, sir.'

Monson acted immedshately and read the note:

Do forgive me, dear. I'm a man short. 1.15 for 1.30. If you *can...do*.
FELICITY

Now, he believed he loved Felicity. He could. He did.

'Telephone immedshately to her ladyship to say Mr Monson will be delighted to lunch today at 1.15,' he gave his answer. And in due course he went.

Further, it lies quite beyond him to explain why all the way to Curzon Street, walking leisurely this fine May morning, he was still aflame with Baalbec, the Pyramids, the Pæstum Temples, and all that sort of delicious, ancient, romantic pagan stuff. Imagination ran that way. He left it at that. Some old-world glamour caught him away into some strange, wild heaven. He found himself suddenly loathing the modern drabness, the senseless speed, the artificial mechanism, the clever, infinite invention that was smart and up to date, and all the rest of the rushing, uncomfortable nonsense. Machinery did everything, the individual nothing. A deep yearning possessed him for the slow, worthwhile, steady liveableness of other days, when a man could believe in a mountain nymph on many-fountained Ida and worship her, by God, with a conviction of positive reaction. He heard the old, old winds among the olives and saw the spindrift blow across great Triton's horn, his sandals trod upon acanthus leaves, the wild thyme stung his nostrils....

In which ridiculous, even hysterical mood, he rang the bell in Curzon Street at 1.15 and waited upon admittance.

So ordinary was the next step, and the routine of the steps following, that he found nothing to remark upon them.

'*So* sweet of you to come and save me. Lord Falsestep had a sudden Cabinet Meeting...I think you know everybody....'

He caught instantly the usual deadly savour. The cocktails and the preliminary chatter shared this deadliness, so that he found himself harking back to Baalbec and Pæstum and his earlier foolishness when, suddenly a late guest was announced, but in such a way that both his eye and ear were caught, held, arrested—what *is* the precise word?— startled is probably the most accurate, but, at any rate, taken with vivid painfulness.

'Painfulness?' Yes, assuredly, because it hurt. A sharp, terrible sting ran through him from head to foot. Something in him blenched, ran hot and cold, with an effect of dislocation somewhere, so that his heart seemed to stop.

Some Bright Young Thing, or its equivalent, chanced to engage him at the moment, though 'engage' is wrong, because the trivial glitter held no power of any sort, and glitter is at best a surface quality. It was, at any rate, while exchanging glittering vacancies thus, that he heard the footman's voice and turned to look.

To look! Rather, to stare. Was it man or woman, this late guest? Such outlines, he knew, were easily interchangeable today. It might have been one or other. 'Or both,' ran like fiery lightning through him, so that he turned faint with the sweetness of some amazing apprehension.

The chatter in his ear seemed suddenly miles away, and not miles alone, but ages. Its tinkle reached him, none the less, distinctly enough: '...so you simply *must* come. It will be too adorable. Without *you* it would be just ashes. Wear anything you like, of course, and doors open till dawn...' The Bright Young Thing's invitation, yes, oozing past her violent lipstick reached him distinctly enough, though it now had a sharply hideous sound—because at the same moment he had caught the voice of the late arrival: '*Thank you for asking me*,' and the words, so softly spoken, had a quality that made them sing above the general roar.

Why, then, did a wave of life rush drenching through him as he heard them? Why did his bones seem to melt and run to gold and silver? Whence came that breath of flower-laden wind across the drowned atmosphere of smoke and female perfume? That tang as of sea and desert air that for a moment seemed too sweet, too strong, to bear?

'...you promise. I'll expect you,' clanged the invitation.

'Of course, I shall be delighted,' came his mechanical acceptance. 'And I'll be there a little before dawn.'

They turned away mutually—he, because he felt curiously shamed a trifle—she, because a young man with a lisping voice approached with a wobbling glass. Shamed perhaps, yet faint as well, faint towards the Mayfair room and atmosphere, but at the same time so alive and exhilarated towards something else that he was intoxicated. He caught at the edge of a sofa to hold him down. He had a fear that he must rise to touch a star, a nebula, an outer galaxy.

There was confusion inextricable, then somehow they were all in the ultra-luxurious dining-room, and Felicity, his friend's wife whom he believed he loved, was dropping a hurried whisper in his ear:

'You are an angel, darling, to come. A woman has failed me too—that impossible Ursula again. Do you mind terribly? No, Lovely, on your left. Just an empty chair...!'

And so it was that the space next to him was unoccupied, an empty chair, just beyond which, he realized with a lift of his whole being, sat the late arrival whose voice, with its singing beauty, had swept Today into the rubbish heap.

Now, until this moment, young Monson—young as well as simple he assuredly was—had held full command of himself, since he had eschewed strong drink and was besides frankly bored, even feeling sorry he had come at all. And boredom engenders pessimism, not optimism. At the same time, contrariwise, it awakens a sense of superiority, false of course, yet compensating, because the mind comforts itself thereby that it is superior to the cause of its boredom. And until that amazing voice had echoed across the room packed with notables and nobodies, young Monson's mood was as stated, below par—bored a little. The Bright Young Thing had exasperated with her affectations. His spirits, though for the sake of politeness to Felicity, his lovely hostess, he had forced them to spurious activity, were distinctly low. There was nothing, therefore, to account for the stupendous, gripping interest he now felt suddenly in that empty space, the breadth of an unoccupied chair, that gaped—otherwise somewhat menacingly—between him and his neighbour. The interest and stimulus lay in this: that across the narrow emptiness the stranger sat. One other thing lay equally beyond his explanation—that, instead of the sense of false superiority referred to, he was aware now of inferiority in himself that wakened a humility of heart so deep and genuine that he found no honestly descriptive words.

How calm, gentle, silent, almost meek, yet never uncomfortable nor out of place, the stranger sat there, and not in any smallest degree embarrassed. Entirely self-possessed, moreover. He might have been the host, a careless, understanding host, whose carelessness and understanding derived from the certain knowledge that all were glad to be there. Yes, it was a *he*, Monson now knew, a guest quite unimpressed by the fact that this was the luncheon of a famous social and political hostess, and that 'those present' would be blazoned tomorrow with photographs in the daily press. Meek, perhaps, yet how strangely powerful, how radiant, and—the words seem childish—how beautiful, with a power and beauty beyond crumbling Baalbec and the windworn Pyramids. And upon some scale of mightiness that dislocated his mind perhaps a little, since a perfect blizzard of unrelated pictures suddenly swept and poured across his thoughts like an immense panorama, pictures all scaled to mightiness, so that his being seemed stretched to capacity to receive them, packed thus into a single flashing second. They roared up, passed, were gone, all simultaneously... great Stonehenge with its ache of grandeur, Pæstum with its rapture, the ghastly loneliness of the Easter Island images, the unanswerable Sphinx and Pyramids, and then, with a leap of terror, to the crystal iciness of the deserted moon, the awful depths of the nine-mile ocean bed... roared past and vanished again, as he stole a glance, wondering how for Felicity's sake, his anxious hostess whom he loved, he might approach his neighbour with a word.

On the stranger's further side, he saw, perched an empty-headed Duchess, avoiding him deliberately. He met Felicity's beseeching eye. He made a plunge across that gaping chair:

'We must bridge this empty space,' he ventured smilingly, leaning over a little. 'Some lady evidently has been detained. The stress of London life just now is hard upon punctuality...'

Something of the sort he said. The words rather tumbled from his mouth. There was a scent of wild thyme as he leaned over slightly.

The other smiled, lifting clear, shining eyes, so that young Monson admitted to something again akin to shock, a singular deep thrill of wonder, beauty, humility. Was it man or woman after all? shot through his mind.

'Not detained perhaps,' the answer floated to him, 'but unaware. Not dead, that is, but sleeping.'

Oddly, there was no shock of surprise at the choice of curious words a foreigner might have found, or one unaccustomed to modern usage, and Monson felt he had merely misunderstood perhaps. The voice was soft as music, very low.

'Late, at any rate,' he murmured in some confusion, his eyes upon his plate, as though in search of steadiness. 'Too late,' he added, his search for the commonplace still operating, 'for this delicious lobster *mousse*—or whatever it may be.'

That sweet, gentle smile again, that scent and purity of wild flowers, as he crumbled his bread and gazed across the narrow space towards his young neighbour, who sat unaccountably trembling before something he had never known before. Trembling, it seemed to himself, with happiness and wonder, yet with a touch of awe due to the new sense of power and splendour that rose in his heart. In his heart alone, yes, not in his mind. He established *that*, at any rate. His mind, if watchful perhaps and steady enough, seemed suddenly inoperative. What happened, what was happening, lay in the heart alone. Thus he found no explanation, as equally no doubt or question, about seeing those slender fingers radiant, the breadcrumbs shining upon the table beneath the other's touch, nor why, though raised repeatedly to his mouth, they multiplied on the cloth even while he took from them...

The eye of Felicity from the top of the long table flared at him. Since the stranger offered nothing, Monson, making a desperate effort to get at his mind, rather than allow his heart full sway, tried again after a moment's interval. To entertain one's neighbour was the acknowledged price of admission to any feast, to sit silent, at any rate, was not permissible. Again, the words fell tumbling from his lips without reflection, or rather from his heart:

'My plans for today were otherwise,' he mumbled, almost stammeringly, leaning over a little as before. 'I didn't really want to come, but I'm *awfully* g-glad I did. It's so difficult to—to live one's own life and—and keep in the swim nowadays.' He paused, watching a smile that opened in those glorious eyes, yet did not travel downwards to the tender lips. 'I was summoned at the last moment because some Cabinet Minister and a lady failed,' he fumbled on, 'but I wouldn't have missed it for—for—everything in the world.'

He stopped dead. The other's lips were moving. There was a light about the face and head.

'I myself was asked indirectly perhaps, but in true sincerity. And none call on me in vain.'

These were the actual words, spoken so low as to be just audible, that floated across the space of the empty chair. It seemed only a glance from Felicity's eye along the table length that held young Monson to his seat.

'Poor hostesses,' he thinks he heard himself murmuring, attempting a smile of charitable understanding. For at the same instant, turning abruptly, he met the other's eyes at the full. One look he saw, a look of fire and glory like dawn upon the Caucasus... and then a sense of fading, the passing away of an intolerable radiance that for a moment had forced his eyelids to drop. Yet in that fraction of a second, before they lifted again, the words came floating in a still, small voice that made them absolutely clear:

'From her heart it came. "Oh, Christ," she prayed, "Do, please, come. I need you." '

There was a stir in the room, a shuffling along the table, as Sir Thomas and Lady Ursula Smith-Ponsonby arrived with many apologies and slid gracefully into the two empty chairs on young Monson's left.

THE MAN-EATER

I'm not sure when Blackwood wrote 'The Man-eater', but it was probably at about the same time as 'At a Mayfair Luncheon'. Blackwood's agents, A.P. Watt, found the story harder to sell. No British magazine was interested and the American agent David Lloyd offered it to the better-paying markets of *Cosmopolitan, Adventure, Liberty,* and *Blue Book* without success. Eventually it was purchased by the pulp magazine *Thrilling Mystery* where it appeared in its March 1937 issue. Blackwood received only $50 for the story. Curiously *Thrilling Mystery* is now a much collected magazine amongst pulp enthusiasts and this Blackwood issue is highly prized easily commanding at least $50 if not more. The story has not been reprinted since that publication and this marks its first appearance in Britain after fifty years.

JOHN PATTERSON, owner of one of the most isolated rubber plantations in all Malaya, sat slowly drinking his evening peg. It tasted good after the long day's work, but there were signs of trouble in his blue eyes that the refreshing drink could not dissipate, and the deep lines about his rather grim jaw had an emphasis that was not caused merely by physical fatigue. He made a good picture of a practical, active man whose mind at the moment was distinctly worried.

To Patterson, it often seemed as if the few hundred acres of the plantation were a kind of island surrounded by the ocean of jungle that was everywhere trying to break in. His eye wandered now beyond the veranda, where the young rubber trees stretched in ordered lines until they were lost in the surrounding forest.

He sipped his cooling drink, he mopped his forehead, he stretched his long legs and lit a cigarette. A mild oath, spoken under his breath, escaped him, as though the thing that worried him now came to the surface of his mind, demanding honest examination.

Since the fall in the price of rubber, he had been hard put to it to keep the plantation going. He had been obliged to cut down his labour supply to the bare minimum. All this he had dealt with over many a long month; it was not new. But now, to add to his troubles, a man-eating tiger had turned up that had already killed two of the neighbouring villagers, and might at any time take some of his coolies who were already, indeed, too scared to leave their huts after sunset.

At this very moment, sitting on his veranda over his evening drink, a rifle lay close beside him in case of any sudden alarm.

There was, however, another thread of trouble that wove itself across the pattern of events his mind had to deal with, something harder to examine than the man-eater and the price of rubber, because it was less definite. As it cropped up now, presenting itself to his thoughts, he was aware that a perceptible shiver ran down his spine.

Though too slight for serious attention, it none the less was there, leaving a faintly unwelcome impression before it passed. For Patterson had a visitor, an Englishman named Norman, and it was something about this visitor that gave him this odd feeling of uneasiness.

Norman had drifted in a fortnight ago, arriving rather casually out of the blue, with only one Malay servant, Saka by name, and a minimum of luggage piled on a rough native cart. He seemed very vague as to where he had come from or where he was going. 'Just roaming about—plant hunting, you know,' was his reply to questions.

With the hospitality of the East, Patterson had not pressed for further information. In some ways he had been quite glad of the man's companionship in his lonely plantation, for it meant someone of his own race to talk to. Yet he could not forget, at the same time, the sensation of something queer and unpleasant that had come with his first sight of the stranger, something the touch of his hand had intensified.

Instinctively, without any reason, Patterson was uneasy. For a passing second, indeed, he had felt an inexplicable touch of fear, of horror almost, yet so utterly unjustifiable that he had dismissed it promptly from his mind. And, giving Norman the freedom of his bungalow, he had been too busy to see much of him, leaving him to his own devices.

This was two weeks ago now, and during the last few days a succession of things, small enough in themselves, perhaps, had suddenly risen in Patterson's mind both in their sequence and all together. That is, he now suddenly connected them all as due to one cause. He saw them as a coherent whole for the first time. And he traced them one and all to Norman, his visitor.

Small enough, indeed, they were, taken separately. There was the attitude of his own servants toward Saka, Norman's Malay compatriot. They utterly refused to fraternize. More—they avoided him, yet at the same time betrayed an air of respect that was rather the respect of fear than admiration.

They were beginning to make trouble in the little household. A couple had left without a reason, the others were uneasy. Toward Norman, the white visitor, on the other hand, their attitude left no room for doubt. They seemed frankly terrified. No satisfactory answers were given to questions—they were just filled with terror, superstitious terror, obviously.

And Patterson, always rather impatient with what he called 'superstitious rot', had not bothered to follow the matter up and press for explanations. They could stew in their own damned juice. He was far too busy to waste his time with them—until they began now to make further trouble by leaving.

What puzzled him even more, however, was the attitude of Spot, his smooth-haired terrier, who was more important to him than any Malay servant. And Spot's dislike and fear of Norman was too marked and persistent to be overlooked.

He ran out with his tail between his legs from the man's mere presence, and no amount of coaxing could make him behave otherwise. Whether Norman noticed this or not was difficult to say, though, at any rate, he gave no sign.

It was these little things, not to mention others, that now all rose up in Patterson's mind as a single whole, while he sat sipping his peg, the rifle ready to his hand. And the reason they thus presented themselves was the fact that it was getting late. It would be quite dark in another ten minutes, and Norman had not yet come back.

Word, too, had come that the man-eater was abroad on the prowl, and Patterson knew that his visitor never carried a rifle. To be out unarmed that late was more than dangerous. And Norman's laughing remark, 'No tiger will ever touch me or Saka,' was too like foolish bravado to be sensible.

'We know them too well, tigers and their little ways,' he had said another time, in reply to a warning. And it was the memory of these silly words, and of this even more silly attitude, that added to the anxious discomfort now in Patterson's thoughts.

It came to him abruptly with something of a shock that Norman's laugh, chilling his blood a little, his language as well were the laughter and language of mania. The man was not sane. He was a crazy man, and it was the jungle that had sent him crazy as many another man before him.

The way he laughed when he boasted of his immunity to tigers—why, that very morning, only a few hours ago!—reminded Patterson unpleasantly of another laugh he had once heard. A memory cell, long inactive, gave up its dead, as he sat there smoking, with his rifle across his knees.

It was a memory of years ago in Africa. He had sat beside his campfire on the Athi plains, much as he was sitting now, listening to the lions roaring in the distance and afraid that they might get one of his donkeys, when a dreadful, snarling laugh had rung out of the darkness, dreadful because it was the parody of a human laugh.

It was only a hyena, of course, and nothing to worry about, but it came back to memory now because—yes—because it held something akin to Norman's laughter of a few hours ago!

He gave a slight shiver as this similarity occurred to him—the crazy and the bestial laughter—then called for his 'boy'; and when Abdul appeared silently, like a drifting shadow, he told him to light the lamps as usual, but to light two extra ones as well.

For the feeling was in him to have as much bright light as possible. Not that the night, now at hand, was darker than it normally was, but that somehow it *seemed* darker and the additional light was welcome. 'God knows what this jungle holds,' ran across his mind. 'Even in daylight it's a menace, but after sundown it's just one damned horror after another.' He was without a trace of superstition, but there was something in the jungle Patterson had never yet made friends with. Frankly, he acknowledged it to himself.

Aloud he spoke to Abdul, who was friend as well as servant, a faithful, understanding fellow.

'It's getting too late to be abroad,' he said, 'and *Tuan* Norman is out without a rifle. There's word from the village that the man-eater is about. Better be ready—in case I need you—'

Abdul moved close without a sound. He looked cautiously over his shoulder before he spoke.

'Have no fear, Master,' he whispered. 'No tiger touch him—or Saka either.'

Patterson stared derisively. 'What d'you mean, man?' he asked.

Abdul held up a warning hand. 'Listen, Master! They come now. Tomorrow I explain,' he whispered, and his whisper was thick with fear. But the fear annoyed, even angered Patterson, because it confirmed something he felt in himself, while at the same time the harsh words he was just about to use did not leave his mouth.

For Abdul was right. His sharp ears had, indeed, caught the sound of footsteps, and as Patterson, rifle in hand, advanced to the edge of the veranda, he saw two shadowy forms moving down the path from the plantation. Norman and his man, Saka, obviously enough.

Why, he wondered to himself in that second—why was it that his sense of relief at their safety was tempered by another extraordinary sense of shrinking dread? It came and went in a flash, perhaps, this other feeling. But, again, he had been definitely conscious of it. Angrily, with quick decision, he dismissed it from his mind. But what the devil was Abdul muttering in his ear?...

'Look, *Tuan*! Look!'

'I am looking, you fool!' he answered crossly. 'I see who it is quite clearly without your help.'

'Look, *Tuan*, look!' repeated Abdul's whisper. 'Their eyes———!' And the man was gone from behind him almost before the words were out.

Patterson, of course, had looked. He had seen—the faint greenish light that glowed in the two pairs of eyes as the men approached him down the path, and he had admitted to himself the sharp, ugly grip of terror that again caught his heart for a passing instant as he stared.

With a decision even greater than before, he suppressed, dismissed it. Eyes always shone when facing a light like that—cats' eyes, animals' eyes, human eyes. Why the devil not? It was all natural enough.

Bah! His nerves were jumpy, nothing more. Yet it was with a certain effort that he then crossed the veranda and met his visitor as he came up the steps.

'Glad to get you back safely,' was what he found to say by way of welcome. 'Getting a bit anxious, you know—after dark, like this.'

His voice, he was glad to notice, sounded quite ordinary. Norman's voice, when he replied, was quite ordinary too.

'Oh, sorry, Patterson,' he said, 'but you needn't have worried. By the way,' he added, 'the tiger has killed again. A woman this time. At sunset. About ten miles up the river. It's feeding now.'

Patterson stared. His breath became oddly irregular for a moment.

'How do you know?' he asked bluntly.

'Oh, it was Saka that heard it,' the other replied, casually enough. 'A man who had passed that way told him.'

Patterson said no more, asked no further questions, at least. He could think of nothing suitable to say at the moment. To hear a white man tell a downright lie shocked him. To lie before a native was worse still, and Saka, standing close, nodding his dark head, had heard it too.

He merely suggested a drink instead, and while he mixed the two pegs, he decided finally in his mind that the sooner he was rid of this unpleasant pair, the better. Though nothing further by way of real evidence had occurred, he was convinced now beyond any question that his visitor was insane.

He was dangerous, too. Patterson had seen men run amok in this strange country before now. He decided to take no chances. And Saka was as unsavoury as his master. As politely as might be, he would get rid of them both before anything happened. And it was to his great relief when that night at dinner Norman himself brought up the subject of his leaving.

Casually enough, with nothing suspicious in voice or manner, Norman referred to his interest in the plant life of the jungle, and his search for a particular species which, however, was not to be found in the district, adding that he really could not trespass on his host's hospitality more than a couple of days longer.

He would push on then to another part of the country. He was very grateful for the pleasant visit and hoped two days would not be too inconvenient—to which Patterson, greatly relieved that the matter seemed to have settled itself so easily, of course agreed with a show of welcome.

He slept well that night, though he did not like Abdul's answer when he informed him of the fact and asked him what it was that he kept secret in his own native mind about the visitors.

'Too dangerous,' whispered the frightened Malay. 'They have long ears, Master. Later I tell you, after they go.' Patterson particularly disliked the phrase 'long ears,' and, the suggestive look on Abdul's face as he said it.

Next morning, however, there was no opportunity for talk. A messenger arrived at dawn from Brent's plantation, ten miles away and his nearest neighbour, saying the man-eater had killed a woman near his place at sunset the night before, and proposing a hunt.

If they started at once they would stand a good chance of getting the beast. Startled by this confirmation of Norman's statement, wondering still more how he could have known of the kill twenty minutes after sunset when it happened, Patterson made his preparations quickly and started off.

For some reason unexplained to himself, he gave his visitor the plausible excuse that he was called away to a neighbour, Brent, who was sick, and Norman, proposing to spend the whole day plant-hunting, asked no questions. Patterson was glad to see his back as he and Saka set off themselves in another direction.

The hunt, however, had no results. In vain Patterson and Brent took up position, while the estate coolies and villagers beat the jungle toward them. The man-eater, his meal finished, had shifted. They found the remains of the woman, but no trace of the beast himself. And that evening after dinner Patterson learned a few facts about Norman from his fellow-planter.

Brent had never run across him, but he had heard of him at different times from other planters. White men, widely scattered and not plentiful in the jungle, were of great interest to each other, and it was odd that no news had come Patterson's way.

He was not the gossipy kind, and his work absorbed him. He now heard from Brent that Norman's wife had run away with Taylor, an engineer who worked on the railway, and that Norman had felt terribly about it. He had become slightly unbalanced, some said. He had sold the little place they had near Klang and taken to a solitary life, wandering about with the jungle Malays.

He had been quite a well-known naturalist before this happened. Apparently, his jungle wanderings were devoted to botany, though it was said his knowledge of wild-animal life, too, was intimate and extraordinary.

Planters, added Brent with a laugh, did not welcome his visits because the servants disliked him and he was apt to upset their households.

'Went a bit out of his mind, you said,' commented Patterson cautiously, who felt it wasn't quite decent to discuss too closely a man who was still his guest. 'And the Malays dislike him—eh?'

Brent grunted. 'Unbalanced, yes,' he repeated, 'though crazy is probably the truth. As for "dislike," that's below the mark, too. It seems he put the devil into 'em.'

And he told a case or two in point when Norman had been visiting other planters—MacDonald in particular—whose dogs went for him and would have torn him to bits if their owner hadn't beaten them off in time.

'Haven't you heard what the natives call him?' Brent asked, filling up the glasses.

Patterson shook his head. He wished the question had not been asked. He wished he had stopped the conversation long ago. He hated, as he hated poison, anything to do with superstition. The jungle was the wrong place for such subjects. He hated it because he didn't believe in it, yet knew it happened. And he had an unpleasant inkling of exactly what was coming.

'They think he's what they call a tiger-man,' Brent said in a voice that was very quiet and had a new note in it.

Patterson made no rejoinder. He sat quite still for a minute, then finished his drink at a gulp. Something went cold in him, cold with horror. He shivered.

'Natives will say anything,' he remarked presently, since a remark of some kind was necessary. He got up from his lounge chair. 'Come on, let's get to bed. I've got an early start in the morning.'

'Get rid of the pair of them,' was all Brent said as they exchanged 'good nights'. 'And the sooner the better. That's my advice.'

But the horrible phrase ran to and fro in Patterson's mind too suggestively and actively for much sleep to come his way. His years in Africa had already made him familiar with the amazing and incredible notion that a man's life and soul may become identified with the life and nature of a savage animal, and that during sleep his 'double' may be projected in that animal's form.

In Africa it was always lion or leopard-men. Astonishing stories by white hunters as well as superstitious natives had been proved up to the hilt. Here, of course, in the Malay jungles it was tiger-men. If the animal, moreover, was injured by knife or bullet, the wound was found reproduced on the body of the sleeping man.

The evidence was as strong as it was utterly incredible, and the whole subject was bathed and soaked in hideous magic and superstition. Patterson's unquestioning, honest mind loathed the whole subject with the intensity of a disbelief that was yet not all disbelief.

He fell asleep finally, however, and luckily he did not dream. It was midday before he left Brent's place for home, for the latter, noticing his disinclination to start, had not hurried him. Had he foreseen what he would find at home, he would probably not have left at all. Abdul, in a state of fear and suppressed excitement, was waiting for him at the door.

'Come, Master, quickly,' he said in a low voice of terror. 'Come to *Tuan* Norman's room.' And he led the way, both men going on tiptoe so as to make no noise. A muttering voice was audible inside the bedroom, which opened off the veranda, and Patterson, peering cautiously round the door, saw his visitor stretched at full length on the bed.

He was talking in his sleep, and Patterson, about to turn away, caught these words: 'Blood, blood, I must have blood.' He stopped dead in his tracks.

He listened spellbound, while horror crept up and down his spine with icy fingers. It was the weirdest, strangest experience of his whole life, passing his understanding, gripping him with nightmare power.

In after years he always declared that some touch of mania must have attacked his mind, inflaming imagination beyond all conceivable bounds. Yet as he stood there, frozen to immobility, it was assuredly no imagination that enabled him to follow a hunting tiger through the words of a sleeping man. And not alone to follow the hunting tiger, but to enter into the very life of the brute itself...

Patterson peered out from the thicket at the edge of an open space, while his eyes swept the glade in search of prey——He stiffened, as the strong smell of a deer came to his nostrils, while with a sickening sensation of reality it came to him that this tiger was not after deer or pig merely—it was after man...

A wave of intolerable excitement swept him from head to foot, and the sleeping man obviously shared this awful lust. The tiger had come on a path leading to a village. With caution the great beast sniffed. The path had been used quite recently. Satisfied, it slipped back behind a low bush and waited.

The sleeping man rolled over. Was he going to wake? Patterson held his breath. No, he was breathing again quite steadily. He had now stopped muttering. He, too, was—waiting.

The muttering started afresh. 'Voices—voices—they are coming——Wait, they are too many——They pass, but others will follow soon——Ah! Here comes one alone, alone—Be ready—Now, you have him!'

The sleeper sprang to his knees on the bed and threw himself with convulsive gestures against his pillow. He woke with a violent start.

As Patterson instinctively stepped back a pace, he felt something thrust into his hand from behind him. It was a kris.

'Kill him, *Tuan*, kill him,' Abdul was hissing in his ear. 'It is right that he should die. We will all swear he died of fever!'

With a great effort Patterson turned to his servant, and with still greater effort he found words to say, for his mouth was so dry that he could scarcely frame the syllables.

'Put up your knife, Abdul,' he commanded in a firm whisper, 'for we cannot slay a man because he talks in his sleep. We do nothing now. I have spoken.'

And as they turned away, moving softly on to the veranda, Norman, his eyes now wide open, was lying on his back staring, staring into space, his body motionless. Had he heard their whispered talk together?

Patterson never knew. He stood there, leaning against the rail, uncertain in his shaken mind what he must do. His heart was pumping wildly, his thoughts and emotions in a whirl.

But he did not stand there long. A breathless runner from the village came bursting into the compound with the dreadful news:

'The tiger has killed again, *Tuan*! Please, come!'

And Patterson's self-control came back at the words. Seizing his rifle, and bidding Abdul follow with another, he was off without an instant's hesitation. The man had been killed only two hundred yards from the village. A crowd of natives had driven the tiger away.

They were already digging a deep pit and covering it with earth and branches, planning to use the corpse as bait, so that the tiger would return and fall into the pit. As no tree was available where a *machan* could be built to watch from, Patterson let them carry on.

And while he supervised the digging, he was horrified to note how closely the ground tallied with the description the sleeping man had given. There even was the bush behind which the tiger had crouched before making the fatal spring, the tracks coming up to it showing plainly. It was all horribly convincing.

But his horror was not over yet. Norman, whom he had left lying on his bed staring into space, appeared suddenly on the scene, approaching with quick, long strides. He wore no hat, his shirt was open, his coat unfastened, his hair wild and flying. He was in a towering rage, as he came striding up, disregarding the threatening looks on the villagers' faces.

'So you think the tiger will be fool enough to fall into that pit, do you?' he roared, a dreadful laughter breaking through the anger.

'I tell you, no! You think he will come for bait like that!' pointing to the dead native covered with tarpaulin. 'Ha! Ha! That tiger is no fool, I tell you. Try him with something younger——!'

His face worked convulsively, as he broke into more of his horrible laughter, and Patterson, taken by surprise at first, saw that he must do something, or there would be violence. The man was certainly mad, whatever else he was.

'You must come home at once, Norman,' he said authoritatively. 'You'll come with me now.' And he seized him firmly by the arm, greatly surprised to find that, far from resenting it, Norman came quietly at once. He seemed to have relaxed a bit, for great sighs escaped him as he obeyed, and his body had turned limp.

The anger was all gone, the laughter silent, he was shivering as though he had the ague. But the muttering continued, though the words were hard to catch, muttering about the sun and sunstroke, fatigue, long trekking, the word 'tiger' cropping up occasionally, too.

Only once did fragments come out clearly, a sort of apology, almost. 'Giving you all this trouble—ashamed of myself—I've struggled so awfully hard against it, but I can't escape—There's no escape...' The voice fell back into incoherent mutterings again.

Patterson put him to bed, gave him strong drink and aspirin, applied ice, and did all he could, watching a long time by the couch until at last the raving man seemed to be quietly asleep.

For himself there was no sleep that night. He did not even take his clothes off. He tossed restlessly under his mosquito net, unable to get the horror out of his mind and thoughts.

It was steamy hot, without a breath of wind—a haunting, nightmare atmosphere. He strained his ears to listen, as the hours passed, but no unusual sound broke the deep stillness of the tropic night, and toward dawn he dropped off into an uneasy sleep.

It seemed to him that he had only slept a minute, when the growling of his terrier, Spot, made him wide awake instantly. He put out his hand to touch him. The dog's hackles were standing up.

Grabbing his rifle, Patterson slipped off the bed, stole silently across the veranda, and peered over the edge. He shivered in spite of the heat. In his bones he knew what he expected to see.

A light mist hung over the plantation, and the young trees wore a spectral look in the faint light. He strained his eyes, holding his rifle ready.

A long shadowy form was stealing through the mist toward the bungalow. It moved silently, sometimes pausing for a minute, then advancing again. Closer and closer it came. Patterson slid up the safety catch on his rifle. He waited. He did not move.

The tiger was sixty yards off. Still Patterson waited. It came on nearer. It stopped at fifty yards, turned its great head, listened. And Patterson, bringing his sights to bear, squeezed the trigger.

In the stillness of the dawn the roar of the heavy Express rifle was terrific. The tiger rolled over as the bullet struck him, but struggled to his feet at once again, snarling savagely. Patterson quickly fired a second time, but though he felt certain he had hit the animal by the way it staggered, he saw to his dismay that it recovered itself enough to slink off through the trees.

But the shots must soon prove fatal, and the tiger would not go far. It was obviously too dangerous to follow up in the half-light.

'Have you got him, Master?' came Abdul's hoarse whisper close behind him.

'I think so,' replied Patterson. 'We must wait till his wounds stiffen and the light gets better. Then we'll go and see.'

'We go *now*,' cried Abdul, within intense excitement.

Patterson was about to stop him forcibly, when to his utter amazement, he saw that, instead of running out toward the trees, Abdul had made a rush toward Norman's bedroom. He followed. They pushed in together.

Norman lay groaning and writhing beneath the mosquito curtains with a jagged hole torn through his ribs. Blood was pouring from another hole in his thigh. He was obviously dying. He was making a tremendous effort to speak. Patterson approached, lifted the curtain, and lowered his head to catch the words.

'Free at last, free—the tiger—tiger-life—free—' And with one long quivering sigh Norman was dead.

For a minute or two Patterson and Abdul faced one another across the blood-soaked bed.

'It was better so,' said Abdul calmly. 'There will be nothing to explain. The *Tuan* Norman died of a fever. All the village know he had the fever last night.'

For a long time Patterson kept silent.

When, presently, he spoke, it was to ask two questions.

'And Saka, Abdul?'

A slow smile crept over Abdul's face. 'Saka, Master, fell into the

tiger-pit last night and broke his neck by mistake.'
'And the tiger under the trees, Abdul?'
Abdul smiled again. 'That tiger, Master, we never find at all!'
And Abdul was right.

BY PROXY

It is true that for the most part the majority of Blackwood's later stories for adults had a bleak and brooding atmosphere. The majority of the stories in *Shocks* had a rather unhealthy fascination for suicides, and that was true of 'The Blackmailers' elsewhere in this volume. 'By Proxy', which I suggest may have been inspired by the rewrite of 'Confession' into 'King's Evidence' is perhaps the bleakest of them all. It was published in *The Bystander* for 17 November 1937 and was also broadcast on the radio in February 1940. This is its first appearance in book form.

T HE November fog drifted in oily spirals over the region of Gorston Square. It hung obstinately, reluctant to be disturbed. In Victorian days the Square had been almost fashionable. Rich merchant princes and rising barristers inhabited its rather grim-looking houses, where now there was hardly a single private dwelling to be seen. The old buildings had sunk into cheap boarding-houses or small hotels of doubtful character, with a few bleak erections converted into so-called modern flats. No wonder the fog lingered and felt at home in Gorston Square. It offered cover to more than one transient who welcomed cover.

On the steps of the dingiest of these hotels, the Gorston Arms, stood a man who had all the appearance of one of these uneasy transients. He seemed part of the fog and gloom and murk: a tall, dark man with hunched shoulders, a pasty, discoloured face and shifty eyes. A scar ran from his jaw across the left cheek almost to his ear, a scar he cursed bitterly because no medical skill had been able to obliterate it. It had been acquired several years before in Denver City from a razor-blade, fixed in a potato, and its grim signature, intended for his throat, had been diverted only because his famous left arm had been a fraction of a second too quick. That famous pugilist's left had saved his life, but for a crook like Lefty Holt it was a damaging mark to carry.

Lefty was glad of the fog that night, as he stood on the steps of the Gorston Arms and sniffed the choking air. Looking right and left, he eyed the street uneasily, watching the few figures that moved so cautiously about their business through the murk. What *was* their business, was the question he asked himself. He preferred to see them moving rather than just loitering. For Lefty knew, with the strange, keen instinct of the hunted, that for days he had been shadowed. The fellow gangsters he had 'let down' in Denver City were on his trail. He was being followed, and this uncanny instinct of the hunted would not let him rest. He had spotted no one in particular, but he was positive they were on his heels. He had been tracked across the water, for they knew that, as a Britisher, he would make for London. The warning whisper ran through his bones and blood: his temporary hotel was no longer safe. A chance caller, and before he even knew what the visitor wanted, the knife would be in his ribs. He must at once find lodgings where he could more easily check new arrivals.

Lefty Holt, crook and double-crosser, hid behind the shelter of the porch and studied the roadway carefully, peering about him into the welcome fog. Few people, thank God, were on the move, but he would not venture forth till he made quite sure there was no suspicious figure loitering on a corner. A postman passed on his rounds, sure of each familiar step; a youth on a bicycle, obviously some clerk hurrying home to his supper or high tea; a blind man tapping along the pavement by the Square railings, safer than any pedestrian, since darkness was his natural condition. A rare taxi crawled slowly by. The outlook seemed safe enough—reasonably safe.

Lefty slipped out swiftly, and in a moment the fog had swallowed him up. In his pocket lay one or two addresses he had sifted that morning from likely papers. He moved rapidly. He did not make the mistake of looking behind him or over his shoulder, but his eyes, for all that, were wide open in his back, nerves and instinct as alert as a wolf's. The postman, the clerk, were gone, and the blind man went as before, tapping his dreadful stick, though the note had slightly changed, and the taps came at longer intervals. He, too, was moving away. Two men slid out from the doorway of an office building lower down the street and disappeared, but they too, went in the opposite direction. The blind man no longer tapped, for he was round the corner. Lefty felt safe. He could go now and inspect the lodgings he had in view.

Nor was the region unfamiliar to him. It was here in boyhood he had learned his first pick-pocketing; the police court a few hundred yards beyond the Square he remembered, too; against these very railings on fragrant summer nights he had courted the girl he took later to Colorado as his wife, a crook even smarter than he was himself. His face darkened at the thought. Meanhearted double-crosser though he was, the knowledge that she in turn had given him the same treatment filled his heart with vicious rage. She had got away with it, too, stones and all, his own share into the bargain. Yet she, too, he reflected, if she ever got clear of the Denver City gang, would make for these same parts and comparative safety. Beasts in danger, he knew, invariably return to their familiar haunts where 'hides' and funk-holes are known to them. Thoughts and memories ran on through his mind in their nasty circle.

He almost collided with a burly figure in blue standing motionless beneath a lamp-post, and instinctively his coat collar went up to hide that scar.

'Evening, mate,' he said gruffly, without turning his face.

'Thick night, ain't it?' came the answer, as Lefty passed on quickly.

But a policeman had no terrors for him at the moment, though it was just as well his face should not be recognized. He was not 'wanted' here. He had done no violence in his early days, only the lesser, meaner crimes ... and ten minutes later he tried the first address in his list, only to find that the room advertised was already taken. Luck failed him at the next house, too; and at the third he rang and rang for some time without an answer. He tried the knocker, for he was getting impatient, and waiting, he felt, was dangerous. Though the fog was now so thick that it was difficult to see even across the street, or ten yards along the pavement, he felt exposed and defenceless, as though he stood naked on the doorstep. Yet he persisted, for some instinct told him this was the house he wanted. The door opened suddenly but cautiously, a few inches only. He liked that caution, it confirmed his instinct.

'What d'you want 'ere?' came a harsh voice in his ear, no face yet visible. It was a woman's voice.

For an instant, Lefty almost lost his self-possession, but for an instant only. If anyone should know that voice, he should. He had heard it last in Denver City some years ago, but he could never fail to recognize it. It went through him now like a flash of steel or fire. The hair on his spine, so to speak, stood up. Questions and suspicions blazed in him. Had she followed him? Had she, too, made her own get-away?

'Who's in there with you—Lizzie?' his snarling voice asked with a filthy oath.

'N-no one,' came the reply, after an instant's hesitation he did not fail to notice. 'But I don't want *you*,' she snapped, trying to shut the door in his face, without success, for his foot had already jammed it. A second later he had forced his way inside and slammed the door behind him, and the horrid pair stood facing one another in the dim-lit little hall.

'It's no good, kid,' said Lefty, in a voice now ominously softer. 'We got to have a show-down, you and me,' and he gave her a cruel blow across the mouth with the famous left that had earned him his name. As the woman, scared to death, staggered back against the hat-rack, protecting her face from further blows that, however, did not follow, Lefty swept the hall the quick, cunning eyes. No hat, he saw, was hanging there, though that did not mean there was no man about. He might just be out. His hand strayed to his left armpit.

'And where's Shearer?' he asked again, in that ominous soft voice.

'Dead,' whispered the woman, white with terror, 'these two years gone.'

Lefty examined her face very closely in the dim light for some seconds.

'He's lucky,' he observed. 'Maybe he had a sweeter death than I had waiting for him.'

The woman, shivering from head to foot, said nothing.

'There's only one thing I want from you, Lizzie,' Lefty went on threateningly, 'but I want it quick. You two sure played me for the blind sucker I was. Where are the stones?' He slipped the gun neatly from his armpit.

The woman's voice had gone, so that it was barely audible. 'Upstairs,' she managed to whisper, pointing overhead with a hand that shook like a leaf. 'I kept your share for you, Lefty, all this time.'

'Like hell you did,' snarled Lefty with an ugly grin.

'I'll get them for you,' came her terrified whisper, with eyes on the pointing gun in his hand, as she began to move. After a moment's hesitation, Lefty decided to let her go alone. Knowing her as he did, he felt her terror was real, and instinct assured him there was no man in the house.

'And move fast,' he told her savagely, fingering his gun. 'No funny stuff, either, or you'll get what's coming to you,' he added, with a flood of blasphemy, as he watched her backing clumsily up the stairs. 'Too hot to cash in, I suppose,' he threw after her, referring to the stones, 'too hot for a —— —— like you!'

A nasty expression ran down his lop-sided face like a streak of fire or poison. He watched her go, counting each step as she stumbled up, yet his eyes simultaneously everywhere in turn, his ears intent for the slightest suspicious sound. He said no further word. He felt certain she still had the stones, or some of them, and would bring them down. He saw her turn the corner along the dark, narrow landing, and when she was out of sight, though still listening closely to the sound of her foot-steps, he turned away and looked cautiously about him.

A door faced him, and he flung it wide open with a rapid sudden gesture, but he did not enter the room till he was quite certain it was empty. He saw a fire burning in the grate, a round table in the centre with books lying open and a few children's toys. A wooden elephant, a golliwog, a tiny aeroplane, lay beneath his eyes. A child's room, obviously.

'She's got a kid, I do believe,' darted across his mind. 'And Shearer's, by God, unless I'm crazy!'

He was surprised at himself. After all this time—what could it possibly matter. But—it did matter. For the blood in his veins boiled up till it almost frothed. Never before had he felt such a storm of wild, animal rage. Ungovernable fury rose in him yet with it something cold as ice, a combination that made the blood ebb and flow strangely, making the scar across his face a livid streak, the face itself a devil's face.

He listened. Overhead he could hear her shuffling about, drawers being opened, furniture moved, but there was no one with her, and only one pair of feet went stumbling across that upper floor. He was quite positive of that. He kept his wolf's ears divided between that upper floor, the corridor outside and the front-door step. His gun was ready pointing for instant use if needed.

Then a door opened suddenly in the hall and he froze to attention.

'Mummie, where are you?'

The reply came down: 'In a minute, darling! Coming!' And a little boy entered the room, smiling and unafraid.

'Are you the new lodger?' asked the little fellow, as he looked the tall stranger over with a fearless eye.

'Well, no—I guess not,' said Lefty in his gentlest voice. 'I just called in to see your ma. You see,' he added, 'I used to know her a long time back.'

The child listened with rather an examining expression, then turned his eyes to his toys on the table.

'Look what she gave me for my birfday,' he exclaimed proudly, unearthing something Lefty had not noticed before among the others. 'A real pistol, like they have in the movies. Isn't it grand? Hands up, or I shoot!' he added, trying to look fierce and determined.

Lefty was watching the child closely, his face working.

'Why, say!' he cried, 'isn't that just fine! It covers the heart every time, don't it just!'

'You bet it does,' laughed the child, playing with it.

And Lefty knew. The same eyes, the same ears, the same set of the head upon the neck. It was Shearer's kid all right. The child of his pal, the pal who had stolen his wife, his share of the jewel-robbery as well, and skipped, leaving him, Lefty, to dodge the cops and make his get-away as best he could without a cent. There was no doubt about it in his mind. The proof faced him here and now, and his blood rose to its maximum of bitter fury. Only one idea lay in his being—revenge.

He heard Lizzie's footsteps stumbling down the stairs.

'Quick,' he said to the boy, with a smile, taking his gun from his pocket, 'we'll play your mother a grand trick. It's a great idea. You take my pistol—it's just a toy like yours, only heavier and bigger—and when she comes in you just point it at her and cry, "Hands up, you villain!" and then fire. And she'll fall down and pretend to be dead just like they do in the movies. And then I'll arrest you, and we'll all laugh together! What d'you say, boy—eh?'

'Oh, that'll be fun!' cried the boy, eagerly taking the automatic Lefty handed to him.

'It sure will,' agreed Lefty, putting the catch at ready.

'Why, it's ever so much heavier than mine,' said the little fellow admiringly.

'Sure. It's the latest toy-model,' Lefty told him. 'Hold it steady against that book now. There! That's fine. Then point straight, and pull the trigger quick, remember. It'll go quite easy!'

The woman came in with a large envelope in her hand. 'Here they are,' she whispered, glancing a moment at her child as though in uneasy surprise.

'Hands up, you villain!' she heard in the boy's excited voice.

The pistol cracked. She slithered to the floor, the envelope fell towards

Lefty's feet. He stared at it a moment, watching the blood pouring from the woman's mouth, then swiftly picked it up, stuffed it into his pocket, and passed out into the hall. The pistol he deliberately left behind him. A moment later he was lost in the fog outside, the excited laughter of the boy still ringing in his ears.

'Shearer's kid,' he muttered, wiping the icy perspiration from his forehead. 'And serve her damn well right! She got what was coming to her at last!' But he was trembling from head to foot.

He moved fast, soon entering Gorston Square. He would find a room tomorrow. The fog was thicker than ever. So much the better, he thought, clutching the big envelope tightly in his pocket and feeling the hard edges of what it contained. There was no single pedestrian about, though he heard again the tapping of that blind man's stick as he fumbled along by the icy railings. And this time he did not like the sound. A violent shiver ran over him. At the corner two other lost pedestrians came towards him. They slipped up uncomfortably close, one on either side. Too late he realized the meaning of that blind man's tapping stick. There was a swift gleam of steel. His hand, whipping to his armpit, found it empty—too late again, for he had lent his gun to a little boy. The two figures vanished in the fog, but Lefty lay quite still against the icy railings.

THE VOICE
and
THE MAGIC MIRROR

These two stories form a short series of tales narrated by the Fat Man on board the liner *Borotania*. They are a little more lighthearted than the last offering. They were both written whilst Blackwood was staying on the French Mediterranean in May 1937. He wrote about them to his young friend Patsy Ainley, daughter of the actor Henry Ainley. 'In Monte Carlo my old pal Wilson gave me two of his queer stories, asking me to write them if I felt inclined. Which I promptly did. And your friend Mr Watt with equal promptness sold them both to *The Bystander*, a queer paper for me to appear in.' Wilson was the same Wilfred Wilson with whom Blackwood had travelled down the Danube in 1900 and is the man transformed into the Swede in 'The Willows'. Wilson (1875-1957) was a large, jovial, bearded man who is represented by the Fatty of these two stories. He supplied Blackwood with the idea for a number of stories, the earliest known being 'The Empty Sleeve' written in 1910. The rare collection, *The Wolves of God* is credited to both Blackwood and Wilson in gratitude for Wilson's friendship and inspiration over the years. I have my suspicions that Wilson may also have suggested the idea for 'The Man-Eater' in this volume, and he certainly provided the basis for 'King's Evidence'. His contribution to fantastic fiction should not be ignored. 'The Voice' was originally published in *The Bystander* for 29 December 1937 under the title 'The Reformation of St. Jules' but the subsequent adaptations for radio, television, and the cinema used 'The Voice' as the preferred title. 'The Magic Mirror' first appeared in *The Bystander* for 16 March 1938 but is better known to pulp magazine collectors for its publication in the September 1938 issue of the legendary *Weird Tales*.

THE VOICE

'FOREIGNERS—they're all mad!'
'Even the English?'
'Mad as hatters!'
'The Germans too?'
'Of course—Jew mad!'
'And what about the French?'
'Well—I guess I used to think them a pretty sane crowd till I came across the St. Jooles affair. After that I saw that they were as mad as all the rest—a bit more, even'

It was the fat man in the corner of the Smoking Room on Deck A who was talking. Why, I asked myself, is there always a fat man in the corner of the Smoking Room on board these liners? I don't know, but there always is.

We were three days out from Southampton on the Borotania. Our particular Fat Man sat in his corner, a huge cigar stuck between his thick lips, and surrounded by a crew of satellites for whom he bought drinks at frequent intervals, provided they would listen to his stories. They did. I am bound to admit that he was an amusing fat man—he had a queer lingo of his very own—and evidently rich. His crowd stuck to him like leeches. I myself constantly took a seat just outside the sacred circle on purpose to listen to his stories, which grew more and more racy as the evening progressed.

On this particular night he was at the top of his form; I could tell by the way he twirled the big cigar and by the flush on his face.

'Tell us about St. Jules,' suggested one of the crowd.

The fat man glanced round to see if the circle was worthwhile. Apparently it was. He blew out a thick cloud of smoke, ordered a round of drinks, smacked his lips, and started.

'Well,' he began confidentially, as the way is with good story tellers, 'I guess some of you boys know the little burg as it is now, but, believe me, three years ago it was some town. Folks talk a lot about Monte, but in those days St. Jooles sure had it beaten to a frazzle. The play at Monte was pretty high, I know, but at St. Jooles it was too high to see the top. And the town was wide open from dark to dawn.

'And I'm telling you—they were a hard-boiled lot when I first hit the town. Everything was going full blast and a bit over. I went to the old Continental Hotel where I always stayed, and the very first person I ran into after checking in was Mossy Mason. And I was sure glad to see old Mossy. Mossy had been my sidekick in a good many deals when we were together back in god's country. We liquored up.

'After a bit, he took me aside to a quiet spot outside on the verandah.

'"Tommy," he says, "you're just in time, but not a minute to spare."

'"And the rest, Mossy?" I enquires.

'"It's like this," he says, "I've got a real good thing, and you must come in with me." And he gives me the quick once-over.

'"Mossy," I told him right away, "I don't want any of your sure-fire-systems-to-beat-the-bank. I have had some and, believe me, I have had a plenty."

'"I'm with you," he explains. "But this is the real thing."

'"Get on with it, then," from me.

'"I've got a wop," he goes on, "with an advertising stunt that will bring in the mazurka every time."

'"Let's have the low-down," I asks.

'"This is the way of it," he tells me then. "The wop has invented a machine that'll throw letters on the sky over a mile long. Bright as god's own fire they are. And they'll knock out all the electric signs that were ever made. They just shake the guts out of you with terror."

"Now, see here," I says. "That's an old stunt. Folks have been trying to do that since Nero played the fiddle, and nothing ever came of it."

'"The scale was too small," he explains. "That was the trouble. Now, tomorrow night we're going back into the hills with a lorry he and I, and, believe me, we're going to show this town something it's never seen before."

'Well, his stuff impressed me some, and I asked what was he going to do it with, this great inventor-wop?

'"A new sort of ray," he tells me.

'I thought it over a bit, but I wanted to see the goods before going in with him.

'"It's O.K. with me," I says finally, for I always make my mind up quick, "but I got to see it first."

'He looks me over. "That's the stuff," he says. "I never knew you miss a real chance. You be down," he goes on, "on the terrace here tomorrow night," he says, "and we'll show you."

'Well, it was after he left me that I bumped into as nice a strawberry blonde as you'll find, and she sure kept me amused the rest of the evening—only that is another story, as they say.

'And next day Mossy introduced me to his wop. He was a cleverlooking guy called Cavallo. He was full of his invention, and, like all inventors, was soon talking in millions of francs. It's a way they have, you know. They could never invent anything unless they were halfbatty to start with. Still, he made me feel there was something in it. He tried hard to explain the thing to me but it was too technical and I couldn't get it. Never mind, I told him. "You show it to me tonight and it will be O.K. with me." And he said "Benissimo" or "spaghetti", or something like that, drank up his mineral water, and made off.

'And about ten o'clock that night, sure enough, a lorry came along loaded with machinery of sorts, and Mossy and Cavallo climbs in. They told me they aimed to get well away into the back country, so that no one could see them doing their stuff. It was a hell of an ascent, all hairpin bends right up to the top of the mountain, and Cavallo turns to me just as they push off. "I'm going to give this town the scare of its life," he says. "They need it."

'"That's all right with me," I says. "They do. Scare hell out of them if you can."

'"I do that," he replies—and they push off.

'I got two hours to fill in, so I go look for my blonde, and we fill in time at the Casino. I run into a streak of luck and the time passes very quickly. So I drag my blonde out of the rooms about a quarter of twelve and we sit on the terrace. We did not know it then, of course, but that was the very last night the Casino was open. Naturally, I didn't say a word about the show I was expecting from the mountains, but as the minutes slipped by I began to get a bit anxious.'

The Fat Man stopped and yelled to the steward to bring more drinks all round. And it was while he was doing this that I noticed, sitting in my corner, that a dark, foreign-looking fellow with a black beard had slipped into the chair beside me. He was obviously French, judging by the Maryland cigarette he was smoking with pleasure. Obviously, too, he had been listening to Fatty's story and was very much amused by what he heard.

The steward having served the drinks, Fatty took a couple of goodsized gulps and went on with his yarn:

'Where was I, boys? Oh, yes; I had the blonde parked on the terrace. Well, I'm telling you I had a job to keep her there. She tried all the time to sting me for a mille and get back to the rooms, but I wasn't having any. I worked hard to get her to look at the lovely night—how the moon shone on the water, how swell a cruise-boat looked as it passed out to sea all lit up, how the lights of the fishing boats in the harbour twinkled. But, I tell you, she was difficult to hold. And all the time the minutes were slipping away and nothing happened. It got to twelve-thirty, and I thought something must have gone wrong with all that apparatus they took up into those steep mountains— accident, maybe, or something. Twelve-forty came, and then suddenly the quiet of the night was shattered. A terrible voice roared from the clouds: "REPENT! REPENT!" and at the same time the words were repeated in flaming letters a mile long in the sky.

'I tell you, boys, I was scared dumb myself. The voice was really awful. It seemed to go right through you, and for a moment I got the appalling notion it must be God speaking. The Frenchies were scared to death, as well they might be. They tore out of the Casino like cattle was stampeding—out of all the restaurants and dance halls they came pouring in a rush and went flopping on their knees in the square by hundreds. A terrible sigh rose from the whole crowd as the voice began to thunder out again, but I can't tell you what it said, as I guess it was Italian, and anyway, I was too scared to take it in.

'Then silence. A silence you could feel. The sky and the night were empty again—just quiet stars and deep blue.

'Was I pleased? I'll say I was, now that my nerves were steady again. I was right on a winner, I knew. I was feeling generous, so I slipped the blonde a couple of notes and told her to beat it. Believe it or not, she was still on her knees, but she kind of regained consciousness when I crackled the notes by her ear. She stopped praying for a moment to shove the notes down her dress—what there was of it—and then went at it again, praying like a loudspeaker.

'I left her to it, and walked to the hotel, treading on air. I felt kind of sorry for all those punks still praying in the square, as I mixed myself a high-ball, but I thought they were a hard-boiled lot and a little spot of praying couldn't do them any harm. I guess most of them hadn't prayed for twenty years, if ever. I got a good laugh when I thought about Charles, the head waiter. Not many guys can boast that they've seen a head waiter pray! Anyway, I would put it all right with them next day. I'd tell them it was only a stunt.

'But that's just where I went wrong. They wouldn't believe me. That's what shook me about the French, as I mentioned at the beginning of this story. I had always thought the French were logical and would listen to reason, but these Froggies all got mad as blazes when

I told them the truth. "No, no!" they cried, and whispered, "It was God"—le bon Doo, as they called Him. Even Charles went on the same way. I told him after breakfast that I'd bring the boys round who had worked the stunt, but he just smiled in a superior way and, by God, he had the last laugh, too!'

'Why? How was that?' cut in some of his listeners.

'Because those two blasted fools came down that mountain road in the dark too fast and had smashed up the lorry and killed themselves. That's why and how it was. Can you beat it for bad luck? And that's why St. Jools still believes in the Miracle of the Voice, as they call it, and how it got reformed. They're building a church now to the Voice. Anyway, the little burg is no use now to any American citizen who aims to see Europe!'

Fatty stopped. The black-bearded Frenchman in the chair beside me was shaking all over, and when I turned I saw tears running down his cheeks. Never before or since have I seen a guy laugh as that Frenchie laughed.

'What's the matter?' I asked him. 'It was a good story. I don't see what's so terribly funny about it——'

He wiped his eyes and recovered his breath. 'Well,' he said in a low voice, 'you see, I've heard it before many, many times——'

'Heard *him* tell it, you mean?' I asked in surprise.

'Mais oui,' he whispered, no longer laughing now. 'He used to tell it every night three years ago when he was staying with me——'

'In your house?' I interrupted.

He nodded. 'I was in charge of him in the St. Jules Private Lunatic Asylum.'

THE MAGIC MIRROR

It was the last night on board the Borotania, as she was due in New York next morning. Most of the passengers were busy packing up in their cabins, so that when I strolled into the smoking-room I found it nearly empty, with only a straggler or two lined up at the bar. Fatty, however, was sitting in his usual corner with his two inseparables, Jimmy and Baldy, whose real names I never discovered.

When I came in Baldy was talking about systems at roulette.

'There are no systems worth a curse,' he was saying. 'It's all boloney to say there are. And most of the wheels are crooked, anyhow.'

'I guess you're right,' Fatty agreed, 'though I did once come across a system that was infallible. The trouble was I couldn't work it long enough to make a real killing.'

'And how was that?' Jimmy enquired.

'Just that the inventor faded away before we could clean up,' explained Fatty. 'Hard luck, you call it! Hard luck isn't the right word. It was a catastrophe. That's what it was, Baldy—a catastrophe!'

'Well, let's have the whole lie, Fatty,' said Jimmy and Baldy together, 'and we'll tell you what we think.'

'It's gospel truth,' came the rejoinder, 'and no lie at all, though I can't blame you if you don't believe it. It was about the strangest thing I ever ran up against—which is saying a lot. To this day I don't know what to make of it. It worked. I will say that for it. But it's got me beat just the same.

'It is some years ago now,' Fatty resumed, delighted to have even what he considered a dud audience of two, 'that I stayed on rather late at Monte. The season was over, and the Sporting Club, together with a whole lot of the better hotels, closed down. I had my quarters in a small pub on the Rue des Moulins, I remember, as my own joint was closed, too. The grub wasn't too good, and I used to drop in now and again at Quinto's to get myself a good lunch.

'One day, after lunch, I turned into the public gardens to smoke a cigar and look at the flowers before creeping home for a nap; and I remember that the cigar, given to me up at the golf course by a millionaire friend of mine, was particularly good. I was enjoying it smoking away and feeling at peace with all the world, when I noticed a curious-looking figure moving along the path towards me. He was an oldish fellow with a straggly white beard, and he was wearing a funny sort of hat on his head. I had never seen a hat quite like it before, but I found out afterwards that it was called a "terai," or some sort of name like that, and that it was worn a lot in India.

'There were plenty of empty seats all round me and I prayed to God the old fellow wouldn't come and sit down within talking distance of me and my cigar. Yet that was exactly what he did. The old bozo comes tottering along till he gets to my bench, and then he parks himself bang down quite close to me. Yes, he parked himself just next door, so that I expected the next minute he would turn and ask me for a match.

'But he had his match all right—his stinking cheroot, too—and he lights up and puffs away without a spot of trouble. Now, as you boys know, if there is one thing I cannot stand, it's the smoke from one of those greenhouse bug-killers, so as soon as he got going I was for going, too. I sort of shifted my legs before getting up, and it was just then he turns and looks at me. Did I say "looks at me"? I can only tell you duds that there was something in his eyes that made me think of lightning. He spoke at the same time. And his first remark somehow took my breath away. I mean by that I hadn't expected it.

'"Could you tell me something about the gambling here?" he asks.

'"Sure," I says, getting my breath back a bit, "sure I can. What's troubling you, stranger?"

'His eyes flashed that queer way again, but all he gives me back was innocent enough. "I understand they play a game called roulette," he says, "but I don't know anything about it. I'd like to."

'"The less you know, the cheaper for you," I tells him, knowing the answer pat. For he didn't look to me like a man to play the tables, what with his "Oxford voice" and his strange face that was half a monk and half, I guess, a scholar. "Keep your money," I adds, "if you've got any."

'"But I want to make some money," he explains straight off the reel and quite honest-sounding. "I've got a plan that's certain."

'And this time I looks him straight in the eye, lightning or no lightning—though I admit there was something in his eye that made me sort of wonder.

'"Now, listen, pal," I tell him, with a fatherly touch that I knew didn't quite come off. "Listen to me, will you? Every train that pulls into this burg has some sucker on it that thinks he's going to make good dough, but only one in ten thousand ever gets away with it. You take my advice and beat it back to Timbuctoo, or wherever you hail from, and just forget it." And I takes a good puff at my cigar for having given good advice for once, feeling easy in my conscience, if you know what I mean——

'"I come from Thibet, not Timbuctoo," he corrects me slap, flashing those googly eyes my way, "and I've got with me a magic mirror. I can't lose. It's a magic mirror from Thibet, you see." And his stinking cheroot puffed across into my face and made me cough.

'Well, of course, I knew then that the old boy was nuts. That Thibet-and-magic business proved it. And yet there was something about him that had me guessing. I had the feeling that he knew a thing or two I didn't know. I can't express it quite. I knew I was on the wrong tack, anyway. He had something I'd never met before. I was underrating him. He was child-like; crazy if you like, but he was something else as well. I only know I let my cigar—that millionaire cigar—go out. That shows you, maybe!

'"What's the great idea?" I says, more easily than I felt. "Are you going to flashlight from the mirror into the croupier's eye and then grab some dough? If so, I can tell you right now that those methods won't work here. Maybe they're all right back in the sticks in your Thibet, but they won't cut any ice here in Monte!"

'He gave me a sort of patient, half-contemptuous look as though I was a kid.

'"The mirror," he says quietly, "shows me what to play—numbers and colours, or whatever the foolishness is." And he pulls down that awful hat over his lightning blinkers, puffs out a poisonous cloud, and looks out over the flowers in the garden. In other words, he showed me plain enough that he thought I wasn't yet born.

'Well, this had me fair flummoxed. I just don't know what to say next. I lit up my cigar again, then threw it away as it no longer tasted good. After a bit I got going again. I asked him how he got his mirror, thinking it a fair question. And he gives me a long spiel about how he had been interpreter with a British expedition into Thibet, and how some Lama gave him the mirror. Good stuff, too, right enough. He did the Lama some service or other.

'"They call them devil-mirrors," he told me.

'"For why?" I asks, wondering what he'll throw me next.

'"Because they bring death and riches," is the answer.

'"Meself," I tells him, "I don't fancy mirrors like that."

'"You've never seen one," he says, knowing all the answers.

'"True," I tells him. "Maybe I don't want to."

'He said nothing for a bit then. I had the feeling he thought I was a nit-wit from Kalamazoo. And that's just what I felt, without knowing why—as though he was giving me the works and I was just dumb.

'Then he gets going again.

'"I am an old man now," he says.

'"I'm over a hundred, if you care to know, and I wish to try this mirror before I die. I promised the Lama I would. I must. Only, I need a helper. I cannot do it all alone."

'Well, this flummoxed me right down to the bone. Either he was nuts or I was! Over a hundred, indeed! Why, those eyes belonged to a young man! I thought it over for a bit. "Where was I?" I asked myself. "In Monte or in some weird Thibetan monastery?"

'"Of course," I says at length, "if that's they way you look at it,

I've got nothing to say. Have you got the mirror with you? I'd sure like to have a look at it."

'"Certainly," he agrees, and pulls out of his pocket a little chamois-leather bag and produces from it a small bronze mirror. I handled it cautiously, giving it the once-over. It had some curious figures twined round the polished surface. Naked men and women and their faces were awful. I'm pretty hard-boiled myself, but, believe me, those faces made me shudder so I could hardly bear to look at them. The old boy's mug, too, had something in common with them, it strikes me.

'"Now," he says, watching me hard, "do you notice anything peculiar about it?"

'I looked carefully and turned the mirror round in various directions so as to get the reflection of the gardens and the trees. "No," I tells him at last, "I can't say that I do."

'"Have you seen your own face in it?" he asked at length, with a smile I didn't care much about. His question gave me quite a shock.

'"No," I tell him—"I have not."

'"Just as well," he says, "for if you did you would die."

'With that I hands him back his mirror as quick as I could, but he only laughs quietly to himself and slips it back into its bag. And then I began thinking things over to myself a bit. After all, I thought, you don't get handed devils' mirrors in Thibet for nothing. I guess the old boy had to do his stuff before the Lama gave it to him—something pretty tough, too, or one of the local gorillas could have handled it. And so I came to the conclusion it was better not to ask any more questions. The only thing that really mattered was whether the mirror would work or not.

'"Go in and try it," I says to him straight. "Why not?"

'But he has the answer to that, too. "I must have someone with me," he explains again. "When I see the numbers in the glass I can't attend to putting the money on as well. I need a helper; someone I can trust. And I trust you."

'I had got this far when a wave of suspicion came over me. The old boy was a conman, and he was sure trying to play me for a sucker. I expected every moment his confederate would come rolling up with some plausible yarn, and that they would start stringing me along to put up some dough. I kept my eyes wide open, but I saw no one. And to fill in time I asked him about Thibet. He told me plenty about the country and certainly seemed to know his stuff all right, but as I couldn't check up on it, this didn't get us very far. It sounded genuine, all the same. He said he had been born at a mission station right on the frontier and that his nurse had been a Thibetan woman. When his parents died he had got a job with the Indian Government, and had now retired with a pension and was on his way to England. He told me a lot too, about having promised the Lama something about the mirror, but I just couldn't make head or tail of that. He wanted, anyway, to use it for getting money, and here in Monte he saw a chance. So I let it go at that.

'"Sure you've never seen a roulette wheel?" I asks him.

'"Never," says he.

'"Well, I'll take you right along and show you one," I says, and I bring the old bird down the street till we get to a shop that has them in the window. Half the shops in Monte stock them, as you know, so that we hadn't far to go. I watches the old fox careful to see if he's going to do an act, but he seems genuinely interested, and he soon got wise to the numbers and dozens and all that, and how it worked. Then I asks him how the mirror's going to show him what to back.

'"I shall see the numbers or the colour in the glass," says he.

'"Well, if you've got any dough." I suggests, "let's go to the rooms and give the thing a whirl."

'"I have a thousand francs," he says, "if you think that will be enough."

'"Plenty," I tell him, "if the mirror's any good. But let's start gently with a hundred-franc stake, just to see how she goes. If we win, we go on; if we lose we don't. How's that strike you?"

'"We shall win," he says, calm as you like, "and half the winnings will be yours. You are entitled to them for your kindness to a stranger."

'Well, this little spiel goes down very well with me, so I just says "Thank you," and takes his hand on it. Talk of a grip. That old hundred-per-center had a fist like iron. Anyway, we wanders over to the Casino and I gets him a ticket for the salle privée and in we goes. And let me tell you, the old bozo was on the up-and-up all right, for when we gets to the rooms he hands over his *mille* and asks me to do the staking while he consults his little mirror.

'Now, as chance would have it, the rooms weren't crowded, and we got a coupla good seats right at the end of one of the tables. I had changed the note into *plaques*, and we were all set. The old guy trots out his mirror and starts staring into it. I watches him close. After a minute or two his face kind of changes. His skin went whiter and his features became sort of fixed and hard. I thought at first he'd dropped off to sleep maybe with his eyes wide open, only I caught a flash of what I call the lightning in them and knew he was just too concentrated to blink. You might have thought he was a flapper going to put the lipstick on with that mirror in front of him. It was sure a queer sight. I notice the croupier nearest to us seems kind of inquisitive and keeps looking at him, but he doesn't say anything.

'They were paying out just when we sat down, but now they spin the wheel and it is time to stake. I glance at the old crank and he mutters "Fifteen", hardly moving his lips. It was fifteen the time before, but all the same, my *plaque* goes on, and sure enough, up she comes—fifteen! Now that, of course, might be just luck, but it gave me confidence, all right, so when next time the old bird mumbles "Twenty-one," I shoves on two *plaques* to see if I can't give the bank a jolt.

'And would you believe it, boys? Up she comes as pretty as a picture, while I rakes in the dough, trying not to grin like a Cheshire cat as I does it. And so it goes on, just as smooth and easy as I'm telling you, and we sure gave the bank a ride that afternoon. But I thinks it wise to stop at last, as the old fellow is beginning to look kind of petered out, it strikes me, so I take him away to the bar and give him a good slug of brandy, and we split the dough as he said, and then I take him back in a *fiacre* to his joint.'

'"How much did you win?" asks Baldy.

'"Sixty *mille* between us up to date," and giving him back his *mille* as agreed.

'Next morning,' Fatty continued, 'I went round bright and early to see how he was making out, and I found him in rather poor shape. So I tried to persuade him to give the rooms a miss that day. Nothing doing!

'"Lead me to the tables," he says, firm as a rock. "It was your brandy that upset me a little, for, you see, I never touch alcohol," and by his voice you mighta thought he was some Professor at Oxford starting up his lecture.

'"Anyway," I suggests, "let's have a good feed first," and I makes in the direction of Quinto's, for there was a bit of time to fill before the rooms opened. But will he eat? Not a damned swallow, I tell you! Not a single bite!

'"I shall see better," he whispers to me, "if I have no food. But please do not let me stop you. I will wait till you have had a meal."

'So that's what happened. "A crank," I says to myself, "must turn his own handle the way he wants," and I left him to it while I enjoyed the best blow-out ever with plenty of good liquor to wash it down, and the old boy doesn't hurry me one little bit, sitting there quiet and silent as an Indian idol. And when I'd lit my cigar we roll away in a *fiacre* back to the Casino.

'We go to the same table again and I notice the croupier recognizes the old guy, and exchanges a quick look with another croupier, and the pair of them watch that mirror pretty close, though there's nothing they can say or do about it, for any guy can look in his pocket-mirror if he wants to and see if his hair's straight. And, believe me, that mirror does its stuff again fit to beat the band. Or, I should say, beat the bank. For it just couldn't miss. Every time my pal mutters his number, up it comes, though sometimes I don't quite catch what he mumbles and so hold back and don't put a *plaque* on. And when that happens he gives me one of those sort of lightning looks that puts the blame on *me* all right. After that I watches his lips. I make no further mistakes, but start playing the dough real heavy, till we'd won so much I swear I couldn't count it, and I could see that the croupiers don't like it one little bit, they don't.

'And so it gets on and on, boys with me watching those mumbling lips like a cat watches a mouse, and making no more miss-hits, till sudden I notice that those lips of his seem kind of white. No blood in them, I mean. I give his face the once-over, and that don't look right to me, either. Made me think of a bladder with the air running out on it. Something was wrong, it seems to me, and I decided we'd had enough for one day and I'd better get him out.

'"Come on," I whispers to him. "Let's go. Give it a rest till tomorrow, pal."

'"One more turn," he whispers back, but the flash from those gig-lamps not quite so bright. "I'm seeing better than ever before."

'So I agrees to that. One turn more can't do us any harm, and he sure was seeing perfect.

'"Thirteen," he mutters. And on go my *plaques*.

'Now it so happens that he can reach the number easier than me, so I hand him the dough while I shove a maximum myself on *impair*, just to give the bank a final trimming before we blow.

'The wheel is spinning lovely when I hear a kind of gasp and a sigh from the old boy, but when I turns quick to look at him he seems okay. A moment later the ball settles nice and comfortable in thirteen, and they pay me on *impair* right enough. Then a strange thing happens. The croupier is in the act of shoving the money over to pay the old guy on his number when he stops, then pulls it back again as though the bank had won. I catches my breath and stares a moment. And everybody stares with me. The room had filled to brim and everybody had been watching our play. There came sudden an awful silence.

'I got my breath back.

'"What's the matter?" I cries out. "Pay the old man his winnings!"

'And the croupier turned to me without a smile.

'"*On ne paye pas les morts*," he said quietly, raking the money in.

'The old boy was dead—dead as a door-nail. He had croaked while the wheel was spinning. Can you beat it for bad luck? I looks round quick to see that no one had pinched the mirror, but I'm damned if it isn't broken into a thousand pieces.

'Isn't life just plain hell?'

ROMAN REMAINS

During the years of the Second World War Blackwood found little inspiration to write new fiction. He concentrated on adapting his stories for radio either as talks or as plays. He even managed to write two new plays, 'Told in a Mountain Cabin' broadcast in April 1942 with Lockwood West and Mary O'Farrell in the lead parts, and 'It's About Time' broadcast in February 1945 and featuring Carleton Hobbs. He did write one new story for radio, 'The Castlebridge Cat', broadcast on 25 October 1944, but it is a little below standard and not worthy of reprinting. His only other wartime writings, 'The Doll' and 'The Trod' were published by August Derleth in the slim volume *The Doll and One Other* in 1946. Perhaps inspired by Derleth's encouragement, and relieved at the end of the war and a chance to return to his beloved Swiss mountains, in 1947 Blackwood completed another story. He wrote to Derleth in July 1947. 'I am asking A. P. Watt to send you a queer little story called "Roman Remains" in case it might suit the magazine. I am not at all sure the story "comes off" but your judgement would satisfy me. It was always my habit to put away a new story for a year or so, then to re-read it when I had quite forgotten it; when I did that I could tell at once whether to tear up or possibly re-write. And I have torn up numerous tales that I realized had not come off.' Derleth liked the story but was unable to afford it for his own literary magazine *The Arkham Sampler* so he forwarded it to *Weird Tales*. It was eagerly accepted and published in the magazine's twenty-fifth anniversary issue in March 1948.

ANTHONY BREDDLE, airman, home on sick leave from India, does not feel himself called upon to give an opinion; he considers himself a recorder only. The phrase *credo quia impossible*, had never come his way; neither had Blake's dictum that 'everything possible to be believed is an image of truth.'

He was under thirty, intelligent enough, observant, a first-rate pilot, but with no special gifts or knowledge. A matter of fact kind of fellow, unequipped on the imaginative side, he was on his way to convalesce at his step-brother's remote place in the Welsh mountains. The brother, a much older man, was a retired surgeon, honoured for his outstanding work with a knighthood and now absorbed in research.

The airman glanced again at the letter of invitation:

'... a lonely, desolate place, I'm afraid, with few neighbours, but good fishing which, I know, you adore. Wild little valleys run straight up into the mountains almost from the garden, you'll have to entertain yourself. I've got lots of fishing rods for you. Nora Ashwell, a cousin you've never met, a nurse, also on sick leave of sorts but shortly going back to her job, is dying for companionship of her own age. She likes fishing too. But my house isn't a hospital! And there's Dr Leidenheim, who was a student with me at Heidelberg ages ago, a delightful old friend. Had a Chair in Berlin, but got out just in time. His field is Roman Culture—lots of remains about here—but that's not your cup of tea, I know. Legends galore all over the place and superstitions you could cut with a knife. Queer things said to go on in a little glen called Goat Valley. But that's not down your street either. Anyhow, come along and make the best of it; at least we have no bombing here ...'

So Breddle knew what he was in for more or less, but was so relieved to get out of the London blitz with a chance of recovering his normal strength, that it didn't matter. Above all, he didn't want a flirtation, nor to hear about Roman remains from the Austrian refugee scholar.

It was certainly a desolate spot, but the house and grounds were delightful, and he lost no time in asking about the fishing. There was a trout stream, it seemed, and a bit of the Wye not too far away with some good salmon pools. At the moment, as rain had swollen the Wye, the trout stream was the thing to go for; and before an early bed that night he had made the acquaintance of the two others, Nora and Emil Leidenheim. He sized them up, as he called it: the latter a charming, old-fashioned man with considerable personality, cautious of speech, and no doubt very learned; but Nora, his cousin, by no means to his taste. Easy to look at certainly, with a kind of hard, wild beauty, pleasant enough too, if rather silent, yet with something about her he could not quite place beyond that it was distasteful. She struck him as unkempt, untidy, self-centred, careless as to what impression she made on her company, her mind and thoughts elsewhere all the time. She had been out walking that afternoon, yet came to their wartime supper still in shorts. A negligible matter, doubtless, though the three men had all done something by way of tidying up a bit. Her eyes and manner conveyed something he found baffling, as though she was always on the watch, listening, peering for something that was not there. Impersonal, too, as the devil. It seemed a foolish thing to say, but there was a hint in her atmosphere that made him uncomfortable, uneasy, almost gave him a touch of the creeps. The two older men, he fancied, left her rather alone.

Outwardly, at any rate, all went normally enough, and a fishing trip was arranged for the following morning.

'And I hope you'll bring back something for the table,' his brother commented, when she had gone up to bed. 'Nora has never yet brought back a single fish. God knows what she does with herself, but I doubt if she goes to the stream at all.' At which an enigmatic expression passed across Dr Leidenheim's face, though he did not speak.

'Where is this stream?' his brother asked. 'Up that Goat Valley you said was queer, or something? And what did you mean by "queer"?'

'Oh, no, not Goat Valley,' came the answer; 'and as for "queer", I didn't mean anything particular. Just that the superstitious locals avoid it even in the daytime. There's a bit of hysteria about, you know,' he added, 'these war days, especially in God-forsaken places like this——'

'God-forsaken is good,' Dr Leidenheim put in quietly, giving the airman an impression somehow that he could have said more but for his host's presence, while Breddle thought he would like to tap the old fellow's mind when he got the chance.

And it was with that stressed epithet in his ears that he went up to his comfortable bedroom. But before he fell asleep another impression registered as he lay on that indeterminate frontier between sleeping and waking. He carried it into sleep with him, though no dream followed. And it was this: there was something wrong in this house, something that did not emerge at first. It was concerned with the occupants, but it was due neither to his brother, nor to the Austrian archaeologist. It was due to that strange, wild girl. Before sleep took him, he defined it to himself: Nora was under close observation the whole time by both the older men. It was chiefly, however, Dr Leidenheim who watched her.

The following morning broke in such brilliant sunshine that fishing was out of the question; and when the airman got down to a late breakfast he was distinctly relieved to hear that Nora was already out of the house. She, too, knew that clear skies were no good for trout; she had left a verbal excuse and gone off by herself for a long walk. So Breddle announced that he would do the same. His choice was Goat Valley, he would take sandwiches and entertain himself. He got rough directions from Dr Leidenheim, who mentioned that the ruins of an ancient temple to the old god, Silvanus, at the end of the valley might interest him. 'And you'll have the place to yourself,' said his brother, laughingly, before disappearing into his sanctum, 'unless you run across one of the young monsters, the only living things apparently that ever go there.'

'Monsters! And what may you mean by that?'

It was Dr Leidenheim who explained the odd phrase.

'Nothing,' he said, 'nothing at all. Your brother's a surgeon, remember. He still uses the words of his student days. He wants to scare you.'

The other, finding him for once communicative, pressed him, if with poor results.

'Merely,' he said in his excellent English, 'that there have been one or two unpleasant births during these war years—in my language, *Missgeburt* we call them. Due to the collective hysteria of these strange natives probably.' He added under his breath, as if to himself, something about *Urmenschen* and *unheimlich*, though Breddle didn't know the words.

'Oh,' he exclaimed, catching his meaning, 'that sort of thing, eh? I thought they were always put out of the way at birth or kept in glass bottles——'

'In my country, that is so, yes. They do not live.'

The airman laughed. 'It would take more than a *Missgeburt* to scare me,' he said, and dropped the unsavoury subject before the old archaeologist got into his stride about the temple to Silvanus and Roman remains in general. Later he regretted he had not asked a few other questions.

Now, Anthony Breddle must be known as what is called a brave man; he had the brand of courage that goes with total absence of imagination. He was a simple mind of the primitive order. Pictures passed through it which he grouped and regrouped, he drew inferences from them, but it is doubtful if he had ever really thought. As he entered the little valley, his mind worked as usual, automatically. Pictures of his brother and the Austrian flitted across it, both old men, idling through the evening of their day after reasonable success, the latter with a painful background of bitter sufferings under the Nazis. The chat about collective hysteria and the rest did not hold his interest. And Nora flitted through after them, a nurse maybe, but an odd fish assuredly, not his cup of tea in any case. Bit of a wild cat, he suspected, for all her quiet exterior in the house. If she lingered in his mind more vividly than the other two it was because of that notion of the night before—that she was under observation. She was, obviously, up to something: never bringing in a fish, for instance, that strange look in her eyes, the decided feeling of repulsion she stirred in him. Then her picture faded too. His emotions at the moment were of enjoyment and carefree happiness. The bright sunny morning, the birds singing, the tiny stream pretending it was a noisy torrent, the fact that 'Operations' lay behind him and weeks of freedom lay ahead ... which reminded him that he was, after all, convalescing from recent fevers, and that he was walking a bit too fast for his strength.

He dawdled more slowly up the little glen as the mountain-ash trees and silver birch thickened and the steep sides of the valley narrowed, passed the tumbled stones of the Silvanus temple without a glance of interest, and went on whistling happily to himself—then suddenly wondered how an echo of his whistling could reach him through the dense undergrowth. It was not an echo, he realized with a start. It was a different whistle. Someone else, not very far away, someone following him possibly, someone else, yes, was whistling. The realization disturbed him. He wanted, above all, to be alone. But, for all that, he listened with a certain pleasure, as he lay in a patch of sunshine, ate his lunch, and smoked, for the tune, now growing fainter, had an enticing lilt, a haunting cadence, though it never once entered his mind that it was possibly a folk tune of sorts.

It died away; at any rate, he no longer heard it; he stretched out in the patch of warm sunshine, he dozed; probably, he dropped off to sleep ...

Yes, he is certain he must really have slept because when he opened his eyes he felt there had been an interval. He lay now in shadow, for the sun had moved. But something else had moved too while he was asleep. There was an alteration in his immediate landscape, restricted though that landscape was. The absurd notion then intruded that someone had been near him while he slept, watching him. It puzzled him; an uneasy emotion disturbed him.

He sat up with a start and looked about him. No wind stirred, not a leaf moved; nor was there any sound but the prattle of the little stream some distance away. A vague disquiet deepened in him. Then he cupped his ears to listen, for at this precise moment the whistling became audible again with the same queer, haunting lilt in it. And he stiffened. This stiffening, at any rate he recognized; this sudden tautening of the nerves he had experienced before when flying. He knew precisely that it came as a prelude to danger: it was the automatic preparation made by body and mind to meet danger; it was—fear.

But why fear in this smiling, innocent woodland? And that no hint of explanation came, made it worse. A nameless fear could not be met and dealt with; it could bring in its wake a worse thing—terror. But an unreasoning terror is an awful thing, and well he knew this. He caught a shiver running over him; and instinctively then he thought he would 'whistle to keep his courage up,' only to find that he could not manage it. He was unable to control his lips. No sound issued, his lips were trembling, the flow of breath blocked. A kind of wheeze, however, did emerge, a faint pretence of whistling, and he realized to his horror that the other whistler answered it. Terror then swept in; and, trying feebly again, he managed a reply. Whereupon that other whistling piper moved closer in, and the distance between them was reduced. Yet, oh, what a ravishing and lovely lilt it was! Beyond all words he felt rapt and caught away. His heart, incredibly, seemed mastered. An unbelievable storm of energy swept through him.

He was brave, this young airman, as already mentioned, for he had faced death many times, but this amazing combination of terror and energy was something new. The sense of panic lay outside all previous experience. Genuine panic terror is a rare thing; its assault now came on him like a tornado. It seemed he must lose his head and run amok. And the whistler, the strange piper, came nearer, the distance between them again reduced. Energy and terror flooding his being simultaneously, he found relief in movement. He plunged recklessly through the dense undergrowth in the direction of the sound, conscious only of one overmastering impulse—that he *must* meet this piper face to face, while yet half unconsciously aware that at the same time he was also taking every precaution to move noiselessly, softly, quietly, so as not to be heard. This strange contradiction came back to memory long afterwards, hinting possibly at some remnant of resisting power that saved him from an unutterable disaster.

His reward was the last thing in the world he anticipated.

That he was in an abnormal condition utterly beyond his comprehension there can be no doubt; but that what he now witnessed registered with complete and positive clarity lay beyond all question. A figure caught his eye through the screen of leaves, a moving— more—a dancing figure, as he stood stock still and stared at—Nora Ashwell. She was perhaps a dozen yards away, obviously unaware of his presence, her clothes in such disorder that she seemed half naked, hatless, with flowers in her loosened hair, her face radiant, arms and legs gesticulating in a wild dance, her body flung from side to side, but gracefully, a pipe of sorts in one hand that at moments went to her lips to blow the now familiar air. She was moving in the direction away from where he stood concealed, but he saw enough to realize that he was watching a young girl in what is known as ecstasy, an ecstasy of love.

He stood motionless, staring at the amazing spectacle: a girl beside herself with love; love, yes, assuredly, but not of the kind his life had so far known about; a lover certainly—the banal explanation of her conduct flashed through his bewilderment—but not a lover of ordinary sort. And, as he stared, afraid to move a step, he was aware that this flood of energy, this lust for intense living that drove her, was at work in him too. The frontiers of his normal self, his ordinary world, were trembling; any moment there might come collapse and he, too, would run amok with panic joy and terror. He watched as the figure disappeared behind denser foliage, faded then was gone, and that he stood there alone dominated suddenly by one overmastering purpose— that he must escape from this awful, yet enticing valley, before it was too late.

How he contrived it he hardly remembers; it was in literal panic that he raced and stumbled along, driven by a sense of terror wholly new to all his experience. There was no feeling of being followed, nor of any definite threat of a personal kind; he was conscious more of some power, as of the animal kingdom, primitive, powerful, menacing, that assaulted his status as a human being ... a panic, indeed, of pagan origin.

He reached the house towards sunset. There was an interval of struggle to return to his normal self, during which, he thanked heaven, he met no member of the household. At supper, indeed, things seemed as usual ... he asked and answered questions about his expedition without hesitation, if aware all the time, perhaps, that Dr Leidenheim observed him somewhat closely, as he observed Nora too. For Nora, equally, seemed her usual, silent self, beyond that her eyes, shining like stars, somehow lent a touch of radiance to her being.

She spoke little; she never betrayed herself. And it was only when, later, Breddle found himself alone with Dr Leidenheim for a moment before bedtime, that the urgent feeling that he *must* tell someone about his experiences persuaded him to give a stammering account. He could not talk to his brother, but to a stranger it was just possible. And it brought a measure of relief, though Leidenheim was laconic and even mysterious in his comments.

'Ah, yes ... yes ... interesting, of course, and—er—most unusual. The combination of that irresistible lust for life, yes, and—and the unreasoning terror. It was always considered extremely powerful and—equally dangerous, of course. Your present condition—convalescing, I mean—made you specially accessible, no doubt...

But the airman could not follow this kind of talk; after listening for a bit, he made to go up to bed, too exhausted to think about it.

It was about three o'clock in the morning when things began to happen and the first air raid of the war came to the hitherto immune neighbourhood. It was the night the Germans attacked Liverpool. A pilot, scared possibly by the barrage, or chased by a Spitfire and anxious to get rid of his bombs, dropped them before returning home, some of them evidently in the direction of Goat Valley. The three men, gathered in the hall, counted the bursts and estimated a stick had fallen up that way somewhere; and it was while discussing this, that the absence of Nora Ashwell was first noticed. It was Dr Leidenheim, after a whispered exchange with his host, who went quickly up to her bedroom, and getting no answer to their summons, burst open the locked door to find the room empty. The bed had not been slept in; a sofa had been dragged to the open window where a rope of knotted sheets hung down to the lawn below. The two brothers hurried out of the house at once, joined after a slight delay by Dr Leidenheim who had brought a couple of spades with him but made no comment by way of explaining why he did so. He handed one to the airman without a word. Under the breaking dawn of another brilliant day, the three men followed the line of craters made by the stick of bombs towards Goat Valley, as they had surmised. Dr Leidenheim led them by the shortest way, having so often visited the Silvanus temple ruins; and some hundred yards further on the grey morning light soon showed them what was left of Nora Ashwell, blasted almost beyond recognition. They found something else as well, dead but hardly at all injured.

'It should—it *must* be buried,' whispered Dr Leidenheim, and started to dig a hole, signing to the airman to help him with the second spade.

'Burnt first, I think,' said the surgeon.

And they all agreed. The airman, as he collected wood and helped dig the hole, felt slightly sick. The sun was up when they reached the house, invaded the still deserted kitchen and made coffee. There were duties to be attended to presently, but there was little talk, and the surgeon soon retired to his study sofa for a nap.

'Come to my room a moment, if you will,' Dr Leidenheim proposed to the young airman. 'There's something I'd like to read to you; it would perhaps interest you.'

Up in the room he took a book from his shelves. 'The travels and observations of an old Greek,' he explained , 'notes of things he witnessed in his wanderings. Pausanias, you know. I'll translate an incident he mentions.'

'"It is said that one of these beings was brought to Sylla as that General returned from Thessaly. The monster had been surprised asleep in a cave. But his voice was inarticulate. When brought into the presence of Sylla, the Roman General, he was so disgusted that he ordered it to be instantly removed. The monster answered in every degree to the description which poets and painters have given of it."'

'Oh, yes,' said the airman. 'And—er—what was it supposed to be, this monster?'

'A Satyr, of course,' replied Dr Leidenheim, as he replaced the volume without further comment except the muttered words, 'One of the retinue of Pan.'

WISHFUL THINKING

'Wishful Thinking' was one of only a handful of manuscripts amongst a mass of items I found amongst Blackwood's papers. It has all the appearance of a story written for radio but there is no record that it was ever broadcast. It may just possibly have formed the basis for one of his television stories. These were never announced in advance in the programme guide because Blackwood would not decide which story to tell until he arrived at the studio. Even then he might change his mind and tell something different. For reasons unknown to me no as-broadcast records of Blackwood's television stories survive in the BBC Archives so there is no way of telling which stories he narrated. Only by chance have I managed to identify a few. Whatever the case, this story has not seen the light of the day for forty years, and it seems rather appropriate to close this collection with a story set, in part (albeit off stage), in Edinburgh, where Blackwood's very first story, 'A Mysterious House' was written, one hundred years ago.

IT is a common enough experience to mistake a stranger in a crowded street for an acquaintance, but on coming closer to find the fancied resemblance hardly exists. Now and again, too, it happens that the acquaintance actually turns up later in the day.

An explanation, some think, is telepathy, but this idea didn't occur to old Colonel Tenders as he pushed along crowded Oxford Street and suddenly caught sight of his nephew some dozen yards ahead and going the same way. Now John was the last person he wanted to see just then; he was always in trouble of some kind, for one thing, and for another John owed him £30; and being a kindly soul he didn't want to embarrass the lad. So he slowed down to peer into a shop window, when John, turning abruptly at the traffic lights crossed the street—and it wasn't John after all.

Odd? Yes, perhaps; but he had known similar experiences. John, anyhow, was living in Edinburgh at the time. Colonel Tenders, distinctly relieved, went on about his business; the fleeting memory, John with it, disappeared completely from his mind.

It was towards the end of a busy day, as he was crossing the park in the dusk that he again saw John, and with the same conviction as before, only this time his nephew was coming straight towards him. He was some fifty yards away, and no evasion was possible. The park was almost empty. This, beyond doubt, was his disreputable young nephew—his tall figure, both hands in the pockets of his uncreased flannel trousers, shirt open at the neck, no tie, no hat either. Here was no room for an absurd mistake, and he braced himself for the undesired meeting. Whatever happened, he meant to be kind, understanding, tolerant.

'Hullo, John! What are you doing down here? I thought you were living in Edinburgh,' he called out, cheerily enough, as they approached one another.

'Yes, I am—I was, rather,' John answered, making no attempt to hold his hand out. His voice was faint, lifeless somehow, and the other felt a sharp pang of pity. Was the lad hungry? 'I wanted to see you,' John went on hesitatingly. 'Oh, *awfully*——'

'Wanted to see me?'

'Yes. Terribly. I—I've been looking for you all day, but couldn't find you.'

'You didn't write to say you were coming, did you? Why didn't you give me a ring? You know my usual haunts.'

'There wasn't time,' John explained lamely.

'Oh, it was sudden, was it?' his uncle asked, a bit puzzled.

'Sudden—er—yes,' was all John said.

There was a betraying touch, a note of despair, almost of desperation in the tense, low voice, and the Colonel took a quick look, but the dusk was growing, and John hung his head; and the other's heart sank a moment. The intention to be kind held good, yet he somehow dreaded the coming request for money, more money.

'Something wrong, John, my boy?' he asked, keeping the exasperation out of his voice. 'In trouble, eh?' He didn't say 'again'. 'Is your wife all right?' Requests for money were usually based on the health of what the Colonel considered a worthless young woman.

'I think—I hope—she's all right, yes. She couldn't get here, you see——' He broke off suddenly, his voice almost a whisper.

'You mean she's in London with you?' his uncle asked, more and more puzzled. They were walking along slowly now, side by side.

John seemed to hesitate. 'I—don't know—quite,' he mumbled, adding quickly as though to himself: 'but I'm sure she's all right.'

The Colonel felt somewhat at a loss. 'You've lost her? Is that it?' he asked; to which came the instant rejoinder: 'Oh, she'll turn up, she can't be really lost. She can't be.'

'Good,' commented his uncle, unable to think of anything better to say, but with the private thought that her final loss would be no bad thing.

'But it's not that I wanted to see you about so awfully,' John suddenly went on, increased urgency in his voice. 'Not about *her*, I mean. It's something else. It's been in my mind so long. Oh, I just *had* to see you——'

'Money, for instance?' the other helped him in as cheerful a voice as he could manager. And John answered at once: 'In a way—yes—money.'

'Yes, of course, John. I understand. You're in a jam, eh?'

'Oh, no, no,' came the surprising reply, 'nothing like that. Though it *is* about money—yes.'

The Colonel felt increasingly at a loss. He couldn't make head or tail of this kind of talk. He disliked the whispering voice. What on earth could be the matter? The young fellow was obviously in grave trouble, but of what kind? Drink was not among his failings; nor could he be starving; the railway ticket south proved that. He remembered the odd, faltering walk when they had met, John coming towards him in a queer, sort of zigzag way.

'You say it's about money, John, and yet you're not in need of any. Is that it?' he asked. 'I don't get you quite, boy.'

'Oh, no,' came the quick reply. 'I'm not in need of money—not of any—oh no,' and he gave a little laugh. A little laugh the other didn't like. It had an odd ring to it. Was the lad's mind affected, he asked himself? He had always been unbalanced, unaccountable, subject to attacks of neurotic kind.

'Come, my boy,' he suggested, as they strolled along. 'Explain yourself. Here let's sit down a moment. Let's take a pew and give me what they call the low-down, eh?'

'Thank you,' said John. 'I'd like to. Do you mind if we go under the trees? There's an empty bench, and it's darker there.' His low voice trembled a little. The Colonel agreed, though he didn't much like the shaky voice, still less the preference for darkness. They sat down. John's next words started him: 'It's that thirty quid I owe you,' he said breathlessly rather. 'I wanted—oh, so awfully—to pay it back,' he repeated with the same intense urgency.

'God bless the boy!' exclaimed the other, relieved in spite of himself.

'What an idea! There's no hurry about *that*. It can wait till your ship comes in——'

'*Now*,' John interrupted, his voice louder suddenly. 'I wanted to repay it *now*——oh, terribly.'

The Colonel was perturbed; his feeling of uneasiness deepened. It was getting quite dark here under the trees; there were no passers-by; John had a screw loose somewhere; his words didn't make sense. If all this was about a trumpery debt, why couldn't he have written? Why come all the way from Edinburgh and just chance a meeting in the streets? And what was the meaning of the uncertainty about his wife's whereabouts?

'I wanted frightfully to repay it,' he heard John go muttering on in that whispering voice. 'You've been so decent to me always. I don't mean only money. I mean your real kindness, your understanding. I know I've let you down every time, but I did so want to repay the money at least—before it was too late—that wish has been so terrifically in my mind——'

'Bosh, John! Bosh!' his uncle interrupted, feeling more and more uncomfortable. 'It's never too late—never. Your intention does you credit, of course, but you didn't come all this way just to tell me that—now, did you?' And, almost without being conscious of the fact, he found himself edging away a little further along the bench.

'No, no, of course I didn't,' he heard John saying. 'I came to pay you. I've got the money with me now. Here, I'm going to give it to you.'

This was too much! The Colonel found no words for a moment, while at the same time the disquieting thought flashed: if it was true, how had he raised £30! Where did it come from?

'Please, please, John,' he broke out; 'you won't—you mustn't do any such thing. And, anyhow, I never lend money, remember; I give it; the little bit I gave you was a present——'

John paid no attention. 'Here it is—thirty pounds exactly,' he said louder. 'Please, oh, please, take it. You must. I beg you.' He held his hand out.

The earnest, pleading voice was so sincere, so urgent, that the other hardly knew what was best to do; various ideas jostled together in his puzzled mind.

'Look here, John,' he said. 'I'll tell you what I'll do, as you make such a point of it. I'll take it and keep it for you any time you need it. Just send a wire, you know.'

'Oh, I do thank you for that,' came the answer. 'I do, I do. Here it is.' And he put his hand out closer. Having come to the point, however, the Colonel shied away from the actual taking. He felt ashamed. He didn't want to take it, not even to touch the packet, or whatever it was being held out. The old boy felt a bit emotional somehow, sentimental perhaps. It was a strange feeling—he didn't want to be *seen* taking it, at any rate. There was turmoil in his mind. Actually, indeed, he doesn't remember exactly what did happen, but he does distinctly remember turning round on the bench and looking squarely, and for the first time, straight into his nephew's face. A shiver ran over him. Dark as it was, he saw something in those distraught and anguished eyes that scared him. Precisely at this moment, too, another thing happened that diverted his attention: a couple of women, chatting volubly about clothes and shopping, passed the bench and went on their way; and it was the presence of these two commonplace people only a few feet away that made him realize sharply—yes, a sense of relief. He wished they had stopped and used the bench. He would have welcomed them. His attention must have been thus distracted for a few seconds from the detail of the money passing from hand to hand. He cannot remember feeling it, touching it, though he does recall patting or tapping something that had somehow reached his pocket. John must have slipped it in.

He got to his feet with a sudden decision.

'Look here, John,' he said firmly; 'I was on my way to my club. Now, you come along with me and we'll have dinner together and a drink. It's only a couple of hundred yards. Come along. I won't take no for an answer. I won't bother you with talk. We'll just eat together.'

And, rather to his surprise, John came with him, moving by his side, his head hanging down as though to pick his way in the dark. It was only five minutes out of the park, and they went in silence, the old Colonel's mind still in a confused turmoil, his thoughts racing, wondering chiefly whether his nephew had a room for the night and how best he could help him. They seemed to reach the club almost immediately without a single word having been spoken by either of them. The

Colonel led the way in and told John to sit down while he went to hang up his coat and hat; and when he returned a moment later to the hall, John was not there. He glanced round, but couldn't see him anywhere. He looked into the Reading Room. The club was very empty that night. There was no sign of the lad. He came into the hall again and asked the Porter where his friend had gone. The Porter looked puzzled.

'Friend, Colonel? I didn't see anyone with you.'

Colonel Tenders insisted.

'Begging your pardon, sir,' said the Porter, 'but you had no one with you. You came in alone.'

The Colonel dined by himself. When in due course he reached home and undressed for bed there was no package of money, no £30, in any of his pockets. He had already looked though his overcoat. It was a day later when information reached him that a certain John Bridewell had formed a suicide pact with his young wife in Edinburgh, as a result of which he had first shot her and subsequently hanged himself.

BIBLIOGRAPHY

Original collections

The Empty House and Other Ghost Stories (1906)
The Listener and Other Stories (1907)
John Silence: Physician Extraordinary (1908)
The Lost Valley and Other Stories (1910)
Pan's Garden: A Volume of Nature Stories (1912)
Ten Minute Stories (1914)
Incredible Adventures (1914)
Day and Night Stories (1917)
The Wolves of God and Other Fey Stories with Wilfred Wilson (1921)
Tongues of Fire and Other Sketches (1924)
Full Circle (1929) one story only
Shocks (1935)
The Doll and One Other (1946)

Reprint collections

Ancient Sorceries and Other Tales (1927)
The Dance of Death and Other Tales (1927)
Strange Stories (1929)
Short Stories of To-Day and Yesterday (1930)
The Willows and Other Queer Tales (1932)
The Tales of Algernon Blackwood (1938)
Selected Short Stories (1945)
Tales of the Uncanny and Supernatural (1949)
In the Realm of Terror (1957)
Selected Tales (1964)

Tales of the Mysterious and Macabre (1967)
Ancient Sorceries and Other Stories (1968)
The Best Supernatural Tales (1973)
Best Ghost Stories (1973)
Tales of Terror and Darkness (1977)
Tales of the Supernatural (1983)

Novels

Jimbo: A Fantasy (1909)
The Education of Uncle Paul (1909)
The Human Chord (1910)
The Centaur (1911)
A Prisoner in Fairyland (The Book That 'Uncle Paul' Wrote) (1913)
The Extra Day (1915)
Julius LeVallon: An Episode (1916)
The Wave: An Egyptian Aftermath (1916)
The Promise of Air (1918)
The Garden of Survival (1918)
The Bright Messenger (1921)
Dudley & Gilderoy: A Nonsense (1929)
The Fruit Stoners (1934)

Plays

Karma: A Reincarnation Play with Violet Pearn (1918)
Through the Crack with Violet Pearn (1925)

Children's books

Sambo and Snitch (1927)
Mr. Cupboard (1928)
By Underground (1930)
The Parrot and the Cat (1931)
The Italian Conjuror (1932)
Maria (of England) in the Rain (1933)
Sergeant Poppett and Policeman James (1934)
The Fruit Stoners (1935) [not the same as the novel listed above]
How the Circus Came to Tea (1936)
The Adventures of Dudley and Gilderoy adapted by Marion Cothren (1941)

Autobiography

Episodes Before Thirty (1923)

ACKNOWLEDGEMENTS

I must first thank Mrs Sheila Reeves for allowing me access to Blackwood's surviving papers, and to the literary agents for the estate, Messrs A. P. Watt, for their co-operation during my years of research. Tracing these stories has been, for the most part, a long, slow but determined trawl of old papers and magazines. Special thanks to Thomas Moriarty who gave me my first leads, and to Richard Dalby who opened up many avenues of research. Thanks also to David Simeon for providing me with further forgotten details, to Neil Somerville for his help at the BBC Written Archives, to Steve Miller for tracing a copy of the elusive issue of *Thrilling Mystery*, and to Michael Pointon, Kenneth R. Johnson, and John R. Colombo who have helped possibly more than they realize. Finally my especial thanks to Patsy Ainley, Barbara Lindsay, and Ella Maillart whose help and personal memories of Blackwood have been a major driving force throughout my research. To these and others too numerous to mention my sincere gratitude.

EQUATION CHILLERS

BONE TO HIS BONE

The Stoneground Ghost Tales of E.G. Swain

Introduced by Michael Cox

'On the edge of that vast tract of East Anglia, which retains its ancient name of the Fens, there may be found, by those who know where to seek it, a certain village called Stoneground.'

The opening words of 'The Man With The Roller' set the tone for this classic collection of antiquarian ghost stories, copies of which are now much sought after by supernatural fiction enthusiasts. Its author, Edmund Gill Swain, was Chaplain of King's College, Cambridge, of which one of the greatest ghost-story writers of the twentieth century, M.R. James, was successively Dean, Tutor, and finally Provost.

Swain was one of the select company present at the famous Christmas readings of James's stories, and after becoming vicar of Stanground near Peterborough in 1905 he began to write his own ghost stories in the Jamesian manner. The result was published in 1912 as *The Stoneground Ghost Tales,* dedicated—appropriately—to M.R. James.

The central character of all Swain's tales is the genial and scholarly rector, Mr Batchel, whilst Stoneground itself is a thinly disguised rendering of Swain's own parish of Stanground. This new edition contains all nine Stoneground tales and makes available again, for the first time in over seventy years, some of the most delicately spooky ghost stories ever written.

As a bonus, six stories concerning Mr Batchel and his haunted world by David Rowlands are included as an appendix.

EQUATION CHILLERS

STORIES IN THE DARK

Tales of Terror by Jerome K. Jerome, Barry Pain and Robert Barr

Selected and introduced by Hugh Lamb

'They thought at first he had died in his sleep. But when they drew nearer and the light fell upon him, they saw the livid marks of bony fingers round his throat; and in his eyes there was a terror such as not often seen in human form.'

These very un-comical words round off a little-known work by one of Britain's most renowned humorists, Jerome K. Jerome—'The Skeleton', one of several tales of terror he wrote, now almost forgotten.

His famous *Three Men in a Boat* has thrown into undeserved obscurity Jerome's fine efforts in the macabre genre. Like many of his Victorian and Edwardian contemporaries, Jerome enjoyed ghost stories and wrote his own from time to time.

Stories in the Dark collects, for the first time, Jerome's major stories in this genre. To complete the volume, a selection of stories is included from two of his friends and contemporaries (with whom he founded the magazines *The Idler* and *Today*), the journalist Robert Barr and the humorist Barry Pain. Like Jerome, their stories of terror and the supernatural have been overlooked for many years.

These forgotten tales from three skilled authors, two of whom are now hardly remembered, combine to make up one of the most unusual and entertaining anthologies in this field of recent years. Jerome, Barr and Pain deserve new recognition for their splendid tales of terror and this book will certainly win it for them.

EQUATION CHILLERS

THE BLACK REAPER

Tales of Terror by Bernard Capes

Selected and introduced by Hugh Lamb

'And for an hour the Black Reaper mowed and trussed, till he had cut all from the little upper field and was approached to the neck of the juncture with the lower and larger. And before us that remained, and who were drawn back amongst the trees, weeping and praying, a fifth of our comrades lay foul, and dead, and sweltering, and all blotched over with the dreadful mark of the pestilence.'

Bernard Capes (1854-1918) was one of the most original and imaginative writers of his day, and yet within a decade of his death his work was virtually forgotten—in spite of critical praise from G.K. Chesterton, who approvingly pointed to Capes's ability to write a penny-dreadful 'so as to make it worth a pound'.

Capes's tales of terror show him at his best, and the stories revived by Hugh Lamb in this new selection will delight all connoisseurs of fantasy and the macabre. Here Capes conjures up a vision of the moon as the repository of lost souls; the soul of a dead glassblower trapped in a bottle; a werewolf priest in a grisly variation of Little Red Riding Hood; a prison cell haunted by a dead man who makes the dust swirl constantly; a wicked ancestor who steps down from his portrait...

Every story in this collection bears the stamp of Capes's fertile and deeply pessimistic imagination—from Napoleonic terrors and haunted typewriters to marble hands that come to life and plague-stricken villagers haunted by a scythe-wielding ghost—and taken together confirm Capes's standing as a first-rate master of the macabre.

EQUATION CHILLERS

DRACULA'S BROOD

Neglected Vampire Classics by Sir Arthur Conan Doyle, Algernon Blackwood, M.R. James and others

Selected and introduced by Richard Dalby

'She was dressed in a long white robe, her teeth appeared abnormally long, and her eyes blazed like cold emeralds... Closer she came, her mouth dripping with saliva in a most repulsive manner. She lifted the bed-clothes and then, like a snake darting upon its victim, she bent down to my neck...' [from 'Princess of Darkness' by Frederick Cowles]

The most famous vampire of them all is Bram Stoker's *Dracula*, published in 1897. But it was not the first piece of fiction to describe the doings of the undead, and it was by no means the last.

This unique anthology gathers together twenty-three rare vampire stories written by friends and contemporaries of Bram Stoker between 1867 and 1940.

Richard Dalby has deliberately avoided stories that have been regularly reprinted and has concentrated instead on reviving neglected examples of the vampire genre—ranging from Frederick Cowles' beautiful but deadly Princess Bessenyei to tales of vampiric trees and fish. A similarly wide range of authors is represented, including Sir Arthur Conan Doyle, Algernon Blackwood, Julian Hawthorne (son of Nathaniel), Vernon Lee, William Gilbert (father of W.S. Gilbert), Eliza Lynn Linton, and M.R. James.

Dracula's Brood provides a veritable feast of pleasure for all lovers of supernatural and fantasy fiction. It also throws new light on a small but fertile corner of Victorian and early twentieth-century literature.